At that moment, all the feelings and desires that Suzanne had considered wanton erupted into an urge that made her lift her face upward to meet Henry's.

The first touch of his lips against hers stole her breath, and the second touch emptied her lungs with a soft sigh. Each touch was as gentle as a breeze, a mere brushing. It was as if he was exploring her lips with his, and it made her want more.

Much more.

She stretched onto the balls of her feet and moved her lips to catch his. He made a low, almost hungry, sound as their lips met full-on, and the pressure between them increased. That happened over and over again, their lips firmly meeting, parting and meeting again.

The unimaginable pleasure that rained down upon her sent her heart racing and the same warm, pulsating need she'd encountered yesterday burst to life deep inside her.

It was a daring, driving need. One that thrilled her as much as it frightened her.

Author Note

Friends are true treasures. I remember being in Girl Scouts and singing, "Make new friends, but keep the old. One is silver, one is gold." That simple rhyme is so very true, and I enjoyed writing each book in the Southern Belles in London miniseries. Annabelle, Clara and Suzanne had been best friends since childhood, and having them reunited in London while finding their happily-ever-afters with noble men was very fitting.

This story is about Suzanne, who thought she knew exactly what she wanted until she meets Henry. He makes her question all she'd ever known, other than friendship. I hope you enjoy their strangers-to-friends-to-lovers story.

LAURI ROBINSON

Falling for
His Pretend Countess

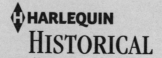

Recycling programs
for this product may
not exist in your area.

ISBN-13: 978-1-335-72385-7

Falling for His Pretend Countess

Harlequin Enterprises ULC
22 Adelaide St. West, 41st Floor
Toronto, Ontario M5H 4E3, Canada
www.Harlequin.com

Printed in U.S.A.

A lover of fairy tales and history, **Lauri Robinson** can't imagine a better profession than penning happily-ever-after stories about men and women in days gone past. Her favorite settings include World War II, the roaring twenties and the Old West. Lauri and her husband raised three sons in their rural Minnesota home and are now getting their just rewards by spoiling their grandchildren. Visit her at laurirobinson.blogspot.com, Facebook.com/lauri.robinson1 or Twitter.com/laurir.

Books by Lauri Robinson

Harlequin Historical

Diary of a War Bride
A Family for the Titanic Survivor
The Captain's Christmas Homecoming

Southern Belles in London

The Return of His Promised Duchess
The Making of His Marchioness
Falling for His Pretend Countess

The Osterlund Saga

Marriage or Ruin for the Heiress
The Heiress and the Baby Boom

Twins of the Twenties

Scandal at the Speakeasy
A Proposal for the Unwed Mother

Sisters of the Roaring Twenties

The Flapper's Fake Fiancé
The Flapper's Baby Scandal
The Flapper's Scandalous Elopement

Visit the Author Profile page
at Harlequin.com for more titles.

To my friend Jennifer.
Your wisdom and encouragement
will always be with me.

Chapter One

Suzanne Bishop had always been told that she was tall for a woman. Well, not always, and not by anyone except Aunt Adelle, who in all fairness had been several inches below five feet her entire life. Therefore, to Aunt Adelle, God rest her soul, a woman who stood five foot four inches without stretching on to her toes was tall.

Truth be, until recently, Suzanne had never paid much attention to her height, or the height of anyone else. There had been no reason to. However, here in England, London to be precise, she noticed because the men were short. Leastwise those who appeared as if it was their mission to seek her out were short.

Men had never sought her out back home.

To be fair, she'd never encouraged them to seek her out.

She wasn't encouraging that here, either, it just happened.

There were a few reasons for that. Clara, her dearest friend, had married Roger Hardgroves, the Marquess of Clairmount, and her other most dear friend, Annabelle, the reason she was in England and not six feet under the earth back in Virginia—thank the Almighty—had married Andrew Barkly, the Duke of Mansfield.

Another reason was that Elaine, Viscountess Voss, Lord Clairmount's mother, had become Suzanne's sponsor, which simply meant that Suzanne was accepted by the *ton* to attend balls and parties during the Season.

Accepted, perhaps, but that didn't mean she felt comfortable. The rules of society here were quite complex and that left her questioning if she should have stayed in London. Both Clara and Annabelle had asked her to live with them on their country estates, but she couldn't depend upon others her entire life.

She'd been raised to be self-sufficient and had done so back home by becoming a teacher.

Therein lay the reason she was here, in London, attending events and functions. It was all quite an adventure and she loved adventures, however, she was also on a mission to become as self-sufficient here as back home.

That meant one thing.

She needed to be introduced to her neighbour, Henry Vogal, the Earl of Beaufort. All these names and titles seemed a bit pretentious in Suzanne's mind, but that was coming from a twenty-two-year-old woman who had no idea what her true surname would have been if she'd been born legitimately.

When a person didn't know who fathered them, there was no way for them to know what their name should have been. She'd been given Bishop as her last name when she arrived at Aunt Adelle's house in Virginia well over a decade ago.

Truth was, Aunt Adelle wasn't her aunt either. She was her great-aunt, or that was the story she'd been told.

Adelle's sister, Jane, had supposedly been Suzanne's grandmother, on her mother's side of course.

Her mother's name had been Lilac and she'd worked in a house of ill repute in Missouri—The Flower Garden. That's what the house had been called and Suzanne wasn't overly sure if her mother's real name had been Lilac, or if her mother had been given that name once she'd become a flower in the garden.

Either way, that's where Suzanne had been born and where Lilac had died. In a house called The Flower Garden. Not knowing what to do with her, Rose, who ran the house, had asked the fine folks of Tinpan, yes, Tinpan, Missouri, to donate enough money to pay for a stagecoach, then train ride, to Virginia. To send Lilac's poor lost daughter to her Aunt Adelle.

Again, that was the story she'd been told and therefore was the only information she had concerning her life. Leaving her to believe there weren't any lords, or earls, or dukes in her family's history.

Yet, here, in England, it appeared as if everyone could be traced back to nobility and titles. All in all, it left her feeling out of place, but that wasn't going to stop her from moving forward with her plan.

To her relief, the music ended and Suzanne pasted a smile on her face for the man whose head she'd been gazing over the top of for the entire length of the overly long dance.

'May I sign your card for a second dance?' the short and portly man asked.

For the life of her, she couldn't remember his name. Mr Horseman, or Hammer, or something along those lines. 'I do apologise, sir,' she said, sounding as sweet as honey even to her own ears, 'but my card is full.'

She'd heard of dance cards, had even attended a couple of dances back home where the host had provided them, but here, they were like the gospel. Luckily, at the first ball she and Clara had attended, Annabelle had told them that if they didn't want to dance, to just scribble names on each line. Annabelle had said that's what Drew, her husband, though he hadn't been her husband at the time, had done for her.

Suzanne hadn't done that at first. However, since that ball, she'd learned that scribbling in a few names here or there on her card made life easier. It gave her time to escape the onslaught of men seeking her attention. She'd had no need of that. Men were an interesting lot and she had never quite figured out the appeal some women seemed to have towards them.

Correct that, she hadn't needed a man's attention. Now she did. She needed to gain the attention of Lord Beaufort.

Her future depended on it.

'Well, then, perhaps I could convince you to share a cup of punch?' the man asked.

The hope in his dull-looking eyes—they were grey, practically colourless—was impossible not to notice, but living through the past five minutes of sidestepping to prevent bruised or broken toes was her limit. 'I do apologise, but I'm not thirsty.' She gave a slight curtsy. 'Please excuse me.'

He said something, but she was already hightailing it towards the curtained door that led to the balcony. That's where Lord Beaufort had disappeared a short time ago and he hadn't yet reappeared.

Besides being an earl, Lord Beaufort owned the publishing house that Suzanne had attempted to sell her story to. Shortly after the Civil War had broken out in America, her hometown of Hampton had been burned to the ground and she'd ended up living with Clara and Clara's daughter Abigail, on Clara's farm outside town. They'd experienced some harrowing times and Suzanne had chronicled every event, every day of their lives up to and including their arrival in England. After rewriting every line, paragraph and page, several times, she'd taken it to Lord Beaufort's publishing house.

That story was her future. Her way of making it alone in the world.

However, that couldn't start until her story was published and Mr Marion Winterbourne, the manager of the publishing house, refused to even read her carefully penned pages. No reason or excuse, just said *no, thank you* and showed her to the door.

There were other publishing houses that she could try, but his was the most reputable, per Lady Voss. Therefore, Suzanne was determined to meet Lord Beaufort and convince him to have Mr Winterbourne at least read her manuscript.

That was another rule of society that was frustrating. Back home, she would have simply knocked on his door and introduced herself to Lord Beaufort, because he lived next door to the Duke of Mansfield's town house where she was staying, but here, it was a rule that she needed to be formally introduced to a man before she could talk to him.

That seemed quite ridiculous to her, but poor Elyse McCaffrey, Drew's housekeeper, had nearly had a heart attack when Suzanne had said she was walking next door to meet the neighbour. The housekeeper had been beside herself while explaining how that wouldn't be proper.

In the end, Suzanne hadn't gone next door, but had asked Lady Voss to introduce the two of them this evening—however, so far, he'd been elusive. In fact, she had the distinct feeling that Lord Beaufort was avoiding being introduced to her.

Therefore, she had an alternate plan.

Heavy gold curtains framed the doorway that led to the balcony and the matching valance looping over the doorway had three-inch-long braided fringes. The opulence of the houses she'd been inside since coming to London was like nothing she'd ever have imagined. The house she'd lived in with Aunt Adelle could fit into a single room in many of the houses where she'd attended balls.

Suzanne stepped out on to the balcony and, ignoring the others who had stepped outside for a breath of cool air—because none of them were Lord Beaufort—she walked to the edge, leaned on the banister and scanned the grounds for any movement.

Several of the other rooms on this side of the house had terraces with staircases that led to the garden, but the ballroom had a balcony, with no stairs. It wasn't far to the ground, yet she questioned why Henry would have leaped down. It was the only way off and Henry had not re-entered the ballroom. She would swear to that.

He wasn't like many of the other men. He was tall. Taller than her by several inches, so a leap to the ground wasn't out of the question. He was also handsome. So handsome, that whenever she caught a glimpse of him, her insides tickled.

His thick, dark hair, which was slightly wavy, was rarely covered with a tall hat like many others wore. She'd surmised others wore those hats to make them look taller. She'd also surmised that she didn't like dancing with men who wore those hats. The wide brims hid the direction of their eyes, but she knew exactly where their gazes went. To her breasts and she now refused to allow a man wearing one to sign her dance card.

Henry was unlike other men in that, too. He didn't sign dance cards.

He hadn't danced with anyone tonight. He had only been at the ball for a little over an hour before he'd sneaked out the balcony door, which meant, if tonight was like the last two balls, it would be hours before he returned.

Music began to play again and the other occupants of the balcony slowly returned to the ballroom. Suzanne watched them out of the corner of her eye, before scanning the garden below again. Near a gazebo, there was a man and woman, who clearly had gone outside for one reason and weren't paying any attention to anyone but each other. There was one other occupant in the garden. A tall man, well hidden in the shadows of a tall hedge near a stone bench.

It was Henry. She was sure of that. Her hesitation lay on the fact that she'd never jumped off a balcony before, but if she was going to do it, she'd better do it quickly, before she changed her mind. Or before someone walked out on to the balcony again. Or before Henry disappeared completely.

Cloud cover hid the moon and a thin curtain of fog was rising up from the ground, but neither impeded Henry Vogal, Earl of Beaufort, from being momentarily stunned by the sight of a woman gathering up her skirt, scaling over the top of the balcony and dropping to the ground as skilfully as any athlete he'd ever met.

Henry eased himself deeper into the shadows of the hedge, flattened his back against the leaves and waited, watching for what she would do next. There was one more thing the darkness didn't impede. His knowledge of the woman's identity. Miss Suzanne Bishop. Her name was being whispered in nearly every corner. Unlike nearly every other man, he had no desire to meet her and had managed to avoid that event.

He had enough woman troubles to last a lifetime.

Miss Bishop glanced left and right, then stayed close to the wall of the house, easing her way towards the hedge.

What was she doing? Other than thwarting his plans. He already had that. He would already be halfway to Whitechapel if not for the couple who had scurried off the library terrace to embark upon some privacy in the shadows of the garden gazebo moments after he'd exited over the balcony—much the same way as Miss Bishop. The couple were still there and the reason he was still hidden in the hedge instead of making his way to Whitechapel, to watch the streets where hansom cabs hid those who didn't want to be seen in the slums, having just left their secret companion's bed, or those on their way to those beds.

He knew the sights of Whitechapel well. Besides the cabs on the streets, drunkards stumbled along the wooden walkways, looking for more ale or a place to sleep off what they'd already consumed, and there were women standing in dimly lit doorways, some wearing nothing more than their underclothes, because getting dressed between companions took too much time.

It was one of the most unsafe regions in the city, yet, that was where he needed to be. He needed information, hints and clues to point him in the direction of the killer. A killer who needed to be stopped.

It sickened Henry to know that because of him, three women had lost their lives and that someone was attempting to pin their murders on him. He was chiefly on his own in discovering the identity of the murderer. There were no peelers or bobbies in Whitechapel. Armed with nothing but truncheons, a constable with a club wouldn't stand much of a chance against the thugs who ruled the streets there. Scotland Yard knew that and constables only appeared when called to action—even then, they didn't offer much hope or help.

Between the enamoured couple and the American woman still easing her way along the wall, Henry was clenching his teeth at the frustration filling him. Was no one remaining inside at the ball tonight? All he needed was a minute to make his way across the garden and slip out through the back gate!

That wasn't going to happen. The couple were too busy to notice him, but Suzanne Bishop, who was still hidden in the shadows, was making her way directly towards him.

Damn it, she was going to cause trouble, that was for sure. She was nosy. He'd seen her peering out the upstairs window towards his house more often than he'd like. He'd also seen her at several balls recently. Between her beauty and her accent, men stood in line to sign her dance card. That had been happening again tonight and she should be inside, blushing under all that attention.

Taller than other women, the way she carried herself was statuesque—add in a pair of sky-blue eyes and honey gold hair, and Henry could understand why the men were drawn to her. Her beauty was unmatchable.

She was only a few feet away and, before he could come up with a plan, a sound came from one of the terraces—a hissed name of sorts. It was clearly for the couple near the gazebo, but Henry leaped forward and planted a hand over Miss Bishop's mouth.

Her gasp was smothered, yet it amazed him that even a gasp could have an accent.

Other than her appearance, and the accent he'd heard from afar, he knew very little about this woman and had no idea what her purpose was for being out here, but he didn't need more gossip about him floating around.

'Shh,' he said near her ear.

A woman, with skirts swishing, rushed off the terrace and hurried towards the couple. 'If your father learns of this, he'll be furious,' the woman said.

'Mother, we were just—' came a reply.

'Don't attempt to lie to me,' the woman interrupted angrily. 'I saw what you were doing! Get inside, and you, sir, take your leave. Now! Through the back gate. I fear for your safety if the Duke learns of this!'

Every nerve in Henry's body was stinging. The Duke of Hollingford was the host of the party and known for his protectiveness of all six of his daughters. Obviously, one young suitor hadn't heeded those reports.

Henry met Miss Bishop's gaze and shook his head, warning her not to make a sound. She nodded and, though he hoped it wasn't a mistake, he lowered his hand from her mouth.

Twisting, she glanced beyond the hedge, to where the young woman was racing for the terrace, and then in the other direction, where the young man was running for the back gate. The very gate he'd planned on using.

The Duchess of Hollingford was standing still, watching the young man, and Henry was at a loss as to what to do. Seconds seemed like hours. The young man was gone, yet the Duchess hadn't moved.

While her husband was known for his protectiveness, the Duchess was known for her ability to gossip. Finding him out here, she could press the chatter already happening about him to the next level. Not to mention what would happen to Miss Bishop's reputation at being caught with him outside alone.

His breath didn't leave his lungs until the Duchess turned and made her way back into the house.

'What are you doing out here?' he asked Miss Bishop.

She let out a long breath as well and then shrugged. 'Following you.'

'Why?'

'Because you seemed quite adamant about not being introduced to me.' She took a slight step backwards and dipped into a graceful curtsy. 'I'm Suzanne Bishop from—'

'America,' he interrupted, still flustered. 'A friend of Drew's wife, Annabelle, which is why you are staying at their town house.'

She nodded as if not surprised he knew all that. 'And you are Henry Vogal, the Earl of Beaufort.'

'Unfortunately, yes.' He glanced towards the back gate, which was out of the question now, and then towards the house. 'You could have broken your neck climbing over that balcony.'

'Not hardly. It wasn't that high.' She glanced down and smoothed the blue material of her skirt with both hands, as if it was the first time that she'd thought about it since scaling the balcony. 'It appeared to be the only way to make your acquaintance.'

'And what was so important about that?' he asked. 'Curious if you are living next door to a murderer?'

Chapter Two

Henry had never wanted to bite his tongue off before and it was too late to do so now. He regretted having said that so bluntly, yet was impressed by how she remained standing in front of him rather than running for the house.

The hints of golden moonlight were shrouding her, making her blonde tresses that were elegantly piled upon her head shimmer. Not a single strand was out of place from her leap off the balcony. She also had a stance about her. One of confidence that told him what he'd said hadn't shocked her.

'I apologise,' he said. 'I wasn't attempting to frighten you.'

'You didn't.'

'So, you've heard the rumours,' he said.

'No, I have not.'

Leave it to him to open a can of worms needlessly.

'I always prefer to hear things directly from the horse's mouth,' she said.

He couldn't stop a slight chuckle. It could have been her accent, or her comment, or simply the entire situation. All he knew was that she was charming and, after his comment, he felt that he owed her an explanation. 'Three women from Whitechapel have been murdered— the first one was my sister.'

She tilted her head slightly to one side and settled a serious stare upon him. 'I may not have been in London long, but I know that Whitechapel is not a district where the sister of an earl would live.'

Henry heard her statement and was still processing the musical tilt of her accent when it dawned on him that he still didn't know why she was following him. 'You could have severely damaged your reputation by following me out here tonight.'

'No one saw me.'

'That's what the Duke's daughter thought, too,' he pointed out.

She glanced at the house. 'Poor girl. Her mother was not happy.' Looking at him again, she said, 'I have more experience sneaking in and out of places.'

He lifted a brow, wondering what she meant by that.

She shrugged. 'I sneaked in and out of army camps, full of soldiers, without ever being seen for months.'

'Army camps?' His tone demonstrated how sceptical he was about her answer. More than sceptical. There was no reason he could imagine for a woman to sneak in and out of army camps.

'Yes.'

'Why? Are you some sort of spy?'

'No, I'm not a spy.'

'Then why did you feel the need to sneak in and out of army camps?'

'It's called survival,' she said. 'We needed food and the area had been cleared of any game.'

'Why were you in such dire straits?'

'Because other soldiers had already attacked the town, burned it to the ground, ransacked Clara's farm and taken everything worth taking.'

Her tone and demeanour had changed. There was no lifting note to her words. Everyone knew America was in the midst of a civil war and war, no matter where, when, or why, hurt people. People from every rank. He knew from Caleb Turner, his manservant, that the Marquess of Clairmount had sent a ship to America and that was how Miss Bishop, along with another woman, who had married Clairmount, had arrived in England. 'Is that why you are here? Escaped to England before you got caught?'

'No, I am here because Annabelle, your neighbour's wife, was worried about us. Myself, along with Clara, her daughter, Abigail, and dog, Sammy, all sailed here on one of Clairmount's ships a few months ago'. She folded her arms, staring at him. 'You have done a good job of changing the subject, so this time I will ask directly. Why would the sister of an earl live in Whitechapel?'

Henry wasn't one to share private information, but it would all come out sooner or later, despite his mother's wishes. 'Heather was my half-sister. If she'd been a full, legitimate sister, she would never have been living in Whitechapel.'

'Legitimate?'

'Yes.' He chose his words carefully, looking for a polite way to explain. 'Her mother was never married to my father. My mother was married to my father when Heather was born.'

'But your father claimed her as his daughter?'

'No.' He let out a sigh. It was quite complicated and complex. 'Not publicly. I knew Heather because I used to come to London with my father when I was young and we would visit the home where Heather lived with her mother. That stopped years ago, but at some point I figured out the truth. Shortly before my father died, I started looking for her, to provide her with an inheritance, but she was murdered before I could give it to her.'

'You don't know by whom?'

'No, I do not.' He considered withholding more, but then decided it might be better if she knew the truth, because tonight she had been in danger. 'However, I believe she died because of me. So did the other women, so following me tonight, being connected to me in any way, is dangerous. Very dangerous.'

Suzanne shivered, yet did her best to hide it. His tone was as serious as a dead rat—it took a lot to kill a rat, so when a person sees a dead one, they should take heed. Henry's expression was serious, too, but he could be acting. Trying to scare her.

Except for the fact that she believed him. Her years of teaching had taught her how to tell when she was being fed a tale. It was all in the eyes. His were dark brown, surrounded by thick, dark lashes, and they were sincere. More than sincere. They looked sad, very sad.

Truth should always beget truth. 'I followed you out here tonight so I could meet you and ask you how I might go about having Mr Winterbourne read my story.'

He stared at her for a long moment before asking, 'What story?'

Sneaking in and out of army camps hadn't been as easy as she'd made it sound. It had been downright harrowing and she'd been scared out of her wits more than once over almost getting caught. She wasn't sorry for what she'd done and would do it again, if need be. Clara and Abigail, as well as Sammy, had needed the food she'd managed to steal in order to live.

Survival was a strong motivator.

In fact, she was still motivated by it. 'I wrote a story about what Clara and I, and her daughter, Abigail, endured during the war, until we arrived in England, and I took it to your publishing house, but Mr Marion Winterbourne refused to read it. He gave it back to me without even looking at it, nor would he answer any of my questions.' Her cheeks grew warm. 'I don't mean to sound like I'm tattling on him, I merely want to know why he's not interested in my story and possibly how I can change it, turn it into one he would be interested in publishing.'

Henry didn't move. Just looked at her.

Her cheeks grew warmer.

'You climbed over a balcony because of a story you want to get published?' he asked.

She lifted her chin, met him eye for eye. 'Yes.'

He was frowning as if he didn't believe her. While searching her mind as to how to convince him that she was telling the truth, she realised a reason why he might not believe her. During her short time attending balls, she had discovered that most unmarried women attended social activities because they were in search of a husband. A titled husband. His name was at the top of the list.

Surely he wasn't thinking that was her reason behind wanting to be introduced to him? Her two best friends had found titled husbands, but she wasn't looking for that. Would never look for that.

However, if she told him that, he might think she was lying for merely bringing up the subject.

Flustered, she threw her arms in the air. 'I refuse to live off the kindness of others my entire life and writing, having my story be turned into a book, could provide me with a way to earn a living.'

'That's why you stayed in London, rather than go to Mansfield with Drew and his wife?' he asked. 'Or to Clairmount with Roger and his wife?'

'Yes.'

For a moment, it appeared as if he was about to smile, but it never quite came to fruition. 'I can't believe that either Drew or Roger would be impressed to learn of your antics tonight.'

A shiver rippled down her spine, because he had a solid point there. It irritated her that he would practically threaten her and the only thing she could think to do was counter. 'I can't believe either of them would be impressed to learn how you sneak over balconies and out back doors, stay away for hours, then return to the balls in time for the meal, pretending you've been there the entire time.'

Neither of them moved, just stood there, staring at each other as though it was some sort of showdown. Perhaps it was and he needed to know that she didn't take being threatened lightly.

'This isn't a game, Miss Bishop, and I suggest you stop now, before you get hurt.'

'I never once thought it was a game, Lord Beaufort.' With that, she pivoted on one heel and headed for the house, choosing to use the library terrace door. Her mind was a dance floor of swirling thoughts, each one about Henry. Annabelle and Clara had already had their fair share of issues and deserved the happiness they'd found. Having either of them worrying about her was the last thing she wanted. It was downright wretched of him to imply that he'd tell Drew or Roger that she'd followed him tonight.

Goodnight and God bless, it wasn't as if she'd done anything dangerous, or that would hurt others.

She would have to find a different publishing house. That's all there was to it.

Men. They were just like Aunt Adelle said—you couldn't trust a one of them.

Henry arrived at her side and grasped hold of her arm, stopping her from stepping on to the terrace steps. 'You should use a different door.'

'Why?'

Before he replied, the hostess of the party, the Duchess of Hollingford stepped out of the open doorway. 'Miss Bishop, Lord Beaufort, I was unaware that you were in the garden.'

'That's why,' Henry whispered next to her ear, then he nodded towards Duchess. 'Only for a brief moment,' he said, while now leading her up the steps 'Miss Bishop was in need of a breath of fresh air.'

'Indeed, I was,' Suzanne said, going along with his story, although she wasn't exactly sure why. She was still irritated at him. Smiling at the Duchess, who had a long face and deep frown wrinkles in her chin, she added, 'It was all the dancing. The music is wonderful. The entire ball has been wonderful. Truly wonderful and your home is beautiful.'

'I'm glad you're enjoying yourself,' the Duchess said, then glanced at Henry, 'You, too, my lord.'

'It's been delightful,' Henry said. 'If you will excuse us, Miss Bishop has a full dance card.'

The Duchess stepped back to allow them to pass.

Henry kept his hand on her arm and escorted her across the library, towards the doorway that led into the hallway and then the ballroom next door.

'How do you know if my dance card is full?' she asked.

'Assumptions.'

The weight of his palm and fingers on her elbow was making her entire arm feel warm. 'One should never make assumptions.'

'If you had, then you would have realised that the Duchess was watching the doorway, making sure that young man didn't return,' Henry said.

'I hadn't thought of that,' Suzanne admitted, wondering if she should pull her arm out of his hold.

'I'd bet she put outlooks at all the doorways,' he said.

Suzanne felt a slump of confidence. 'She'll know we hadn't gone out another door.'

'She might,' he said. 'And we might have just created the opening line for another round of gossip.'

She twisted, looked him in the eye. 'How so?'

He lifted a single brow, making him look even more handsome than his dark suit and white shirt did. 'Surely you understand what being alone outside with me means.'

She shook her head. 'That you escorted me outside for a breath of fresh air?'

'I could only wish that was all,' he said, glancing around the room as they walked into the ballroom.

The tone of his voice sent a shiver up her spine. 'What do you mean?'

He didn't reply, merely gave her a nod and released her arm. 'Goodnight, Miss Bishop.'

Anger filled Henry as he left the ball and made his way home. He had more than enough on his plate without Miss Suzanne Bishop. He could have let her walk into the house alone. She probably wouldn't have mentioned being outside with him. He simply hadn't wanted her to face the Duchess of Hollingford alone.

Now, people were going to believe he was as smitten with her as half the other men in London.

Would his life ever again be the quiet calm that it had been at one time? He couldn't see how, but he could hope, couldn't he?

When a knock sounded on the front door mid-morning the following day, he half expected it to be the Duchess Hollingford. He'd considered paying her a visit to explain that there was nothing significant about him and Suzanne being in the gardens together, but figured his protests would only provide fodder for her gossip.

He could use what he'd witnessed with her daughter to discourage any of the Duchess's gossip, but that wasn't his style, and again, would merely increase her suspicion about him and Suzanne.

Henry rubbed at the ache in his temple as he rose from his chair and made his way to the doorway of his office to watch Caleb walk across the hall and open the front door.

'Good morning,' the caller said cheerfully. 'I sincerely hope this isn't too early to call, but I just made this rum cake and wanted to deliver it while it was still warm. That's when it's at its best. Warm. It is quite delicious.'

Henry bit his lips together to keep from smiling at the southern accent, until he realised no one could see if he smiled or not and released a full-blown smile.

'It's not the kind of rum cake you have over here,' Suzanne continued to tell Caleb, 'with fruit and such.

Mrs McCaffrey—she's the Duke of Mansfield's cook and housekeeper, because all the other servants are at Mansfield and I said the three of us would get along just fine next door, that's where I'm staying, in the Duke's town house. His wife Annabelle, the Duchess, is one of my dearest and oldest friends. We grew up together, back in Virginia. In America that is—anyway, Mrs Mc-Caffrey told me about the rum cakes you make here at Christmas time. This isn't one of them.

'It's a butter rum cake made from good old flour, sugar and eggs, and a few other things, like a little dash of salt and baking powder, and of course lots of butter and rum. Not a lot of rum, just enough to make it delicious. That's what my Auntie Adelle always said. Just enough to make it delicious. It's her recipe that I used. I know it by heart. Auntie's been gone going on five years now—God rest her soul and all the others we miss so dearly—but I memorised her recipe years ago.'

Henry's smile grew, wondering if she'd yet to take a breath. Not that he'd heard and she clearly wasn't finished yet.

'I baked it this morning to bring over here to be neighbourly. That's what we always do back home, in Virginia, whenever a new neighbour moves in, people bake them things, or bring them canned goods or flowers from their gardens, just something to say welcome, it's good to meet you, and I figured it was high time I did that, too. Is Lord Beaufort home so I can deliver the cake to him personally? '

Henry couldn't see her, so had no idea if she was batting those thick lashes surrounding her sky-blue eyes or not, but could imagine that her charm alone was making the usually stiff and proper Caleb, who always carried himself as rigid as a board, grow weak at the knees.

'Oh, goodness me,' she continued before Caleb could respond to her question. 'I didn't introduce myself, now, did I? I'm Suzanne Bishop, from Virginia. Hampton, Virginia, and I'm staying right next door in the Duke of Mansfield's town house for the time being. I do believe I already mentioned that. I'm just so pleased to make your acquaintance that I'm rattling on, now, aren't I? Do forgive me, I really just want to be neighbourly.'

'It is a pleasure to make your acquaintance, miss,' Caleb said, the first words he'd managed to get in since he'd opened the door. 'But I am afraid—'

'Oh, forgive me, but what is your name?' she asked. 'Did I miss it?'

'No, forgive me,' Caleb replied. 'It's Caleb, miss. Caleb Turner.'

'Aw, Mr Turner. It is wonderful to meet you. Just wonderful. It's so nice to know who is living next door. Did I mention that this cake is best served warm? The butter and sugar glaze just melts in your mouth then. It's tasty any time, but warm is the best. I'm sure Lord Beaufort would appreciate tasting it while it's at its best, don't you think?'

Henry covered his mouth to keep his chuckle silent as he stepped into the hallway, feeling empathy for his manservant. This woman could talk her way into Buckingham Palace. The guards wouldn't stand a chance. Neither did Caleb.

'I'm sure he would, miss, but His Lordship is—'

'Please show our guest in, Caleb,' Henry interrupted as he walked towards the door. 'And ask Mrs Turner to brew a pot of tea to be served with the warm cake in the drawing room.'

'Yes, my lord, right away,' Caleb said, as he stepped out of the doorway and gestured for Miss Bishop to step into the entranceway.

Henry had thought he was prepared to see her again, especially after listening to her for the last several minutes, but his breath stalled as she stepped around the door. Her dress was more yellow than gold, but shimmered as brightly as the honey-gold hair she had neatly pinned up, except for several corkscrew tendrils that framed her face. A very memorable face. Although she'd been on his mind all night, his memory hadn't done her beauty justice.

He'd noticed her beauty before last night, everyone had, but it was her personality that really shone through this morning. She was not only a very lovely woman, but also a delightful one.

He wasn't delighted easily and shouldn't be this time, but couldn't deny how she'd captivated his mind last night, and she was doing a good job of captivating him right now, too.

'My lord,' Caleb said. 'Please allow me to introduce Miss Suzanne Bishop.' He then turned to her. 'Miss Bishop, please allow me to introduce the Earl of Beaufort.'

Before Henry had a chance to acknowledge the introduction, or explain they'd already met, she handed the cake to Caleb and stepped forward, hand out.

'Good morning, it's so nice to be properly introduced,' she said. 'Please, call me Suzanne and I believe Drew calls you Henry. It's such a fine name, don't you agree?'

Henry took a hold of her offered hand, not in a hand-shake as she'd clearly expected, though. Instead, he made a show of raising her hand and kissing the back of it. 'I agree, Suzanne is a fine name.'

'I meant, Henry, but thank you all the same,' she said, with a slight, yet graceful curtsy.

Fully aware that his manservant was still standing there, cake in hand, and fully enthralled by this walking, talking, ball of sunshine, Henry said, 'We'll be in the drawing room, Caleb.'

'Yes, my lord.'

Henry could swear he'd never seen Caleb blush before, but the man's cheeks were definitely red as he pivoted about and carried the cake down the hallway towards the kitchen.

'We need to talk,' Suzanne hissed under her breath.

Her accent was still there, but not nearly as pronounced as she'd made it while speaking with Caleb, and Henry wondered why he felt a bit miffed by that. He shouldn't be. She was quite the actress, one he still needed to investigate concerning her tale of submitting a story to the publishing house. That had been one of his family's businesses that he'd invested time and money into, with the hope of building it back into one that could maintain itself with little input from him. It had been at one time, but, like others, it had been pushed to the sidelines and had been hanging by a thread for a few years.

'Why?' he asked. 'Has something happened since last night? Other than you baking a cake, of course.'

Chapter Three

This was another one of those ideas that she'd come up with and thought was quite splendid—much like her one to follow him last night—until she'd knocked on the door a moment ago. That's when Suzanne had wondered if she should have thought a bit deeper and longer about coming over to see him this morning.

She'd barely slept a wink, thinking about what had happened after he'd left the ball last night.

'Well,' she said quietly as they walked towards an arched doorway off the hall, 'I've been thinking.'

'Lord help me,' he muttered.

Not impressed, she shot him a glare and, head held high, walked into the drawing room. The walls were painted white, the upholstered furniture was dark blue and there were several cream-coloured tables. Small ones near a sofa flanked by two chairs and a large table near the window, with four chairs surrounding it. The curtains as well as the large carpet that covered the centre of the room contained several shades of blue, which was her all-time favourite colour.

'Please,' Henry said, gesturing one hand towards the sofa.

She sat and watched as he moved to one of the chairs. He wasn't wearing all black this morning. His trousers and boots were brown, his shirt white. And his thick brown hair seemed to have more waves than she'd noticed before. Prior to last night, she'd only seen him from a distance and had to admit that he was the most handsome man she had ever met.

'Dare I ask what you've been thinking about?' he asked.

'You,' she replied, doing her best to sound as disgusted as he had. He, of course, was referring to when she'd told him that she'd been thinking, not what she was currently doing, but the answer was the same either way.

'Me?' He shook his head while leaning back in his chair and crossing his arms.

'Yes. You need me.' She had come to that conclusion last night. Actually, it had been in the wee hours of the morning when her plan had struck.

'I. Need. You?' He pronounced each word slowly and forcefully.

She rolled her eyes at his exaggeration. 'Yes, you do. You need a diversion. And that is me.'

'I'd say you are more of a distraction.'

'Distraction, diversion. It's the same and I can provide it.'

He uncrossed his arms and rubbed his forehead before leaning forward. 'Miss Bishop—'

'Suzanne,' she corrected. 'We'll need to be on a first-name basis.' It had all made perfect sense this morning and she'd added to the plan while baking Aunt Adelle's rum cake that everyone back home loved and would do practically anything for, but now that she was about to voice her entire plan out loud, she was having second thoughts.

'Why do we need to be on a first-name basis?' he asked.

She swallowed the lump in her throat and glanced at the doorway, half wondering if she should leave and re-think a few points.

'Suzanne?'

'Because people who are courting call each other by their first names,' she said before losing her nerve.

'Courting?' He sounded shocked. Probably was. His eyes had certainly widened.

'Not for real,' she said quickly.

He rubbed the back of his neck.

'Just pretend,' she said, just as quickly. 'Pretend courtship. I'm not looking for a husband. Not at all, but I do need my book published. Or another book, if that's what Mr Winterbourne would prefer. And you need a diversion so you can catch the real killer.'

While letting those words sink in for him, Suzanne rubbed her hands over the shimmering gold material of the dress covering her knees, the dress she'd chosen specifically for meeting him this morning because Clara said she looked like a ray of sunshine in the dress. That's what she wanted to be. A ray of sunshine, of hope. She liked helping others and he needed help.

So did she and this could work if he'd agree.

He blew out a long, slow breath of air before asking, 'How would pretending to be courting you, as you put it, help me catch the killer?'

She hadn't completely come up with all the details. In truth, she'd been hoping he might have some ideas that would make it all work. Choosing to start with the facts, the inevitable facts, she said, 'I've often seen you sneak out of balls, like you did last night when you jumped over the balcony.'

He remained silent, as if refusing to admit anything. She didn't need him to admit it. She knew she was right. But there was more to it than that. 'I'm assuming, and correct me if I'm wrong, that you are doing that—sneaking out and then back into balls—so you can go to Whitechapel and look for the killer, hoping the ball provides you with an alibi. However, if no one is able to vouch for you being at the ball the entire time, your alibi is no good. I could provide that alibi for you.'

'You could?'

'Yes. We could arrive together and leave together, and I would make sure that no one notices your absences during the time that you are gone.'

One of his perfectly arched dark brows lifted. 'By using the same country charm that you used on Caleb to get through the front door?'

She had purposefully enhanced her accent while speaking with his servant at the front door. 'That is how people here expect me to sound.' She'd figured that out at the first ball she'd attended. People didn't care what she said, they just wanted her to talk. Which was irritating. Her accent wasn't any funnier sounding than the accents over here, however, she would use it as a tool in this situation. 'It holds their attention.'

Nodding, he said, 'I can agree with that.' He then held up a single finger on one hand and looked towards the doorway.

Momentarily, Caleb pushed a white rolling tea trolley into the room, all the way to the where she and Henry sat. The cake she'd baked, sliced and set out on china plates with tiny blue flowers, was on the trolley, along with a tea set that matched the plates. A fine mist of steam swirled out of the spout of the teapot.

Without a word, Caleb set the cake, along with forks, on the short table in front of her, as well as a side table next to where Henry sat. The servant then poured tea into cups and asked her if she wanted milk or sugar.

Aunt Adelle used to say that she could talk an Eastern diamondback rattler out from under a rock and Suzanne wanted that to be true now. This plan she'd come up with could work and it would give Henry a reason to help her get her story in front of Mr Winterbourne. 'No, to either, thank you, Caleb, and please know that the cake is for everyone in the household, so I do hope you will help yourself to a piece and encourage others to have some as well.'

'Thank you, miss,' he said quietly, while setting her cup of tea on the table in front of her. 'It smells delicious.'

'Oh, it is quite delicious. I don't wish to sound boastful, but I've never met a person who didn't like this cake. Auntie Adelle used to make if for all kinds of occasions besides giving it to new neighbours. Community picnics and dances, weddings and funerals—everyone wanted the recipe. She wouldn't give it out, though. Said it was a secret she'd take to her grave. She didn't, though, because she taught me how to make it.'

Suzanne chose not to reveal that the thing her aunt took to her grave was that the bottles of rum she bought regularly were not all used for her cakes. Most of that was what Aunt Adelle had sipped on day in and day out. Suzanne did cover her mouth briefly with four fingers from one hand, and let out a tiny and what she hoped was a charming giggle.

'There was one time,' she said, attempting to sound very cheerful, 'Auntie made a cake for Jess Cramer's birthday, and two men got into a fisticuff fight there at the party over the last slice. Auntie felt so bad that she sent me home right then and there to make another cake. It doesn't take long. The longest part is the baking and the most important part is knowing how long to let it cool before pouring the sauce over the top. If the cake is too warm, the glaze just runs off, doesn't soak or stiffen properly. Oh, and once it cools, just pop it in a warm oven for a few minutes and it'll warm up and taste as good as when it was first made. It'll melt in your mouth. It surely will.'

'Thank you, miss,' Caleb said, his elongated face pinking slightly. 'I'll remember that.'

'Please do, and please let me know if you like it, because I can whip you up another one in no time. Any time. Just come on over and knock on the door. Feel free to knock for other reasons, too. It'll make me feel like I'm back in Virginia. Back there we were always sharing a cup of sugar or flour, and an egg or two, with our neighbours.' It didn't take much for her to let her smile slip away. 'That, of course, was before the war, but I'm hoping it'll be that way again some day.'

'I'm sure it will, miss,' Caleb said. 'And you have my deepest condolences for the troubles happening there right now.'

She met his gaze with all the sincerity filling her. 'I truly do hope it will be that way again one day and thank you, Caleb, your kind words mean so much.'

He gave her a long, sympathy-filled look, as if he wanted to say more, but didn't, before he turned to Henry. 'Will there be anything else, my lord?'

'No, Caleb,' Henry replied while he picked up this plate and fork. 'I believe we have everything we need. Go and have a piece of this melt-in-the-mouth cake.'

Suzanne knew Henry was mocking her, but didn't mind, because she knew that the cake on his fork would be melting in his mouth in a moment and she couldn't wait to see it happen. The cake was undeniably delicious and everything else she'd said about it was true, too.

A sweet second later, a great sense of satisfaction filled her as she watched Henry's eyes widen and his chewing slowed as he savoured the buttery sweetness. She sipped on her cup of tea as he swallowed and took a second forkful of his cake and, once again, appeared to be savouring the flavours.

After swallowing that piece, he pointed his fork at her. 'You baked this?'

'I did.' Her cake was untouched. Though she knew how delicious it was, and would probably never grow tired of eating it, she was certain that he'd want a second piece. It most likely wasn't prudent to be so self-righteous over something, but a cake was justifiable.

So was helping him if he'd agree to it. This truly could work out perfectly for both of them.

Henry finished the rest of his cake and the look on his face as he glanced at his empty plate was nothing shy of disappointment. She slowly leaned forward and pushed her plate across the small table, towards him.

'Are you sure?' he asked.

'Yes, I'm sure. I can make another one.'

He picked up her plate. 'How often do you make one?'

A little humph escaped before she could stop it, because earlier, while baking the cake, she'd realised it had been a long time since she'd made one and that had left her a bit melancholy. 'Until this morning, it had been over a year. Since before the war struck Hampton.'

She wasn't trying to make him feel sorry for her, just stating the truth. It was hard to think about, to remember, a town that no longer existed. People who were gone for ever. She tried not to focus on it, to remember, because there was nothing that she could do about it.

He was eating this piece of cake slower, as if he'd accepted how delicious it was and was now simply enjoying it.

'I offer my condolences, too, for what your country is experiencing,' he said.

'Thank you,' she said.

'Are you anxious to return?' he asked.

'Yes, and no,' she replied in complete honesty. 'I want to know how the country is faring, but I don't want to be in the midst of it.' She'd felt guilty over that. 'If I'd been alone, I probably would have gone north, helped at a hospital or done something to show my support. At least I want to believe I would have, but Clara needed my help. I couldn't leave her. Mark, her husband, died in battle, and Abigail, her daughter, was just a baby. Their dog, Sammy, just a puppy. They are the only family I have.'

He finished his cake and set the plate on the table beside his chair. 'No parents? Siblings?'

She shook her head, in part as an answer to his question and in part to herself for bringing up the conversation. Her own past was also something she didn't like to think about. However, she had to admit that she had been doing just that ever since he'd said that his half-sister had lived in Whitechapel and how he'd been attempting to help her to change her life, before she'd been murdered.

'It was just you, alone? What about your aunt? The one with the cake recipe?'

Clearing her mind as best she could, Suzanne replied, 'I lived with Auntie Adelle from the time I was seven. She died about five years ago. Just died in her sleep one night. Annabelle and Clara had been like the sisters I never had from the moment I moved to Hampton, to live with Aunt Adelle. I met them on my first day of school.' A smile formed at that memory.

'I was somewhat tall and gangly for my age, and a boy, Jeb Wright, called me a name, I think it was beanpole or string bean, I can't remember for sure, but Annabelle heard it and she retorted. With words and a shove. Within a flash, half the school yard was rolling on the ground, kicking and pulling hair. Miss Wayne, the teacher at the time, called across the street to the dry goods store for help to break up the fight.'

'Who won?' he asked.

A tiny giggle formed and she let it out, not only because of the memory, but also because of all the school yard fights she'd broken up as a teacher. 'I don't think any of us won,' she said, 'because we were all in trouble, at school and at home, but in the end, I came out a winner because Annabelle, Clara and I were best friends from that day on.'

'That was in Virginia?'

'Yes.'

'Is that where you'll return to?'

She hadn't thought so, up until last night. Once she had a way to earn money, she would be free to return to America if she chose. She'd never wanted anyone to know about her birth, her early years, but perhaps she should learn more about her parentage, other than what Aunt Adelle had shared.

There was so much nobility here in England, generations of family that went back centuries. She didn't have that, but she had recognised there was an empty spot that was inside her. One that had been there since Aunt Adelle had passed on and had become stronger again since Clara had married. It was strange, and sad, knowing that she wasn't connected to another living person anywhere.

Thinking about him and his half-sister last night had made her wonder if there were others in her family that she hadn't ever known about. That wasn't completely accurate. Thinking about him, which she had done for hours, had made her nervous in a way she'd never experienced.

He was so handsome, so… She couldn't put her finger on exactly what she felt about him, thought about him, and that was disconcerting. A man had never taken up so much of her thoughts before and she had to protect herself from that. It wouldn't be that hard. She'd been protecting herself from men for years. 'I don't know,' she said. 'I may go further west. To Tinpan.'

'Tinpan?'

'Yes, Tinpan. Tinpan, Missouri. That's where I was born.'

'Interesting name for a town.'

'It was named that because if a person didn't have their own tin pan, they couldn't eat. No cook had enough dishes for all the rail men.'

His frown made her smile. Prior to last night, she hadn't thought about Tinpan in ages. 'I might go there if the town still exists.'

'Why wouldn't it still exist? The war?'

'Possibly, if the battles expand that far west. But more likely because it was a rail town. People followed the building of the railroads westwards, creating towns at the rail heads. When the rail was completed, the town packed up and moved with the rail workers. Unless, of course, a depot had been built, then it became a permanent town. The rail wasn't done when I moved to Virginia, so I'm not sure what happened.'

'Did you have family there?'

'Only those who died.' Suzanne picked up her cup and drank the last bits of tea. Long ago, she'd decided to only look forward, embrace the adventures awaiting her rather than reliving things that no longer mattered, but now she was questioning that.

Sitting her empty cup back on her saucer, she said, 'So, back to our original conversation and the reason I'm here. I will keep everyone's mind off whether you are in attendance or not during your absences from balls and other events.' Confidence that her plan would help both of them once again felt solid inside her. 'If you agree to have Mr Winterbourne read my story. Just read it. I'm not asking you to make him publish it.' She would take care of that. All she needed was a foot in the door.

Henry's mind was processing several things at the same time. One, that had been the most delicious cake he'd ever tasted. The unique, buttery sweet flavour was still lingering in his mouth. Two, Suzanne was undeniably the most charming woman—correct that—the best charmer, he'd ever met. And three, he never again wanted to see the sadness that had briefly reflected in her eyes when she'd spoken of Missouri. It had taken all his control to stay seated, to not move to the seat next to her and engulf her in a hug. He had two younger sisters and knew that, sometimes, a hug helped them.

He cleared his throat because it felt tight and reached for the teapot. 'More tea?'

'No, thank you,' she said, lying a hand over the top of her cup.

He'd had his fill and set the pot back on the tray while shifting his thoughts to her proposition. 'I thank you for your cake and I will ask Mr Winterbourne to read your manuscript, but I'm not in need of the assistance you offered.'

She let out a slow sigh and grimaced. 'Yes, you are. Shortly after you left last night, the Duchess of Hollingford suggested that if any one saw two people in the gazebo, it had been you and I.'

Henry silently cursed as his jaw tightened with anger. 'To you?'

She shook her head. 'I overheard her, but she knew I heard.'

'I shouldn't have left when I did,' he said, furious at himself. 'I apologise for putting you in such an uncompromising position.'

'I apologise as well, for I am the one who followed you,' she said. 'Thinking about that last night is when I came up with this plan. Pretending to be engaged would limit her gossip and it would give you the opportunity to search for the real killer, stop him before he can strike again.'

That was his goal and she most likely could convince anyone and everyone that he was nearby, whereas in reality he'd be on the streets of looking for clues about the real killer, but it wouldn't be right to involve her in all this. Although, a false engagement would salvage her reputation. It would also save her from having other men lure her outside at other balls. Men who would have only one thing in mind.

Or the murderer himself.

'I understand if you need time to think it through,' she said. 'I thought about it for a good portion of the night and I commend you for wanting to help your half-sister. Not only for trying to find her real killer, but for wanting to help her before then. Not everyone would do that and I'd be honoured to know that I'd helped you in that process.'

He looked at her for a moment, then smiled slightly. 'But you also want to have your manuscript read.'

'Yes, of course,' she said. 'That is what started it all. Why I jumped over the balcony to follow you.'

'That is true,' he said.

'It is and the other thing that is true is that I am not interested in anything else, as in marriage. I know that most women here are seeking a husband, a titled husband. I assure you, that's not what I want. I merely want a way to provide financially for myself. This plan could be a win for both of us.'

Chapter Four

Henry was in the midst of processing how every one of her explanations, how everything she said, made sense, while also questioning his own inner thoughts. He wanted to know everything about her, which was unusual for him. Women rarely caught or held his attention. She certainly did. He was willing to ask Marion Winterbourne to read her manuscript, because he wanted to read it himself. To learn all she'd been through and more.

'There is something I would like to know,' she said. 'If you don't mind.'

'Oh? What is that?' he asked.

'Were you shocked or embarrassed when you discovered you had a half-sister, one born out of wedlock?'

'No. I was angry though. Still am.'

Her expression never changed—in fact, it might have softened. Most people would be shocked by what he said and the truth of it. Other than he, that is, because ever since his father had become incapacitated by a stroke, Henry had been discovering disarrays caused by family. Pilfering from companies, squatters overtaking buildings, causing long-term tenants to flee, farm ground left unattended and unproductive managers.

'I felt that Heather had been cheated out of a family,' he explained, 'had suffered because of others. However, my mother didn't want Heather to receive an inheritance. She said it would ruin our family if people were to discover that her husband, my father, had fathered a child out of wedlock.' The entire conversation had angered and disgusted him. The entire ordeal. 'There are numerous children born out of wedlock. That's not a choice they make, nor should they suffer because of it.'

He was a firm believer in that and, because he knew others who had produced an illegitimate child and had left them unacknowledged, he'd made a vow that would not happen to him. A man had needs, he wouldn't deny that, but he would not become his father, losing interest in a wife, forgoing his vows and seeing his needs met elsewhere.

Therefore, every companion he'd ever chosen had known up front that if a child was produced by their actions, even with the precautions he deemed necessary, he would raise that child. Him alone. There would be no offer of marriage, no money exchanged. The child would become his property free and clear. To provide for and raise. He wasn't concerned if no child was ever produced. If he never had an heir. There was no doubt in his mind that one of his younger sisters would produce a nephew for him to pass down the family title and properties to for the next generation.

'It's understandable that your mother would have been upset when she learned about Heather,' Suzanne said.

'That must have been a long time ago, because she

wasn't surprised when my father confirmed my conclusions shortly before he died.'

'Did he want Heather to receive an inheritance?'

'I believe so. He said that he was glad I'd found her.'

'For who? You, him or her?'

She was as insightful as she was smart. 'I'm not sure,' Henry admitted.

'How did you find her?'

'One of the businesses that my family owns is a milliner's manufacturing company, the assembly plant is in Whitechapel.' Like the publishing house, his father had allowed his uncle to oversee the milliner and it had been full of bookkeeping discrepancies as well as mistreatment of employees. 'It was as I was leaving the district late one night that I came upon Heather.'

His stomach tightened at the full truth of that. She'd been selling her wares—selling herself—and had attempted to flag down his coach by stepping into the street in front of the horses. It had sickened him then, and still did now, to know that had been the life of one of his flesh-and-blood relatives. 'I didn't recognise her, but later realised who she was.'

He shook his head at the memory of how she'd shouted, *'Heather will treat you right, my lord.'* The name had stuck, so had her mass of red curls, and during the ride home he'd compared her to a memory of a little girl with curly red hair and a mass of freckles. That memory had stuck, made him search for more information.

'I found her a few weeks later, explained who I was.' He made no mention of the seedy room or the overall condition of the building where Heather had lived, but he would never forget it.

'She remembered my father. Remembered me. I was just two years older than her. She turned twenty-five earlier this year and explained how her mother had died when she was ten. Her mother had told her who her father was, but she had no proof. I told her that she didn't need any. I knew and I gave her money. Told her that there would be more and that I'd be back. I wanted her to be able to change her life.'

Suzanne was silent, but the empathy filling her eyes spoke louder than words.

'I told my father what I was doing,' he continued, 'and that's when he confirmed that she was his daughter. He died a short time later. I contacted a barrister to petition a sizeable amount of money for Heather, as a legal heir. Heather was killed before his petition cleared the courts.'

'And the other murdered women, did you know them?' she asked quietly.

This wasn't a conversation he wanted to have with her. It had already gone further than he'd planned, but perhaps, if she knew the truth, she'd realise the dangers of her offer of help. 'No, but I believe they were all committed by the same person.'

'Why do you think that?'

'Because their demise was identical to Heather's,' he said. Strangulation. For all Henry knew, that could be how many girls died, because the death of a *working girl* in the Whitechapel district often went unreported and was rarely, if ever, discussed within society. People claimed it was simply a reality of the life of a prostitute that she could be attacked or murdered. It was a chance that those girls took.

That attitude infuriated him.

'How so?' Suzanne asked.

'With Heather's death, and the other women's, the murderer reported them to Scotland Yard, described the cause of death, and the location of the bodies. All three were found in the park. Hyde Park. Whether they'd been killed there or not isn't known, but I believe the women were murdered in Whitechapel and their bodies transported to the park.'

'How has the murderer reported them and not been caught?' she asked.

'By letter, written on expensive stationary. I know a detective at Scotland Yard and he's provided me with all the information they have.'

'Are there any significant clues as to who the murderer might be?'

Henry debated answering. As far as he knew, no one but Adam Hendricks, his insider at Scotland Yard, knew what had been placed by Heather's body. A cufflink. One of his father's. Adam had shown it to him because the Beaufort insignia was engraved in the gold. Heather might have been in possession of it, or the murderer might have left it behind. He hadn't yet been informed if a cufflink had been left behind by the other bodies or not. Ultimately, Henry chose to keep that information to himself and shook his head. 'No.'

'When you go to Whitechapel at night, what are you hoping to discover?'

'Clues.'

She grinned. 'I figured that, but what precisely?'

'I'll know when I see it.' That's all he could hope for, to discover something or someone in the act.

'Is your detective friend searching there, too?'

'No, a death in Whitechapel, or one of a certain profession, doesn't interest Scotland Yard.'

'Why not?'

'Because if they investigated one, they'd have to investigate them all and that wouldn't leave any time for them to respond to reports of stolen baubles from wealthy homes after they've hosted a ball.' He knew that sounded insolent, but it was the truth.

'What do you mean? Stolen baubles?'

'Many hosts station servants at doors of their homes during balls on the off chance that a guest might attempt to sneak out with the family jewels, candlesticks, or other such treasure.'

'Oh, goodnight and God bless,' she muttered. 'Put that stuff away, or don't even have a party if that's what you're worried about.'

He didn't hide his grin. Couldn't. Her accent gave every sentence a sing-song cadence. 'I'm not worried.'

'I wasn't talking about you specifically. I was talking about the hosts.' Her shapely brows knitted over her eyes. 'Why would they host a ball if they are worried about someone stealing their belongings?'

He gave a slight shrug. 'A ball is one of the ways to show off family treasures.'

'So they want to show them off, but not have them stolen. If anyone were to ask me, I'd suggest that maybe, just maybe, if they let people go home at a decent time, they wouldn't need to worry so much about their belongings.'

'A decent time?' he questioned.

'Yes. This idea of eating supper at three o'clock in the morning—who, in their right mind, thinks that's a good idea? Babies get their days and nights mixed up, not adults. How do they get up and go to work in the mornings?'

'Most of them don't,' he said.

'I have discovered that,' she said. 'It is certainly a life-style for the elite.'

Once again, he agreed with her, yet attempted to defend his countrymen. 'It is mainly during the Season.'

She made a scoffing sound. 'I don't believe that and you don't either. After the Season are the post-Season balls, then the Christmas and New Year balls, then the pre-Season balls, and then, once again, it's the Season balls.'

He chuckled at the truths in her explanation. 'How long have you been in London?'

'Only a few weeks, but it didn't take me long to catch on to the pattern.' She grinned. 'Don't worry, though, we won't have to pretend for a full year of Seasons. With my help, you'll catch that killer. Hopefully, before he strikes again.'

Henry still wasn't convinced that a pretend engagement was the best of ideas, but he didn't want to be the reason for her reputation to be soiled. At the same time, he didn't want her any more deeply involved.

She sat quiet for a moment, looking at him thoughtfully, before she said, 'Everyone needs help at one time or another. If Clara and I hadn't had each other back home, after the war struck, neither of us would have made it through it all. I'm certain of that, and without Annabelle's help in asking Roger to send one of his ships to find us, we wouldn't be here.' Then with a slight shrug, she said, 'I suggest we start our plan as soon as possible.'

He still hadn't agreed to any plan, yet asked, 'As soon as possible?'

'Yes. Perhaps the Hampshires' ball. Elaine says it's one of the most anticipated ones.'

'The Viscountess Voss, Roger Hardgrove's mother, your sponsor,' he said, just to waste time before disappointing her with his answer.

'Yes, but it won't be an issue for me to drive with you instead. I've had Mr McCaffrey drive me to and from most of the balls I've attended. I know some might find that unconventional, but I don't mind being unconventional. I simply do not see a reason for Elaine, I mean, Lord and Lady Voss to drive all the way across town just to pick me up and then bring me back home.'

She might not mind being unconventional in travelling alone, but her actions could be deadly. No woman should be out alone right now. Hiram McCaffrey, Drew's butler and groom, was nearly the same age as Caleb. Though competent, Hiram wouldn't be much protection should someone decide to overcome her coach.

That was merely one more thing that conflicted with his need to inform her that they would not be creating a courtship between them. Not even a false one.

'I suppose I should be returning home,' she said. 'Some might think I've been here an inappropriate amount of time.'

He assumed she was referring to Elyse McCaffrey, Hiram's wife and Drew's housekeeper and cook. Much like Caleb's wife, Anna, his housekeeper and cook, Elyse was a stickler for rules and decorum. He'd been surprised that Anna hadn't sent Caleb in on the pretence of collecting the tea trolley, whereas in reality it would be to check on them considering the amount of time Suzanne had been here. Like Drew, he limited the number of staff in London to two. It kept life simpler, and he liked simple.

Rising to his feet, he said, 'I can imagine that some people didn't approve of you baking a cake and bringing it over, either.'

Her smile made her eyes sparkle. 'The cakes were already in the oven by the time Elyse realised I was in the kitchen. I explained to her that I had made two, one to keep and one to share, and how I used to do that back home. She is far too proper to tell me that for me to share one with you would be most inappropriate.' Suzanne stood and her smile brightened even more. 'However, once she tasted the cake, she thought giving it to your servants would be fine. She and your housekeeper are good friends.'

'I am aware of that, but you came to the front door,' he pointed out.

Her giggle was soft. 'I do hope I didn't cause Elyse to have a fit of vapours again.'

He held out an arm for her to rest her hand on while he walked her to the door. 'Again?'

She shrugged. 'Your customs take some getting used to.'

'I'm sure they do.'

'It was nothing bad. She steered me out of the kitchen upon catching me washing dishes, then caught me weeding the flower beds in the back garden. Evidently, *guests* are not to perform anything that might resemble a chore or work. Again, she is too proper to actually tell me that. She attempts to redirect my attention on to other activities, such as reading or embroidery. I enjoy both, but I'm not used to sitting idle. Even before Aunt Adelle died, taking care of everything around the house was up to me.'

Once again, he believed her every word. She was a unique woman. Beautiful and unique. He also believed that if there was one woman who could be his alibi, it would be her.

He didn't want to admit that her plan was growing on him, but it was. It could be exactly what he needed to be able to be in two places at once.

'I told Elyse that we formally met last night,' she whispered as they stepped into the hallway, 'but I don't believe that she was convinced that was enough for me to walk next door, cake or not. She's probably biting her nails waiting for me to return.'

He certainly didn't envy the housekeeper. Not in the least. However, he also had to admit that he was intrigued by Miss Suzanne Bishop. More intrigued than he'd ever been by a woman.

As they entered the hallway, he was sure ears were listening. 'Thank you for your visit, Miss Bishop, and for the cake, it was quite delicious.'

She grinned up at him, fully understanding his change of subject. 'You're welcome, I'm glad you enjoyed it.'

They walked the rest of the way to the door in silence and, once he opened the door for her, he said no more than what was necessary to bid her goodbye. He would find another time, well before tomorrow night, to inform her of his decision not to accept her offer of assistance.

It was too dangerous. He was too dangerous. Regrettably, because he'd like to get to know her better. If things were different he would do that, but right now, he needed to keep his focus on catching the murderer.

His family had been through enough lately and it was his job to protect them from more.

Suzanne had the distinct feeling that Henry hadn't bought into her plan of helping him and wasn't sure what to do about that. Her impulsive reactions were not always the best, so she forced herself to keep her mouth closed and nodded her response to his goodbye, but as he stepped back inside to close the door, her resolve broke and she caught his arm with one hand. 'I was considering attending the Exposition again this afternoon. Would you care to join me? It's quite the sight to see.'

'That it is,' he said, not looking directly at her.

Afraid he was about to decline her offer, she tried harder. 'Say three o'clock?'

His grin was truly an amazing sight to see, because he acted as if he didn't smile very often, saved them for only certain times or people. He bit his lips together and glanced down at the floor, before looking up at her. 'I believe I could fit that in my day. I will have my carriage ready and call on you at three.'

'Very good. Until then, Henry.' She released his arm and then hitched up the hem of her skirt as she pivoted and hurried down the steps. Between now and three, she had to think of a solid way to convince him that her plan would work.

She wholeheartedly did not believe that he'd murdered anyone. He was far too kind. Just looking at him made her heart pitter-patter, which was highly unusual. However, she'd never met a man who needed her help before. He certainly did. If he wasn't willing to let her help him find the real killer, she'd do it on her own.

There was one other thing that she was certain about.

He was a complicated man. A very handsome one. She had been to the Exposition a couple of times already, yet was overly excited to go again.

With him.

For the next few hours Suzanne balanced her thoughts between all he'd told her about the murders, his sister, father and mother, with what she could do to convince him that he needed her help.

All he'd told her made her sympathise for his sister and him, for the position his sister had found herself in. It was also making her think more deeply about her own family, about her mother and what had driven her into living the life she had, being a flower in the garden.

If Aunt Adelle had known her mother's circumstances, she'd taken it to her grave. Suzanne had questioned her aunt, several times, but Aunt Adelle had stuck to the same story. That Adelle's father, Jonas Bishop, had been heavily invested in the building of the railroads across the nation and that when Adelle had been a young woman, her parents and sister had taken a train west to explore the expansion. Her parents had returned, but her sister, Jane, hadn't. She'd met and married a man working on the railroad and had stayed out west.

Her parents had not been happy about that and had disowned Jane. Years later, after their parents had died, Adelle had attempted to find her sister, but never had been able to find hide or hair.

Adelle had said that she'd given up hope of ever finding her sister, but had also refused to move out of their family home in Virginia, so that if Jane ever came home, she'd be there. Adelle had lived off the money left by her father's death her entire life, never having married herself. She claimed that she'd been shocked when she had received a letter from Rose that had stated a great-niece of hers had been left an orphan in Missouri and enquired if Adelle would take responsibility for the child.

Apparently, per Rose's letter, a man who had been connected with the railroad knew of the family connection. It was all hearsay, with no real proof, but Adelle had said she hadn't needed proof. She had immediately written back to Rose, saying to send Suzanne to Virginia.

Suzanne was grateful to Adelle for taking her in, accepting her as family, but she couldn't help but question if they truly had been family. It made her think harder about going to Missouri when the war was over. Whatever the truth might be, it was worth knowing.

Would knowing more make a difference in her life?

She'd spent most of her life telling herself to look forward, not backwards, but discovering the truth was moving forward.

Wasn't it?

There were things standing in her way. The war, her current location, and the money she'd need to travel back to America and then on to Missouri.

She had hope that the war would end soon, not only for herself, but her fellow Americans. Henry had said that he'd have Mr Winterbourne read her manuscript. That alone was worth any help he needed from her. If Mr Winterbourne liked it and published it, he might want more stories from her and that could provide her with an ongoing source of income.

Aunt Adelle had been a stickler that every woman should have her own source of income.

Due to the generosity of the men that both Annabelle and Clara had married, she currently didn't need to worry about finances. She had a safe place to live, food to eat and a wardrobe that was larger than she'd ever owned.

That thought sent her to the mirror, where she questioned if she should change her dress before Henry arrived. The yellow gown she wore was extraordinarily lovely with its gold stitching and white piping, and she certainly hadn't soiled it, but women here didn't need a reason to change their clothes. Lady Voss had changed her gown for every meal when they'd been at Roger's country estate, Clairmount, before coming to London.

Suzanne walked across the bedroom to the wardrobe and opened the door. A lilac gown called to her. Its simplicity made it perfect for a visit to the Exposition. The skirt wasn't layered or covered with rows of lace, nor was it so wide it needed a bustle, which got in the way of riding in a carriage. It did have short puffed sleeves, a fitted bodice, and a matching hat that made it as fashionable as some of the more elaborate gowns.

Decision made, she quickly changed gowns, hoping that Henry would like it. That was odd for her. Then again, she'd never gone anywhere with a man before.

Still standing at the mirror, she positioned and pinned a hat that matched the gown at a slight, elegant angle on her head. The soft lilac colour was enhanced by a deeper purple ribbon tied around the brim of the hat. All in all, she found the ensemble quite fetching, especially since it included a matching lilac parasol.

There were times, like now, where she wondered if she should pinch herself, just to make sure that she wasn't dreaming. That she and Clara weren't still back in Virginia, trying to survive. Those had been months of misery, but neither of them had voiced that, because neither of them had believed that would help.

Suzanne had seen the worry and fear on Clara's face daily and had vowed to never let her own show. That had been wearing, crippling at times, but had also been what had made her surge forward each and every day, whether that had been searching for basic necessities, or information pertaining to the war.

Being rescued had not been something she'd prayed for, because she hadn't believed that anyone could save them.

She had to wonder if that was how Henry felt. That no one could help him. That he was completely on his own.

There was a driving force inside her to prove him wrong. She was proof that miracles happened. To her way of thinking, she'd been saved twice: once as a child by Rose sending her to Aunt Adelle and, again, by Roger sending Captain Harris to find her and Clara.

It seemed only fair that it was her turn to save someone and that someone could be Henry.

Chapter Five

The clock struck three at the same time a knock sounded on the door. Suzanne was in the front parlour, and had seen the black coach arrive out of the front window. Still not fully used to having servants take care of certain tasks, she had to force herself to remain still until Hiram had answered the front door, then walked to the doorway of the parlour to inform her that Henry had arrived.

'Thank you, Hiram,' she said and collected the parasol she'd set on the chair near the parlour doorway.

Though a few men back home had shown an interest in her, she had never been courted. Henry wasn't courting her, either. She had been the one to ask him to attend the Exposition with her. That was a first.

She hadn't reciprocated any of the attention from men back home because she knew better. Knew how to stay aloof. Men, marriage, had never been something she sought. Aunt Adelle had never married and had highly suggested that it was far healthier and more rewarding than waiting on a man hand and foot. She claimed that women had very few freedoms and should never consider giving any of them up for someone else.

Suzanne felt that her aunt's thoughts had been very logical and a good fit for her as well, which was why she'd obtained her teaching licence as soon as she'd completed her schooling. It had been difficult for Hampton to keep teachers. They often married mid-year, or left town. She'd promised the school board that she wouldn't marry, wouldn't abandon her students, and hadn't for over four years. Right up until the school house had burned along with the rest of the town.

'Good afternoon,' Henry greeted from the hall as she stepped out of the parlour.

All of her thinking since they'd departed on his front step this morning had been normal, for her thoughts always ran a bit wild, but seeing him had a different effect on her. It caused a rapid pounding of her heart and a quick shortness of breath.

For years, she'd prided herself on being practical and for never allowing her emotions to overrule her sensibilities, and suddenly wondered why she couldn't control some things when it came to him. Was it because he was the most handsome man she'd ever seen? Or was it because she hoped his publishing house would buy her book? Or was it because, for the first time in her life, she was lonely?

That realisation hadn't happened until this very moment. Back home, even after Aunt Adelle had passed away, she'd had Clara and Annabelle. Then her students, which had helped tremendously when Clara had married her first husband, Mark, and later when Annabelle had left town.

Even after arriving here, she'd had Clara, but the past few weeks, she'd had no one. The McCaffreys were kind people, but as Drew's servants, there was a barrier between her and them than she'd never experienced and didn't know how to cross.

Perhaps that was why she'd become so engrossed with Henry. She was lonely.

'Is something amiss?' he asked.

Pulling her thoughts together, she shook her head while searching for an excuse to have been staring at him. 'No, nothing's amiss. I was just wondering if I needed my parasol.'

'We can always leave it in the coach if you decide it's not needed,' he suggested.

'You are correct,' she said, doing her best to hide her sudden attack of nervousness. He looked so sophisticated and manly. His trousers were grey, his shirt white. Both were rather unnoticeable compared to his shimmering gold vest and burgundy-coloured frock coat and matching cravat. He held himself with such confidence and nobility that, for a split second, she questioned how she'd ever thought that others might truly believe he'd be engaged to her. She certainly was not of his class and never would be.

'Shall we?' he asked.

She nodded. Both to him and to herself. Another thing Aunt Adelle had insisted upon was a healthy amount of self-righteousness. Just enough to remember that everyone has a choice to believe in their own abilities. Suzanne did believe in herself and believed she could pretend to be engaged to him, despite her lack of social standing.

They spoke of the Exposition, mainly which building they would visit as they exited the house and settled themselves inside his coach. The leather curtains were pulled back, letting the sunshine and fresh air fill the interior.

'Is there an exhibit you have not seen yet?' Henry asked, continuing their conversation as the coach began to roll along the street.

'No, but many of them I've merely walked past,' she replied. 'The crowds were too large to get close enough to actually see anything.'

'Hopefully, we'll be able to see some of those today, but I'm sure it will still be crowded. The newspapers are touting the attendance numbers daily. It appears to be a destination for people from around the world.'

'I've read that as well.' Once again being able to read a daily newspaper was another significant shift in her life lately. She would never take such simple things for granted ever again. 'What are you looking forward to seeing today?'

Seated across from her, his shoulders squared, his face clean shaven, he stared at her with those dark eyes for a quiet, still amount of time. She wanted to know what he was thinking, but at the same time, felt a slight blush on her cheeks and a quiver in her stomach, knowing that he was appraising her. Her lilac gown, perhaps, or the hat upon her head, or perhaps, he was seeking something deeper. Her thoughts, like she was his.

'I have nothing specific in mind,' he finally said.

It was her turn to eye him and try to figure out what might interest him the most. 'Perhaps you'd like to see the chess tournament. It's quite interesting to see how thoughtfully and methodically the players choose their moves. Or the machinery and industrial displays. They have a cable that can be laid beneath the water for telegraphing and a unique machine that prints designs on wallpaper, as well as one that weaves rugs. Or the art gallery. It is quite extensive and covers displays from several mediums.'

'All of that sounds interesting,' he said. 'I suggest we simply start at the western dome, near the piano player, and make our way through as many exhibits as possible before we grow tired.'

She grinned at him, wondering if he knew that the piano player was a favourite of hers. 'They are selling sets of stereograms taken of all the displays and it's been reported that those photos are delivered daily to the Queen so she can view the exhibits from her seclusion.'

'I've heard that.'

'Have you seen the stereograms?'

'No, I have not. Have you?'

'Yes, they have some for people to sample before purchasing. When looking through the stereoscope, you see two identical images, and they are three dimensional. It's quite fascinating.'

'Have you purchased a set?'

'No, I was just curious as to what they looked like.'

'You are a curious person, aren't you? Interested in a variety of subjects and topics.'

'I have to be,' she replied.

He lifted a brow. 'Have to be?'

'Yes. I am—was—a teacher, back home. Therefore, I had to be curious enough to learn bits and pieces about nearly everything so I could entice the children to want to learn more. Teaching isn't about telling children what they need to know, it's about exposing them to a variety of things and allowing them to discover what they want to know more about.'

The corners of his mouth turned up in a slight smile. 'You enjoyed teaching.'

A soft fluttering happened inside her. 'I did.'

'And you miss it.'

There was no shame in admitting that she missed it, even if she wasn't interested in returning to the profession. 'I did.'

'Did that end when the war started?'

He wouldn't know all of what happened, nor was she interested in telling a tale that she didn't know the end to. 'Not right away. Not until the town was attacked and burned. I believe it will be rebuilt some day.'

'Do you want to be a part of that rebuilding?'

'Perhaps.'

His grin grew and once again a flutter happened inside her. More than a flutter. His features were well defined, but not harsh, and when he smiled they merged into a face that, for a man, could be considered beautiful. At the same time, he held somewhat of an intimidating presence, one that said he couldn't be easily cajoled.

That flutter inside her could be a warning to watch her step, because she had never gone up against someone like him before. No one, not a single person, had made her feel topsy-turvy before.

Her breathing grew tight, short, and she glanced out the window, watched the unending rows of shops and buildings flow past. She did want to help him, for she liked helping others and was good at it. She could easily cover for his absences at balls, but if he didn't want that, it would never happen.

'I apologise. I did not intend to bring up sad memories,' he said. 'I don't believe that I can even imagine the difficulties you have faced.'

She turned, saw the sincerity that was now softening his features. 'No need to apologise. I have more wonderful memories of Hampton than of sad ones.'

He gave her a slight nod, then said, 'Tell me one of your good memories.'

'About what?' she asked. 'Teaching?'

'If you like.'

At that moment, she liked the way he looked at her. With interest. Not because of her accent or looks, but real interest in her. Who she was. What her memory might be. She had several, and chose one she thought he might enjoy.

'Well, I had this young student, Seth Wayne. He was in the earliest grade and on the small side, and therefore not always included in some of the games the older children played during recess. One day, while exploring the yard around the school alone, he discovered a small animal skull. Quite excited, he brought it over for me to look at.'

In her mind, Suzanne could still see Seth's small face, with his big blue eyes sparkling and his fuzzy blond curls fluttering in the breeze. 'I told him that he'd made quite a discovery, and that I had a book inside the classroom that would help us identify what type of animal the skull was from. I then called the end of recess so all of the children could see his find.'

'You took the skull into the school building?' Henry asked.

'Of course. It was simply a skull, bleached white from the sun—furthermore, it was a way for Seth to be included by all of the children. With the help of the book, the students assisted Seth in determining that it was a rabbit skull. He was very proud of his find and I told him that perhaps he'd grow up to be an archaeologist.'

Suzanne had to pinch her lips to contain a giggle. 'He then asked me, "What's that?" and I explained that an archaeologist was someone who studied history by excavating artifacts such as bones and identifying them. To which he quickly replied, "But, Miss Bishop, I already did that".'

Henry laughed. 'He had a justifiable point.'

She had so many wonderful memories like that, of things the children had said and done. 'Yes, he did and, before long, the entire town was calling him the young archaeologist.' Even though Seth was halfway around the world and she had no way of knowing how he was doing, in her heart she chose to believe he was still alive and well. She leaned across the space separating her and Henry and whispered, 'They called him the little archaeologist at first, but I encouraged them to say young instead, due to his size.'

Henry had leaned closer to her and whispered, 'I see.'

'Everyone agreed with me, other than Mrs Leeds. She and her husband owned the dry goods store and she told me that I shouldn't encourage any child to claim that they were something that they were not.'

'I must know what you said to that,' Henry said.

'Well...' her face grew warm '... I told her that I was sorry.'

'You did?'

'Yes. Very sorry that no one had ever told her that she was pleasant as a child.'

Henry had spent the past few hours going over options in his head and, ultimately, came to the conclusion that a fake engagement was his best option when it came to keeping her reputation intact and in finding the killer. It was also the only way he could make sure that she was safe. That had become a very integral part of this entire scenario.

He also spent a lot of time convincing himself that he was not attracted to her.

But that was a lie.

He was attracted to her and was enjoying every bit of her story telling. How could he not? She was so animated and so likeable.

There was one other thing that he had to admit. His ability to smile at her didn't feel awkward. His life of late had not been one where happiness, and smiles, came easily. With her, they simply formed, not only on the outside. She made him smile on the inside. He'd nearly forgotten how that felt.

'I must admit,' he said, leaning back in his chair, 'that I never had a teacher who would have taken a skull that I'd found on the ground inside for me to examine.'

She'd leaned back in her seat and tilted her head slightly sideways. 'I find that extremely sad. Learning can't just come from books. It comes from life, from experiences.'

'I agree with you and I think your students were extremely lucky to have had you as their teacher.'

Her cheeks pinkened slightly. 'Thank you.'

The warmth inside him grew stronger and, when Caleb opened the door, Henry felt the warmth of Suzanne's hand spread up his arm as he escorted her out of the coach.

The area was crowded with people, coaches, carriages

and men on horseback, so he held on to her hand until they were clear of the traffic.

'My goodness, it's busy here today,' she said.

'It is.' He grasped her elbow to keep her close as they manoeuvred through the crowd and into the building.

The inside was nearly as crowded, and full of people from all walks of life, including a few that were anything but savoury and who clearly noticed Suzanne in her pale purple dress and fashionable hat. A protectiveness rose up in him and he walked closer to her side, while casting looks in several directions, letting several know they had best take their interests elsewhere. 'Who has accompanied you on your previous visits?'

'Hiram and Elyse,' she replied. 'The piano player is this way.'

He considered himself a gentleman when it came to women, but not all of his thoughts right now could be considered gentlemanly. Her nearness was causing more than warmth and protectiveness in him. The fresh, flowery scent that drifted off her couldn't be ignored. It went straight into his nostrils and the impulses created inside him flared with desire.

He released her elbow and placed a palm against the centre of her back, allowing them to walk even closer. A dangerous act considering the urges that were building with every step.

'Have you heard the piano player before?' she asked.

He had, but he chose to shake his head simply because of the excited shine in her eyes.

'You are going to enjoy it,' she said. 'I certainly did.'

What she had was an advantage over him. He'd escorted beautiful women before, to numerous and various events and celebrations, but Suzanne Bishop was different. Unique, and her charm was only surpassed by her beauty.

She was also at ease, fully enjoying her surroundings, whereas his every sense was heightened and she was the reason for it.

'Listen,' she said as the music began to override the noise of the crowd.

He smiled down at her and guided her closer to the stage where the pianist was performing. The music filling the air seemed to fill her. She began to gently sway to the beat of the music. Her eyes were closed and the smile on her face was one of pure pleasure.

They stood there throughout the recital, her swaying to the music and him considering what an odd circumstance this was for him. He'd attended the Exposition previously out of necessity. It was expected for someone of his rank and peerage, and to see the few displays that pertained to the businesses within his family's holdings.

There was no reason for him to be here today, other than for her.

When the clapping ended and the pianist left the stage, Suzanne looked up at him with a very dazzling set of eyes. 'Now we shall see something of interest to you.'

'This was of interest to me.'

She looped an arm through his. 'You tolerated that because you are a very polite man.'

He found no reason to argue that point as they walked away from the stage. 'The pianist was very good.'

'That he was,' she agreed.

'Do you play?'

'No.' A tiny frown formed between her eyes as she looked up at him. 'Do you?'

'No, but there is a piano at Beaufort and both of my sisters play.'

'Sisters?' She stopped and stepped in front of him. 'You didn't tell me that you had sisters.'

He grinned at her. 'You didn't ask.'

She shook her head, while asking. 'Older or younger? What are their names?'

'Younger. Rosemary is twenty-one and Violet is eighteen.'

'Are they in London? Where do they live? Are they married?'

With what was becoming a permanent grin when she was near on his face, he remained silent.

'Why aren't you answering me?'

'Because I was waiting until you had asked all of your questions.'

'That's not how it works,' she said. 'I ask, you answer, I ask again, you answer again. It's called questions and answers.'

With her arm still linked to his, he began walking again. 'Is that a game Americans play?'

'It's called conversation,' she said.

'Well, then, no, they are not in London. Violet lives at Beaufort. Rosemary is married to Judd Woodsworth and they live at Hemlock, an estate near Beaufort. Violet will be wed to Carter Moores next spring and they will move in with his family, who live several miles away from Beaufort.'

'Is that why they aren't in London for the Season? Because they are married and engaged?'

'Yes.'

'So, I was correct in assuming that women only attend balls in order to snag a husband.'

'Why had you assumed that?' he asked.

'Because it was obvious, for the younger women that is. All they talk about are the bachelors and their titles.'

'Is it?'

She leaned closer, so their upper arms touched. 'Yes, and you are on the list of eligible bachelors.'

Chapter Six

Henry was fully aware of his status and the goals of the unwed ladies looking to snag a titled man. He'd avoided being snagged or even enticed and would continue to for years to come. His saving grace had been that there had never been another woman like Suzanne. Despite the circumstances and all he knew, he liked her. It was impossible not to.

'Does that bother you?' she asked. 'To be so sought after?'

'It might if I was interested in such things, but I'm not. I find myself quite busy with family and business issues.' Pressure to marry had been put upon him for years, but since his father's stroke and subsequent death, his mother had eased off the subject. 'How about you? You are sought after. Men stand queuing to sign your dance card.'

She smiled at him. 'Our agreement will benefit both of us in that aspect. Not being expected to produce a dance card will be heavenly.' She pointed ahead of them. 'Oh, look. The queue to see the inside of the train isn't very long. I haven't seen that yet, have you?'

'No, I haven't.' He was still questioning if he should accept her offer, but her reply had struck curiosity. 'You don't like having men sign your dance cards?'

Leaning closer, she said, 'I don't like men.' She pulled him towards the queue to see the train. 'Do you travel by train very often?'

'Occasionally, when I'm required to visit my business interests near the Channel.' He lowered his voice to ask, 'Why don't you like men?'

'The only time I was on a train was when I moved from Missouri to Virginia. It was a long time ago so I don't remember much about it.' She then shrugged and whispered, 'I've never held a lot of trust in men.'

'So you were seven the last time you were on a train?' he responded first, then asked, 'Yet, you're willing to trust me?'

She eyed him for a moment, as if surprised he remembered she'd told him how old she'd been when she went to live with her aunt, or maybe she was questioning if she should trust him.

'Yes, seven,' she said, 'but Aunt Adelle told me that my grandfather had loved trains and she had a small model train that had been his.' Glancing at the locomotive, she added, 'I'm trusting you because we will both have something to gain. I see our agreement as a partnership. I gave it considerable thought before suggesting it.'

He nodded, 'I believe you did.' Then, he asked, 'How big was the model train?'

Her face took on shine and her eyes shimmered as she went on to tell him about the model and how she used to pretend there were little people inside the train. That set off a variety of topics that they discussed while not only viewing the train, but many other displays. She spoke passionately about many things and her knowledge on various subjects was unsurpassable.

Their conversation didn't return to their fake engagement and he didn't mind that. The idea had grown on him, yet he had always been cautious and certainly would need to be in this instance.

Hours later, when they walked beneath the large tower clock run by weights and on display by its maker, Henry was surprised to see how late it had grown. That was also when he noted the crowds had diminished and even some of the exhibitors had left their display areas.

Time had ceased to exist as the two of them had ambled through the massive buildings with towering, massive domed ceilings. He couldn't remember a day he'd enjoyed more and credited that to her. Her enjoyment of seeing each and every display had been contagious. He'd been as interested as her, or perhaps it would be better to admit that she'd made every display interesting. Even things he'd thought he'd have no interest in, but had once she'd started talking about them.

A sense of disappointment filled him as he said, 'I believe we are among the few stragglers and need to leave before we are locked inside for the night.'

Her eyes lit up and she bit her bottom lip before whispering, 'Wouldn't that be amazing? We could explore until we got tired and then sleep in the train. The seats looked quite comfortable.'

He chuckled at her enthusiasm and couldn't deny that spending the night with her sounded very adventurous and dangerous, considering his attraction to her that had continued to grow all day. Therefore, he pointed out, 'And be arrested in the morning, ending up in Newgate.'

She let out an exaggerated sigh. 'You might be right.'

'Might be?' he asked, leading her towards the exit with his hand on her back.

She glanced up at him. 'I suspect you are correct and it's my goal to keep you out of prison, not have you sent to it.'

He'd nearly forgotten about all of his issues today.

'Furthermore, I am hungry,' she said. 'Aren't you?'

'I am,' he admitted.

'Good,' she said. 'You can join me for the evening meal. Elyse is an excellent cook and there's rum cake for dessert.'

Before he could respond, someone shouted his name.

Suzanne glanced up at Henry, then at the man who had shouted his name and was walking towards them. There was no outward sign of disgust on Henry's face, but she felt him stiffen and that alone made her question who the man might be and why Henry didn't like him.

'I planned on stopping by the house this evening,' the approaching man said to Henry. 'See if you were up to visiting a gentleman's club with me.'

Henry's lips pursed in a tight line as the man stopped next to them. 'What are you doing in London?'

'I have some business in town,' the man replied, while staring at her. 'And decided to have a look at the Exposition while here.'

There were some people Suzanne instantly knew she didn't want to spend time with and that's how it was with this man. He was younger than Henry, younger than her also, and thin. Very thin and he had a shifty set of eyes, which had her instincts saying he wasn't to be trusted. For all she knew, he could be the murderer.

'This is my cousin Bart—Bartholomew Vogal,' Henry said to her.

Cousin! Oh, goodnight and God bless. Here she was thinking he was some character who was up to no good and he was Henry's family. That's why she shouldn't jump to conclusions.

'Bart,' Henry continued, 'may I introduce Miss Bishop.'

The man removed his light grey bowler hat that matched his suit and held it in his hand as he gave her an exaggerated and formal bow.

'It's a pleasure, my lady,' he said, as he straightened and held a hand out towards her.

Suzanne then understood exactly what she found disconcerting about Bart. She'd seen young boys acting as if they were older than their age. That's what Bart was doing, pretending to be sophisticated, mature beyond his age. It wasn't working for him, he looked far too young. However, because he did remind her of some of her past students, she chose to be lenient and didn't correct him on the way he'd addressed her. She also chose not to offer her hand because he might take the liberty of kissing the back of it. With a nod, she said, 'Mr Vogal.'

'Bart, if you please.' He grinned, showing a row of straight white teeth, and let his arrogance take another step by saying, 'It's rare to see my cousin in the company of a lady. Especially one so lovely. That's usually my department.'

'How long will you be in town?' Henry asked.

'Not long.' Bart slid both hands into his trouser pockets as he rocked on his heels. 'Just arrived this afternoon.'

Suzanne felt the need to keep her gaze averted, due to

how Bart kept looking at her and wiggling a brow. She was having a hard time getting past her first impression. Family or not, Bart was not very likeable.

'Where are you staying?' Henry asked.

'An hotel,' Bart said. 'I didn't want to intrude upon you.'

'You will check out of the hotel and go straight to my house,' Henry said. 'I'll expect you there within the hour.'

'I—'

'Within the hour, Bart,' Henry interrupted.

Suzanne couldn't stop herself from glancing between the two men. Animosity was clearly building between them and she had no doubt who would win in any contest.

Henry looked at her, gave her a glimmer of a smile and then put pressure on her back to step forward.

He didn't bid farewell to his cousin and she didn't look back as they walked to the coach that had rolled to a stop. Caleb had already climbed down and held open the door for them.

Once inside, Henry watched his cousin out of the window until the coach turned the corner. 'I apologise,' he said. 'I won't be able to accept your invitation for this evening's meal.'

'No need to apologise,' she replied. 'I can tell your cousin's arrival was a surprise.'

He shook his head. 'A frustrating surprise. My cousin has been quite coddled since birth, which increased after his father, my uncle, died, and now that has resulted in Bart rarely, if ever, accepting responsibility for his own actions. He's too young and immature to be in London alone.'

'Is that why you'd prefer that he stays with you rather than at an hotel?'

'Yes, and it is why I will be taking him back to his home first thing in the morning.'

The intimidating persona she'd imagined Henry had was coming through and a part of her felt sorry for Bart. The younger man's attitude was no match against his older cousin's, she was sure of that.

She was also sure that the disappointment filling her needed to be contained. They'd had a wonderful day and she hadn't wanted it to end. She glanced out the window at the sky that was streaked with yellow and orange as the sun slowly lowered to meet the horizon, where it would disappear. Perhaps it was best that their time together ended now, before supper, because she needed to do some serious thinking. She was feeling far too many different things when it came to Henry.

She still wasn't convinced that he thought her idea of their pretend courtship would work and needed some time to come up with a way to prove that to him.

In the twenty-four hours between when Henry had brought her home after the Exposition and now, she had looked out a window towards his house well over one hundred times. Mayhap two hundred. First it had been in curiosity as to what might be happening between Henry and Bart, but this morning, after she'd seen them ride away, she'd kept checking, hoping to see a sign that Henry had returned.

He hadn't.

She truly wished she could talk to Annabelle or Clara about the things she was feeling for Henry, but even if they were close at hand, she'd have a hard time describing what was happening inside her.

It was quite ridiculous, this infatuation she'd acquired when it came to him, but the fact was, she couldn't deny that she liked him. Liked him more than she'd ever liked a man in her entire life. Today had confirmed that, for she'd miss him. Missed knowing he was next door. Missed knowing that she wouldn't spy him from afar.

A heavy sigh escaped her and she crossed the room, then sat down on the bed.

Why was that? Why was she feeling so much for him?

When he'd dropped her off yesterday evening, he'd stated that he would collect her manuscript upon his return to London and personally deliver it to Mr Winterbourne.

That should have thrilled her, for it was what she'd wanted. It did make her happy, except that it felt as though she was getting something for nothing. This was meant to be a partnership, her help in return for his.

She couldn't accept his help without giving some in return.

A knock on her door interrupted her thoughts. It also increased her heart rate—had Henry had returned?

Hiram was on the other side of the door. 'Excuse me, miss. You have a visitor.'

'I do?' Suzanne attempted to remain calm as she asked, 'Who might it be?'

'The Duchess of Hollingford, miss,' Hiram said. 'I've shown her into the sitting room.'

A sense of dread washed over her, yet she lifted her chin and walked through the open doorway. 'Thank you, Hiram.'

The Duchess of Hollingford, with her permanent

frown wrinkles, was standing near the fireplace, examining the gilded framed picture of Drew and Annabelle from the mantel when Suzanne walked into the room. 'My Lady,' she said, with a slight bow, knowing it was expected.

The Duchess replaced the frame on the mantel. 'Miss Bishop. I do hope it wasn't too late to call upon you.'

'No, not at all,' Suzanne replied. She might not be of noble birth, but she knew how to play hostess. 'Would you care for a cup of tea?'

'No, thank you. I only require a moment of your time.'

Suzanne waved a hand to the cream-coloured sofa. 'Please.' She waited until the woman took a seat before sitting down in the opposite chair.

'I'm sure you've found London different from America,' the Duchess said, folding her white-gloved hands in her lap. 'Very different.'

'The scenery is different,' Suzanne replied, withholding her opinion about other things.

'Well, my dear…' the Duchess lifted her double chin high '…due to you being new to London, I felt it necessary to take it upon myself to see to your well-being.'

'As you can see,' Suzanne said pointedly, 'I am fine.'

The other woman's smile was far from genuine. 'It has been brought to my attention that you are residing here, alone.'

'I am not alone. Mr and Mrs McCaffrey reside here as well.'

'The McCaffreys are servants.'

Suzanne told herself to not let her feathers get ruffled. 'I consider them friends.'

'That's quite impossible, my dear. As is you residing here alone. I am here to let you know that I will be contacting Lady Voss and requesting that you either reside at her residence or go and stay with...' she cleared her throat slightly '...one of your American friends.'

Goodnight and God bless, who did this woman think she was? 'Why?'

'Surely, even as an American, you understand how improper it is for you to be living alone?'

And that right there was what this was all about. Suzanne leaned forward in her chair. Met the woman eyeball for eyeball. 'There is nothing improper about where I am living.'

Setting her chin firmly, the Duchess said, 'I assure you there is; society agrees with me.'

Who exactly was society? Suzanne wanted to know, but refrained from asking because it didn't matter.

Wiggling in her seat while stiffening her spine, the Duchess continued, 'I chose to give you the opportunity to move without me asking Lady Voss to see to the event and I'm sure we will both agree that we can keep this conversation between the two of us.'

Suzanne doubted the woman had ever kept anything to herself. Outsider or not, she wouldn't be bullied, nor told what to do. Furthermore, she didn't like the Duchess. The woman was too big for her breeches, that's what Aunt Adelle would have said. 'All you needed to do was ask,' Suzanne said.

A slow smile grew on the Duchess's face as she nodded. 'Thank you, my dear. I was hoping you'd be agreeable.'

Suzanne smiled in return, mainly because the other woman thought she'd won. She hadn't. There was too much of Aunt Adelle roaming about in her head for that. 'You could have even asked me that night,' Suzanne said.

'I would have assured you that I do not trouble myself with gossip, so wouldn't have mentioned seeing your daughter and her friend outside in the gazebo.'

The Duchess wheezed while sucking in air.

'Instead, you chose to insinuate to others that Henry and I had been outside for more than a breath of fresh air and now you are attempting to tell me where I can live, and with whom.'

'I am merely trying to protect your reputation,' the Duchess stated.

'No, you are not. Had that been the case, you wouldn't have made mention of Henry and I being outside.'

'The Earl is only toying with you, Miss Bishop. When he marries, it will be to a woman of noble blood.' Sticking her nose in the air, the Duchess added, 'Not a foreigner.'

Therein lay the real reason she was here. She wanted Henry for her daughter. For one of them, she had several. Suzanne wasn't exactly sure what struck her right then. It could have been thoughts of how Aunt Adelle would have responded, but something inside her stung. She stood and did her best to keep her tongue civil. 'Thank you for your visit. I'll have Hiram escort you to your coach.'

The Duchess glared at her for a moment, then stood. 'I wasn't going to mention it, but there have been some unexplained and quite dastardly deeds that have happened recently and—'

'I refuse to listen to idle gossip,' Suzanne interrupted.

'It is more than gossip. Three women of ill repute have been murdered, which isn't out of the ordinary. Women in their profession rarely live to old age, rightfully so.'

Suzanne balled her hands into fists. If felt as if the Duchess was talking about her mother, though that wasn't possible. She'd never told anyone, not even Clara or Annabelle, about her mother and the Flower Garden. 'Rightfully so?'

'Yes. Being attacked or murdered is a chance they take.'

The Duchess not only sounded unkind, she sounded cold-blooded. 'Those women are human beings. Often put in circumstances beyond their control.'

Nose held high, the Duchess tsked before saying, 'Sympathising with such unsavoury women is most unladylike.'

'I'd say being so cold-blooded is unladylike.'

The Duchess glared at her. 'I dare say you Americans are uncouth.'

'I dare say you English are downright rude and prudes to boot.'

The Duchess drew in a deep breath. 'I did not come here to exchange insults.'

'Why exactly did you come?' Suzanne knew the answer, so she continued, 'To warn me off Henry? To tell me that he murdered those women? I can assure you that he didn't. I happen to know that Henry was not in the vicinity of Whitechapel on the nights those girls were murdered.'

'How could you possibly know that?'

'Because I was with him.' Then, because she was about as furious as she'd ever been, she added, 'We're engaged.'

The Duchess opened her mouth, but didn't speak, instead merely sucked in air.

Suzanne felt a chill ripple over her entire being. What

had she just done? Having little choice to change anything, she gave a curt nod. 'Hiram will see you out.'

At the door, she waved for Hiram to escort the Duchess outside, then hurried up the stairs and shut herself in her room.

Chapter Seven

Henry and his Aunt Minerva had never seen eye to eye and this time was no different. If she wasn't such a fool when it came to her son, she would be happy that he'd been hauled home before he'd caused any problems. Instead, she'd defended Bart by saying she'd sent him to London to look into a few business dealings.

That had been a lie. They had no businesses or dealings. But for the sake of all the family businesses, Henry didn't want to alienate family. As the second son, his Uncle Emmet hadn't inherited the wealth that his father had, nor had he chosen to make a life on his own for himself and his family. Instead, he'd begged his older brother to allow him to oversee a section of Vogal investments. One had been the milliner's manufacturing company that Henry had already spent years working to make profitable and a safe, healthy place for employees again.

Another had been the publishing house that had been nearly drained of all its resources.

His father had already been too ill to even understand the disarray that Emmet had caused and Henry had seen no reason to burden his father by telling him the issues that he'd uncovered.

Both companies were now thriving and Henry knew that Minerva expected they'd be turned over to Bart to oversee. Henry had already informed her that if that was to ever happen, it would only be after Bart could prove he'd matured and become a responsible adult.

That still hadn't happened. From the moment he'd arrived at his house, after checking out of the hotel, Bart had acted like an insolent adolescent.

'I apologise if you believe I'm being harsh,' Henry told his aunt. 'I assure you that my concerns take all family members into consideration. It's my duty to see that everyone has all of their needs met. At the present time, all dealings and issues with any holdings are my responsibility.'

'I'm aware of that, Henry,' Minerva said, huffing out an exaggerated sigh. 'But you have to see Bart's side. He's a grown man and wants to provide for his family.'

In Henry's opinion, eighteen did not make a grown man—furthermore, if Bart was a grown man and if he had those ambitions, he'd be looking to do something besides spending his family's monthly allotment by pretending to be rich. 'Perhaps at some point in time, when he proves himself competent, I'll assign Bart business duties, but until then he does not have permission to discuss any dealings other than with me.'

Clearly angry, Minerva narrowed her green eyes at him from where she sat on the edge of the orange brocade sofa in her drawing room. The house had been built for them—Emmet and Minerva—on the edge of Beaufort property when they had married. His own father, Edward Vogal, the Fifth Earl of Beaufort, had known that his younger brother would never branch out on his own, even back then. He'd said as much, more than once, but, as the older brother, had also felt obligated to provide for everyone in the family.

Henry knew that feeling well.

'How is he supposed to prove himself if you don't give him a business to run?' Minerva asked.

'If you recall, I have given him ample opportunities, of which he has not followed through on a single one.'

'Those were jobs for a child,' she insisted.

Henry held his tongue when he'd wanted to point out that even as a child Bart hadn't been capable of overseeing anything. Not even a pet. Several dogs and horses had been brought over to Beaufort after Bart had tired of them and begged for a different one. He could also point out the times he'd arranged to have Bart employed by one of the family investments, farms and companies, only to have the overseers and managers contact him to say that it was not working out.

The bottom line was that right now, Henry did not have time to deal with Bart or with Minerva. He had more important tasks. Standing, he extended a serious gaze to both Minerva and Bart, sitting a chair next to the sofa. 'Until further notice, Bart is not to travel to London without my permission.'

'Mother! You can't let him keep me prisoner here.' Bart slammed his glass on the wooden table so hard it shattered, raining shards of glass on to the floor.

Minerva leaped to her feet and rushed towards her son. 'Oh, darling! Did you cut yourself? Here, let Mother see.'

Henry had to grit his teeth together to keep his opinion of Bart's behaviour, and hers, to himself. Both were what kept Bart from ever growing mature enough to become responsible for anything or anyone.

Not bothering to wait for the cooing and whining to end, Henry left the room, collected his hat and gloves from the butler, and exited the house. Even if he rode hard and fast, he wouldn't make it back to London before midnight. Furthermore, Barley had already made the long trip from London and needed to rest before returning, so he mounted his horse and steered him towards Beaufort.

Henry wasn't looking forward to a visit with his mother, but wouldn't mind checking in on Violet and to learn the latest news from Rosemary.

Having travelled the route numerous times, Barley let out a nicker and set the pace for the short ride. Not only did the horse know the way, he was probably looking forward to his comfortable stall in the stable and the care he would receive there.

Grey-haired Samuel saw them coming and was waiting outside the stable with a carrot in hand. The groom and horse were old friends. Samuel had been there when Barley had been born and had given the horse his name as a colt when the cheeky horse had broken into the store of what was still his favourite grain.

'Weren't expecting you, my lord,' Samuel greeted.

'It wasn't a planned visit,' Henry admitted while dismounting. 'I had to bring a wayward family member home.'

'Young Bart,' Samuel said, shaking his head. 'I'm afraid there's not much hope for that boy.'

Henry agreed and voiced it. If anyone knew a family's secrets, it was the servants. 'I will be leaving first thing in the morning.'

'Very well,' Samuel said. 'I'll see that this old boy is ready.'

There wasn't an animal on all of Beaufort property that didn't receive the best care possible, Samuel made sure, which was why Bart's dogs and horses had always found a home here when they'd been cast aside.

Henry wasn't yet to the front steps when the large, arched door opened and a squeal filled the air as his sister ran towards him.

Laughing, he caught Violet as she leaped off the last step and gave her a solid hug before setting her back down on her feet. She looked a lot like their mother, with near-black hair and brown eyes, but Violet was always smiling.

'I'm so happy to see you,' she said, hooking her arm with his as they walked up the steps. 'It's so dull around here without you.'

He laughed. 'I seem to recall hearing you say that I was dull on more than one occasion.'

'You can be dull, dear Brother,' she said, giggling. 'But it's extremely boring around here when you're gone.'

'In that case, I must warn you, I'm leaving again in the morning.'

She made a pouting expression, then grinned. 'Oh, well, at least I'll have one evening of fun.'

'Why are you so bored? Isn't the young Mr Carter Moores still calling upon you?'

Her cheeks flushed red. 'Of course he's still calling on me, or was, until he left for Scotland last week. He'll be gone all month.' She sighed. 'I miss him so much, Henry.'

He leaned down and kissed the top of her head. 'I'm sure you do.'

'Maybe I could go back to London with you.'

The hope in her voice was clear and he hated to disappoint her, but had to. 'Not this time, maybe in a month or two.'

'A month or two? You'll still be in London then?'

'I'm not sure.' He wasn't sure of a lot of things, including how long it would take to catch the murderer. The urgency to get back to the city had been growing in him since before he'd left. He'd been worried about leaving Suzanne, which was strange because, last week, he'd had no thoughts about her, one way or the other. That, of course, had been before she'd climbed off the balcony, before tasting her rum cake and before escorting her to the Exposition.

It was also before she'd suggested that they work together by pretending to be *courting*. Every time he thought about that word, the way she said it, with her southern drawl that cut off the 'g' at the end echoed inside his mind. That was enough to make him smile.

'You can be happy about being gone so long, but I don't have to be,' Violet said.

He licked his lips in order to remove the smile and crossed the threshold into the house.

'Welcome home, my lord,' James, their long-standing butler, greeted him and held out his hand.

'Thank you, James.' Henry handed over his hat and gloves and, for a brief moment, felt hesitant. Normally, when he arrived home, it was for a purpose. Today it was merely because Barley needed to rest.

'Hello, Henry, dear.'

He turned towards the sweeping staircase and watched as his mother gracefully descended the steps.

'See you later,' Violet whispered and made a fast exit down the hallway leading to south wing where the library and conservatory were located.

Both of his sisters were well aware of the distance that had occurred between him and their mother the past few months. 'Hello, Mother,' he said, moving towards the bottom stair and held out a hand for her to take. 'I hope you are well.'

She laid her hand in his and stepped off the staircase. 'I am fine, thank you, and you?'

He kissed the cheek she offered. 'I'm happy to hear that. I'm doing well, thank you.'

She gestured towards the hallway that led to the sitting room in the south wing. It was where she always entertained callers and was her way of letting him know that the argument they'd had months ago was not forgotten and was still making her point by not going to the less formal drawing room where family usually gathered. 'To what do we owe this unexpected visit?'

'Bart,' he said as they walked to the room. The piano along the far wall instantly made him think of Suzanne. Again. He had to work out what to do about that and her.

'What has that impudent child done now? Your father worried about how Emmet and Minerva coddled that boy.'

'He did,' Henry agreed as he led her to a chair. 'Father also used to say the apple doesn't fall far from the tree.' Henry believed that to be true, which was why he was so cautious about his own behaviour, hoping to catch himself prior to becoming like his father in certain ways.

'That he did.' Settled into the highbacked chair with

sculpted wooden arms and legs, his mother eyed him directly. 'However, Emmet was simply lazy. Bart's lazy and sly. I never trust when he appears for no reason.'

Concerned, Henry asked, 'Does he do that often?'

'No more than usual. I've just never trusted him. Remember that dog he had, the one you found tied in the woods?'

Henry sat in the chair opposite her. 'Yes.'

'How he claimed that he hadn't tied it in the woods. Emmet accused you of stealing the animal and how upset your father was by all of that.'

Henry nodded. The poor dog had been skin and bones, which his father had pointed out to his uncle, and declared the dog would not be returned to Bart. Samuel had named him Hound and for the next ten or so years, he'd been part of the family.

She had to have the same memories arising as him, because she then asked, 'Remember when Bart claimed Hound had bitten him?'

'Which time?' Henry asked.

'That dog never forgot who had been mean to him and who'd treated him kindly.'

Henry wondered if there was double meaning in her statement, considering the shaky ground between them. Eventually, he hoped, they'd be able to bridge that gap, for she was his mother.

'Yes, well, I ran into Bart in London and escorted him home,' he said.

'What was he doing in London?'

'He said he had some business to see to.' Instead his cousin travelled there, thinking that he would be accepted into the men's clubs, where he would drink and play cards. Henry knew the only acceptance Bart would have received would have been from men who would easily have taken advantage of Bart's age and naivety.

With her shapely brows knitted tightly together, his mother asked, 'Surely you haven't given him any businesses to oversee? You've worked so hard to repair Emmet's neglect.'

'No, I have not. That is precisely why I brought him home.' Bart's last name would have allowed doors to open and Henry made a mental note to contact several managers upon returning to London, to warn them about his young cousin.

'How long will you be here?'

'Only until morning.'

His mother nodded slightly, then looked down at the folded hands in her lap, before looking back up at him. 'Have you attended the Exposition? I was at the one years ago and would like to see this one, but with the family kerfuffle, I don't know that I could hold my head up.'

Anger tightened his lips. 'There is no family kerfuffle, Mother. In fact, in case you haven't heard, Heather did not receive any monies.'

Her lips parted, but she didn't speak as her eyes went from being round to narrowing. Then, with an accusing glare, she asked, 'Why not?' Before he could respond, she continued, asking, 'Did the courts see the foolishness in your actions?'

'No,' he said. 'Heather received no money because she was murdered.'

Suzanne rubbed her aching temples and opened one eye. Sunshine filled the room, announcing a new day, one that was sure to bring Henry home. And that meant that she'd have to tell him that she had said more than she should have to the Duchess of Hollingford.

She flipped off the covers and then let her frustration out with an overly exaggerated amount of kicking to get rid of the sheet still covering her legs. Still annoyed she grabbed a pillow and tossed it off the bed.

By then she was sitting up and let out a hard huff of breath.

Why had she let the Duchess get under her skin like she had? All she'd wanted was to have her story read.

Still sitting on the bed, Suzanne covered her face with both hands and groaned. 'You had the option to not say anything,' she told herself aloud. 'But did you make that choice?'

She climbed off the bed and threw her arms in the air. 'No! You didn't!'

How had she got herself so embroiled in someone else's life?

That wasn't the question. She knew how. She should have minded her own business from the beginning.

Why, oh, why hadn't she?

Hours later, Suzanne still didn't know the answer to that question when, in the early afternoon, she saw Henry ride in on his big, white horse. Tall, with a broad chest and muscular legs, it was a regal-looking animal. The two black ones that pulled his coach were fine looking, too, but that white one suited Henry. A large, powerful horse for a large powerful man.

She pressed a hand to her stomach, wondering how she could be thinking about his horses at a time like this.

As if he knew she was watching, he turned and looked across up towards the window on the second storey of

Drew's house. Afraid to move, she stood there, watched him dismount and lead the horse inside the stable. A moment later, his man, Caleb, hurried from the house to the stable.

She left the window then, took a brief moment to assess her reflection in the mirror. Other than smoothing the dark blue material of her dress over her churning stomach, she made no adjustments to her image and turned away from the mirror. Then she picked up the manuscript and left the room.

Once downstairs, she informed Elyse—who surely knew what had happened last night via Hiram who had been close enough to hear every word, yet had been kind enough to not say anything—that she'd be back shortly and exited the back door.

The distance separating the houses was not far and at the sight of Henry leaving his stable, her heart began to pound. Nerves could do that to a person, make a person's heart race, and right now, she was nervous. Very.

He smiled and that made her heart pound so hard her breathing stopped. She had to close her eyes and tell herself to breathe, because if she dropped dead right now, he'd probably be blamed for her murder, too.

'Hello.'

She ripped her eyes open, shocked that he was already standing directly before her.

'Is that your manuscript?' he asked.

She nodded.

He stood quietly, looking at her, for several still moments, then said, 'Would you like to give it to me?'

She nodded, cleared her throat and pressed the manuscript over the racing of her heart. 'We—we have to talk,' she said swiftly.

'Very well,' he said, with a slight grin. 'Your house or mine?'

'Yours.' Hopefully there would be less chance of being overheard there. She'd already had enough of that.

He waved a hand towards his property, then rested his palm in the small of her back as she took a step. He'd done that while they'd been at the Exposition and she'd liked the feeling, the security of knowing he was right at her side when they'd manoeuvred through the crowd, walking from exhibit to exhibit.

Memories of that day had mingled in and out of her thoughts yesterday while she watched for his return, and again today, while doing the very same thing, just with a very different sensation churning her stomach. 'How was your trip?' she asked as they walked across the manicured lawn.

'Fine, thank you. How was your day?'

'Fine.' Might as well jump right in and either sink or swim. 'Until last night.'

He glanced down at her, brow raised.

She drew a deep breath to calm her jumping nerves. 'That—that's what we need to talk about.'

'Do I dare ask what happened?'

Once again, her heart didn't want to beat, her breathing stalled and suddenly there was a humming sound in her ears.

'Suzanne?' He grasped both of her upper arms. 'Suzanne, what happened. Dear Lord, there wasn't another murder, was there?'

She shook her head, chasing away the reactions of telling him the truth of what she'd done. 'No, it's not that bad, but it's not good either.'

'What is it? Was someone hurt? An accident?'

'No. I—' They were still in the garden, but it was as good of a place as any. 'The Duchess came to see me and she made me so mad that I told her we were engaged.'

Chapter Eight

Half an hour later, Henry turned from the window of his study, where he and Suzanne were sequestered behind closed doors. She was sitting in one of the brown leather chairs that flanked the desk. Her hands were in her lap, fingers laced and white from how hard she was squeezing them together.

He bit the inside of his cheek, for none of this was a laughing matter and was certainly going to take some finesse to get everything squared around. Yet, seeing her sitting there, looking so solemn and distressed, filled him with nothing but the desire to comfort her. Assure her it wasn't the end of the world.

If it was possible, she was more beautiful than he remembered. The two days since he'd seen her seemed much longer. He'd thought of little else on the way home, except for her, and had told Caleb to give Barley an extra rub down and grain for how hard he'd pushed the horse to get home in the shortest amount of time.

Henry ran his hands the length of his arms as he unfolded them and stepped forward. 'So, the most logical way that I can see to move forward is for us to announce our engagement.'

She closed her eyes, shook her head. 'I'm sorry, Henry. So sorry.'

'It is what we'd discussed,' he said, silently questioning if she'd changed her mind.

'I know, and I know that you weren't completely taken with the idea. I swear that I didn't mean to say those things. To call her cold-blooded and rude, and a prude.' She shook her head. 'I shouldn't have done that, but she was acting as if those girls deserved to die because...'

'I know. I've encountered that attitude myself.'

'That's not right,' she said.

'No, it's not.'

She stood up, paced the floor. 'Women should be able to earn a living just like men, in many different ways, and they shouldn't be judged on that.'

'I agree.'

'Aunt Adelle said that women shouldn't have to depend on men to take care of them, that they should have their own money. Their own lives.'

'I agree with that, too,' he said, with a new understanding of her desire to get her story published. 'I would have liked to have met your aunt. She sounds like a very clever woman.'

'She was.'

'Was she on your mother's side, or your father's side?'

'My mother's.'

'But she didn't live in Tinpan?'

'No, she lived in Virginia her entire life.' She rested both hands on the back of a chair. 'Adelle was actually my grandmother's sister. Jane. That was my grandmother's name and when she was a young woman she went west along with her parents. Her father was a railroad man, that's what Aunt Adelle called him, and when he and his wife came back home, Adelle said that Jane had stayed west. She'd met herself a railroad man, got married and never returned to Virginia. Aunt Adelle always hoped she would. She never left the family home, so she'd be there if Jane ever returned.'

'Did you know your grandmother?'

'Not that I can remember.' She pushed off the chair and walked around it, then sat down. 'That's all beside the point. What are we going to do now that I've angered the Duchess, because she was furious. I could tell.'

He crossed the room, sat down in the chair on the other side of the table from her. 'We will carry out our plan of a pretend engagement.'

She looked at him, with concern etching her face. 'You could be imprisoned for the rest of your life if you can't prove you didn't murder those women.'

At the moment, he wasn't as concerned about his future as he was hers. The Duchess of Hollingford could severely damage Suzanne's reputation with bold-faced lies. Unfortunately, people would believe whatever they wanted to believe whether it was about an engagement or a murder.

'The Duchess wants you to marry one of her daughters,' Suzanne said.

He shook his head. 'The Duchess wants each of her daughters to marry a titled man. Who that man might be isn't as important as their titles.' He picked her manuscript off the table. When it came to her, there wasn't any of the coldness he'd often felt towards women, and he wasn't convinced that was favourable on his part. There wasn't time to contemplate that. For her sake, the situation at hand had to remedied as soon as possible. 'We have a few things to do before we attend another ball.'

'Such as?'

'Delivering your manuscript to Mr Winterbourne and shopping.'

'Shopping for what?' she asked.

'An engagement ring.' Henry took a long breath, let it settle in deep. If it was any woman other than Suzanne, he might question if she was tricking him into an engagement. For her own gain. Suzanne, however, had nothing to gain by marrying him—in fact, being connected to him could cause the exact opposite.

'An engagement ring?' She shook her head. 'That's not necessary. We can just pretend.'

'We will be pretending,' he said, 'but must make it appear to be real. Engagement rings have become very popular, therefore you will have one, and we will need to have a party. We will ask the Viscount Voss if he and his wife would host one for us, formally announcing our engagement.'

'Don't you think that would be too much?' she asked, with her cheeks turning red.

'No, I don't. An engagement ball would be expected.'

Sighing, she shook her head. 'You won't be able to sneak out from a ball announcing our engagement.'

'I won't leave that one.' There were a lot of things he needed to think through about this situation. He stood. 'Let's take this one step at a time. I'll have Caleb hitch the team to the coach. Is there anything you need to collect from your house before we leave?'

She grimaced and rubbed her forehead. 'Courage. The ability to think straight.' She then slapped a hand over her mouth. 'Oh, dear.'

He looked at her, waited for her to say more.

'Annabelle and Clara,' she said. 'I can't have an engagement party without them being in attendance. Lady Voss will demand that.'

'For this to work, we can't tell anyone the truth.' He trusted both Drew and Roger. The three of them had known each other as children, become friends before they'd each inherited their titles, but involving even them was out of the question. 'Long engagements are not unusual,' he said. 'Once the war has ended, we will break our engagement and you can return to America. It will provide the perfect reason, because it will be true. You're an American and will never be happy here and, due to my responsibilities here, I can't travel to America, so we'll part amicably.'

The look on her face held a touch of confusion, which made him ask, 'Isn't that correct? It's what you told me the other day.'

She shook her head. 'No, I mean, yes, it's completely correct, but the war might not be over for years.'

He was fully aware of that, but would deal with it after other things had settled. 'I know.' Holding out a hand to assist her off the chair, he asked, 'Shall we?'

Though she laid a hand in his, her gaze was as hesitant as her slow rise from the chair. Her eyes were so blue, he thought about how easy it would be to get lost in them. Lost in thinking about ways to make them sparkle, shine and glimmer. He'd seen them do all of that, at the Exposition, and before then, when she'd brought over her rum cake. She'd been full of confidence then and he wondered where that was now.

'I am sorry, Henry,' she said quietly. 'I can't shake

aside the feeling that I've made everything worse instead of better.'

He tucked her hand inside the crook of his arm, and walked towards the door. 'Plenty of things get worse before they get better.'

'You could stop being so nice about all this,' she said. 'Call me a ninny or tell me that you're mad and need time to think about what I've done, or, I don't know... something.'

He'd learned years ago that being rational, accepting things and moving forward was the best action in nearly all circumstances. 'Would any of that make you feel better?'

'No,' she answered demurely.

'Me neither.' He paused long enough to open the door and then escorted her into the hallway.

There were several jewellers in town, but only one that he'd patronised in the past for gifts for his mother and sisters. Jon Mathers had rented space in one of the buildings that Henry's family had owned for years. That was where he instructed Caleb to drive to after the horses had been put in harness and the coach brought around to the front of the house.

Upon arrival at the large brick building that housed several shops, Henry exited the coach and took Suzanne's hand to assist her down the coach step. Though lovely in her blue gown, her face bore the expression of someone about to face the headmaster at a school after being caught red-handed in a despicable deed.

'Thank you,' she said, after stepping upon the ground, while pulling her hand from his and not meeting his gaze.

He gestured to the door of the jewellery shop with one

hand and rested his other on the small of her back. 'This is merely the first move in the game,' he said quietly.

She frowned, glanced at him. 'Game?'

'Yes, this one that we are playing concerning our courtship.' It was one hell of a way to look at things, but he didn't know how else to make her feel more comfortable about it. 'Do you play chess?'

'No, I never learned.'

He stopped near the door. 'But you watched them play at the Exposition, we both did the other day.'

She nodded.

'For most, chess is not overly logical until the final few moves. Before then it's intuition, spontaneous decisions and passion for the game, or the win. For the master player, it's all about logic and calculations right from the start. There are only so many moves a player can make at any one point during a game and calculating which move an opponent will make and how to respond to each move is what gives master players the upper hand.'

Her gaze grew thoughtful, then she shook her head. 'I think it's too late for us to gain the upper hand.'

'I beg to disagree. You and I already know how this game will end. That in itself is having the upper hand.' He then opened the door, and escorted her inside the jewellery store.

Jon Mathers recognised him instantly. 'Lord Beaufort, what an unexpected pleasure. How may I be of assistance?'

'Good day, Mr Mathers,' Henry replied. 'Allow me to present Miss Suzanne Bishop.' Looking at her, he continued, 'Suzanne, this is Mr Jon Mathers, renowned jeweller.'

'Miss Bishop,' Jon said, with a bow. 'It's my pleasure.'

'Hello, Mr Mathers,' she replied.

'We are in need of an engagement ring,' Henry said.

The jeweller's eyes widened beneath his bushy grey brows. 'Lord Beaufort, you have my congratulations and I'm honoured you have chosen my meagre establishment to serve your needs.'

Henry purposefully glanced at Suzanne and realised the smile he'd pulled up for the jeweller hadn't been needed. A real smile pulled at his lips at the way a blush had turned her cheeks pink. He might be taking advantage of the circumstance, but the urge struck and he couldn't deny the opportunity. Reaching up, he used a single finger to brush a long tendril of blonde hair away from one of her eyes. 'I know your work, Mr Mathers,' Henry said, 'and want only the best for my bride-to-be.'

The shimmer that appeared in Suzanne's eyes told him that she knew what he was up to and that she was up to the challenge. When it came to acting, she had him beat with her southern accent and charm, or so she thought.

A slightly smug smile formed before she shifted those sky-blue eyes to Mr Mathers. Pressing a hand to her breast bone, she shook her head. 'I would not consider this a meagre shop by any means. So many things have already caught my eye. I can tell that your work is truly exquisite.'

Henry bit the inside of his cheek as she continued showering the man with praise and how Mr Mathers, old enough to be her grandfather, nearly melted behind the counter as he hung on to her every word.

Suzanne had walked into the shop with the intention of not accepting an engagement ring. She truly saw no need for Henry to spend that kind of money on a pretence. That had been before he'd challenged her. She'd seen that in his eyes when he'd called her his bride-to-be. If he thought that he could play this game better than her, he'd soon discover he was wrong.

She might not know how to play chess, but she knew a person got more bees with honey than vinegar. Every teacher knew that. Children who liked their teacher was more apt to like school and learn more than those who didn't like their teacher, and over the years she'd learned how to make even the most stubborn child like her.

It was not the same as pretending, or acting—children could easily pick that out. It was about being personable and real and finding interests to share. That was easy with the jeweller. His work was amazing and what woman didn't like jewellery? She always had, even though she'd never owned any herself. Aunt Adelle had owned a few pieces that she'd let Suzanne wear. Along with everything else, Aunt Adelle's jewellery had all been lost in the fire. All that was left of the house were a few charred boards and the big cook stove. If she'd been home that night, perhaps she would have been able to save a few things, but she'd been at Clara's house, comforting her friend who had just learned that her husband had died while fighting in the war.

Months ago, she'd accepted the loss of her home, knowing she'd lost far less than many others, and kept her focus on the reason she'd thought about Aunt Adelle's jewellery.

Mr Mathers had taken out a tray lined with velvet and holding several rings. Though each and every one of them was gorgeous and she complimented the jeweller on his workmanship, Suzanne couldn't imagine owning any of them. The genuine jewels in their settings—diamonds, rubies, emeralds, sapphires, and the like—had to be so very expensive.

Knowing that Henry had his mind set on buying a ring and also knowing that she might not be able to change his mind, she turned her attention to a smaller tray inside the glass cabinet that held simple gold bands. They were wedding rings, not engagement ones. She truly wouldn't be needing either, but a simple band had to be far less expensive.

Still playing along with Henry's game, she smiled up at him. 'It's simply too hard for me to choose.' Then, gesturing to the plain bands, she said, 'Perhaps we should just buy one of those.'

Even though she knew they were play acting, the way he looked at her made her heart flutter. And nearly fluttered right out of her chest when he leaned closer and placed a tiny kiss on her temple. The gesture was false, simply part of the act, but his lips were so warm and soft she had to close her eyes and swallow hard, otherwise she might humiliate herself by fainting right then and there.

'We'll buy one of those, too,' he said softly. 'Another day.'

This man might be the death of her yet. She told herself to gather some strength, or steam, or whatever it was that she needed in order to be the one to make him swoon, not the other way around. 'Silly me,' she said, doing her best to sound as sweet as honey. 'I'm just so excited to become your wife, I find myself quite addlepated. Perhaps we can do this another day. I can't possible choose one today.'

One of his hands was still on the small of her back

and he ran it upwards to the spot between her shoulders blades and rubbed the area softly. 'Then I shall help you decide.'

Her entire being felt overheated, as though she'd spent too much time in bright sunshine. She needed something to remind herself that this was all pretend and easily found it. Back at his house, Henry had said that they would break the engagement and she could return to America. She hadn't fully decided if that would happen, mainly because it would depend upon her finances and her story being accepted. That had to happen now and she had to return to America. It was what Henry wanted. A way to end the plan that she had created.

He picked up a ring, an overly lovely one with a sparkling sapphire surrounded by several small diamonds. It had been the first one that had caught her eye.

His other hand left her back and took hold of her left hand. Fully aware that he was about to slide the ring on her finger, to check for sizing, she willed it not to fit. Either too large or too small would be fine. She wasn't choosy, just hoping it wouldn't fit on her finger.

It fit.

Perfectly.

And was even more gorgeous on her hand than lying on the black velvet.

'I think that one is quite perfect,' Henry said.

'Oh, I agree, Lord Beaufort,' Mr Mathers said. 'It looks stunning on her hand. Utterly stunning.'

'I think so, too,' Henry said, still staring at her, with one brow lifted.

For the first time in her life, Suzanne couldn't think of anything to say. Not a single word and the grin on Henry's face said he knew that. He was so close to her that she could practically see herself in his eyes. He smelled good, too. Like cinnamon or ginger, an aromatic, woodsy, yet warm, sweet smell that heightened every one of her senses.

Her breath caught as he leaned closer again and, this time, placed a tiny kiss on her cheek. The desire to turn her face, feel those warm lips against hers, was enough to make her question the good senses she'd always credited herself for having.

He straightened, and looked down at her with a smile that could have melted butter. At that moment, she might as well have been made of butter.

One of her hands grasped his forearm as if she was afraid that he'd move away. That was exactly what she should want. She'd never kissed a man, nor let one kiss her, and here he'd gone and done that twice within a matter of minutes.

Mr Mather's cleared his throat softly, but loud enough that it broke whatever had been holding their gazes locked together, and both she and Henry turned to look at the man at the same time.

'If you would be interested, my lord, that ring has a matching necklace and earrings,' Mr Mathers said.

'Oh, no, no,' she protested, quite breathless.

'Yes, I am interested,' Henry said at the very same time.

'One moment, please,' Mr Mathers said. 'They are in the back room.'

Suzanne felt hot and cold at the same time and Henry was the reason. She released her hold on his arm and grasped hold of the ring on her other finger. Henry's hand covered hers before she had time to remove the ring.

'If you take that one off, you'll have to pick out another one,' he whispered. 'We are not leaving here without an engagement ring.'

'We don't need one so elaborate,' she hissed. 'And most certainly don't need a matching necklace and earrings. I've never worn earrings in my life.'

'You've never been engaged before, either,' he said.

'We are not getting engaged for real,' she reminded him. 'It's pretend.'

'You've never been engaged for pretend before, either, have you?'

'No, and you haven't, either,' she whispered, glancing towards the doorway where Mr Mathers had disappeared.

'You're right, I haven't.' Henry touched the tender skin beneath her chin. 'But I believe I'm doing a better job of pretending that it's real than you are.' He tilted her chin upwards. 'Perhaps you need some lessons.'

He was staring at her mouth, making it tingle, like her temple and cheek had after he'd kissed them. *No*, she mouthed, because her voice didn't want to work.

A thud sounded and, with a chuckle, Henry released her chin and turned to the counter as Mr Mathers walked through the doorway with a wooden box in his hands.

The necklace had three large sapphires and too many diamonds to count, yet it was delicate and elegant rather than showy. The earrings matched the ring with one sapphire, surrounded by diamonds, and dangled off a thin wire that attached to silver ear clips with diamonds embedded in them.

Henry took the necklace from the box and held it up, looking at her.

There were two ways she could respond to his silent request that she try it on. To deny would further his acting of being the happy soon-to-be bridegroom, therefore, she took the second option. Sucking in a deep breath, she turned about in order to allow him to fasten the necklace behind her neck.

Her entire being tingled as he lowered the necklace over her head and then fastened it at the back of her neck. It took a long deep breath before she dared turn around and face him.

'Perfect,' he said, picking up the earrings.

She put the earrings on herself and forced herself not to flinch at the unusual feeling of having something clipped on to her ear lobes. It wasn't uncomfortable, just different. She took solace in that. Told herself that none of this needed to be uncomfortable, just different from what she was used to. That was something she could deal with. Things had been very different since she'd arrived in England.

That gave her an avenue to use in all of this. She could let Henry take the lead and simply play along. Due to the fact that she had absolutely no experience in courting, that could be her best route and, once he realised what she was doing, it was sure to make him not be so diligent in his acting. They didn't need to act as though they were overly smitten with each other. Did they?

Not overly sure about that, she twisted, looking up at him with what she hoped looked like devotion, or some other such overly exaggerated emotion, because the jeweller was watching them closely. Due to that, she also copied what Henry had done earlier. She had to stretch on her toes in order to reach his cheek and the moment her lips encountered the warmth of his skin, a unique and heady thrill shot through her body.

The division that struck inside her was shocking. A

part of her wanted to press her entire body against his, feel the warmth of him from head to toe, and the other part of her wanted to run because what she felt had been wanton.

Her only saving grace was that she'd never run from anything in her life. Lowering back on to her heels, she forced herself to meet his gaze.

Saying nothing, he placed his hands on her shoulders and searched her face for what felt like an eternity. The swirling heat deep inside was poignant and something she'd never felt before, and her mind was certainly thinking things that she had never thought before.

Without looking away, Henry said, 'I believe we've found exactly what we were looking for, Mr Mathers. Please add them to my account.'

Chapter Nine

Suzanne couldn't say how long it took to travel from the jewellery store to the publishing house. It wasn't until Caleb opened the coach door, revealing that was where they'd arrived, that she finally found her tongue. She needed her story published so badly, yet was unsure of the route she was taking to make that happen. Laying a hand on the manuscript that was on the seat beside her, she said, 'I will wait here, but please don't tell Mr Winterbourne that we are engaged.'

Henry nodded. 'I will only be a moment.'

As the coach door closed behind him, she took a deep breath. She was still wearing the ring, necklace and earrings and had been in some kind of a stupor from the direction her mind had taken back in the shop, when the desire to feel his lips upon hers had been undeniably overwhelming.

Since then, she'd been trying to figure out how and why she felt that way. Those feelings weren't going away and they should. She had to remember why she was doing all this. Yes, it was to help him, but it was also to help herself, to ensure that she wasn't dependent upon anyone.

Yet, right now, it appeared as if she was dependent upon everyone in order for that to happen. Especially Henry.

The door opened and, while stepping inside, he said, 'Mr Winterbourne will send a response within a few days.'

'Thank you.' She wanted to ask if Mr Winterbourne had remembered her, but chose to remain silent.

'I've asked Caleb to take us to the Voss residence.'

'Why?'

'To enquire about their interest in hosting a ball for our engagement.'

'Today? Shouldn't we—?'

'The faster we make our moves, the better,' he said.

She could see the need in that and knew she was the reason they had to take these measures. If she'd held her tongue the other night, their fake courting would have been a lot less complicated.

Everything would be a lot less complicated.

As gracious as ever, Lady Voss welcomed them into her home upon their arrival and she, along with the Viscount, immediately agreed to hosting a ball. With a pulse on the Season, Lady Voss insisted that a ball at the end of the week would be ideal. It appeared that a ball had just been cancelled due to an illness in the hosting family, leaving the night open for an engagement ball that many would be interested in attending.

Suzanne did her best to act overjoyed, including when Lady Voss claimed there would be significant time for both Clara and Annabelle to travel to London to be in attendance, whereas in truth, she was ready to run all over again. All the way back to America. Henry was right. She did need to return. Living in the midst of a war raging around her would be easier than the one battling inside her. She didn't know what had happened inside her, but something had. Otherwise, she wouldn't be questioning things she'd always known about herself and about men.

Henry was surprised by the ease with which he could act the smitten bridegroom. Albeit Suzanne was adorable, charming beyond description, and any man would be honoured to have her on their arm, but he wasn't any man. He knew the engagement was pretend, but his concern for her wasn't.

The truth behind that had struck a nerve when Lady Voss had asked when his family would be arriving and if his mother would like to assist in the planning. He hadn't taken that into consideration and should have. He couldn't have an engagement ball without his mother and sisters in attendance.

He had assured Lady Voss that he'd have his mother call upon her as soon as she arrived in town and had agreed to nearly all of her other suggestions before he and Suzanne had taken their leave.

'I will have accounts set up for you this afternoon,' he told her as they travelled back to his town house and he considered all the tasks he'd need to complete, including sending a messenger to Beaufort.

'Accounts for what?'

'Whatever you need.'

'I don't need anything.' She sighed heavily. 'I'm sorry, Henry. I feel as if I've made things harder for you.'

He could see how distraught she was and sincerely wanted to ease that for her. 'You haven't. You provided me with alibis for the times I sneaked out of balls by what you told the Duchess, and one thing that is very true is how short an attention span many of the gossipers have. News of our engagement could very easily override chatter about the murders.'

'It could also take time away from your search.'

'Which will make it more difficult for someone to suggest that I have time to be conducting devious acts elsewhere.' It was a long shot, but what they were doing with their fake engagement might draw out the murderer. Perhaps he'd been doing things wrong before in trying to sneak around, looking for clues to find the murderer. In a sense, that had been playing into their hands.

Suzanne was frowning, clearly not following his line of thinking.

'Think about it,' he continued. 'The murderer wanted to arouse suspicions about me. When that didn't happen, they figured they had to murder again and again.' That was such a sickening thought. 'And I'm afraid that they will continue to until they can pin it on me. That will be more difficult when I'm with you all the time.'

She shook her head. 'If no one knew Heather was your half-sister, there was nothing that would have aroused suspicion. There still isn't, other than rumours, which have no basis.'

He'd chosen not to tell her earlier, but she was the one person he could trust in all of his. 'Yes, there is something. By Heather's body, they found a cufflink. It had the Beaufort insignia on it.'

She glanced at the cuffs of his white shirt sleeves.

'Not mine. My father's.'

'That's what your friend at Scotland Yard found and told you about?'

'Yes, it is. He found it in the grass after the body had been removed.'

'Were any Beaufort items found near the other victims?'

Henry shook his head. 'I haven't heard if anything was found near their bodies or not.'

'Do you know how someone would have had your father's cufflink?'

'No. I considered asking my mother. She is very particular. There is nothing that is ever out of place, nothing unaccounted for. If one of my father's cufflinks had gone missing, she wouldn't have stopped looking until she discovered where it had gone.'

Henry drew in a deep breath, before he continued, 'But the less anyone knows about this, the better.' He didn't want his family to know about the rumours, though he had shared news of Heather's death on his most recent visit home. 'My mother prides herself on having a scandal-free family. That's why she didn't want Heather to receive an inheritance and why she and I have been at odds the past few years.'

'You created a scandal?'

'She was afraid that I would when I took over the businesses that my uncle had been managing. My father had his first stroke while I was at university and my mother insisted that he'd get better soon, that there was no need for me to come home.'

'But he didn't get better?'

'Somewhat, but the doctors had warned he could have a second stroke at any time. After I left university I discovered that the family businesses my father had allowed my uncle to run had been in disarray. My uncle had died several months before in a carriage accident and I had some serious financial decisions to make. In order to save the companies, I had to sell off some other properties and invest that money into the failing business.

'My mother felt that by selling off properties, people would question if we were in dire straits financially. She argued that we had other choices, but we didn't, and I sold a few rental properties, reinvesting the money in the companies. The investments were paying off when my father had his second stroke and died a few months later.'

'After you'd told him about Heather? And told your mother?'

He nodded, but explained, 'My mother had known about Heather for years, she admitted that. She just didn't want her to receive an inheritance.'

'Because of her profession? How it would cause a scandal?'

The financial burdens he'd taken on, that of making sure everyone in his family was well taken care of, had been extended to Heather. It was only fair. 'Not because of her profession. Simply because of who she was. A Vogal. My mother didn't want anyone to know that my father had been unfaithful to her.'

That had been so frustrating to him and what his mother and he had argued over. She had obviously forgiven his father, because there was no animosity between them, never had been, that he knew of. He'd worked hard, given up everything else to focus solely on making sure the family's finances would be viable for years to come and felt that Heather's wrong had needed to be made right.

'Who else knew that Heather was your sister?' Suzanne asked.

'My mother and my barrister are the only people that

I know of. Obviously, someone else did, or does, I should say, and I'm beginning to think this is about more than me wanting to see that Heather received an inheritance.'

'Like what?'

'I'm not sure, yet, but hopefully that will come out in the wash as our engagement and activities become the subject of conversations.'

She sat back in her seat, stared at him for a long moment, clearly mulling over what he'd just said. He was mulling it all over, too. This could draw out the murderer and that was his number one goal, but he still wasn't completely comfortable putting her in this position. It could be more dangerous than before. She could now become the target of whoever had become his number one enemy.

'What will your mother, and your sisters, think of our engagement?'

That was easy. 'They will be delighted.'

Less than twenty-four hours later, that was confirmed. His mother and both sisters descended upon his town house shortly after noon the following day.

'Why on earth didn't you mention this while you were home?' Violet asked, slapping his chest as soon as she'd stepped inside the house. 'Mother nearly fainted dead upon reading your message last evening.'

Rosemary was slightly more reserved. She gave him a solid hug before saying, 'You, dear Brother, owe me a night of sleep. I received the message from Mother after dark last night, telling me to be at Beaufort before sunrise, with baggage to travel to London.'

His mother was the third one through the door, which was her way. After he'd given her the customary kiss on the cheek, she eyed him critically while removing her white gloves. 'You can imagine my surprise.'

'I can,' he acknowledged. The less he said, the better off everyone would be.

His mother handed her gloves to Caleb. 'When can we expect to meet her?'

He'd assumed they would arrive this afternoon when he'd sent the messenger yesterday and had planned for that. 'Suzanne will join us for a tea later today and we will be dining at the Viscount Voss's house this evening, in order for you to be involved in the engagement ball preparations.'

Lips pursed, she stated, 'I could have hosted the ball at Beaufort.'

'I am aware of that, Mother, however, the distance would have impeded the number of guests who would have been able to attend.'

His mother huffed out a breath. 'I barely know Lady Voss.'

'She is Suzanne's sponsor,' he stated.

'Sponsor? Why does she need a sponsor? Has she no family?' His mother pressed both hands to her bosom. 'Is she a commoner?'

Henry shouldn't be enjoying this as much as he was. His mother could be a snob and, for years, that had irritated him. It was almost as if he'd dreamed up this very moment. 'Miss Bishop is an American, Mother. She arrived in England a short time ago, along with a friend of hers, who recently married the Marquess of Clairmount. Another one of her American friends is married to the Duke of Mansfield.'

'Well,' she said, stiffly. 'I had heard both the Duke and the Marquess had married Americans.' Huffing out a breath, she uttered, 'Good Lord, are we under invasion?'

Choosing to ignore her muttered question, Henry said, 'They did.' Then he pointed out, 'With the blessing of the Queen.'

He wasn't as acquainted with the royal family as Drew or Roger, but Suzanne's connection to Annabelle and Clara was certainly enough to impress some and his mother wouldn't mind that.

'Your sisters and I will require a resting period before tea.'

'Of course.' He made an extravagant gesture towards the stairway. 'Your luggage will be brought up immediately.'

His mother was the first to march forward, followed by a grinning Violet.

Rosemary was next, shaking her head at him as she whispered, 'Oh, dear Brother, I do love you.'

'Rosemary!' their mother snapped.

'Coming, Mother,' Rosemary replied. 'I was merely telling Henry that Judd will be joining me here in a few days.'

'Carter is still in Scotland,' Violet said from where she climbed the steps and while smiling over her shoulder in her own show of being in on Rosemary's cover-up.

If she needed support of any kind, Henry was certain that Suzanne would find it in his sisters and that pleased him greatly. Along with those thoughts came one that said if anyone could ever win over his mother, it very well could be Suzanne. Whether or not that could work in his favour was something he needed to take into deep consideration.

Marriage, a real marriage or a pretend one, would not

be the outcome of this engagement. He hadn't needed to remind himself of that, but took note of it just the same.

Thankful that he'd understood her gestures from the window moments ago, Suzanne caught hold of Henry's arm and pulled him behind the tall hedge that separated their properties.

'We need to talk,' she said.

He looked at her for a moment, then shook his head. 'Do you start all your conversation that way, or just those with me?'

'I don't—' She huffed out a breath. 'I think I've changed my mind.'

'You think you've changed your mind about what?'

'Us.' Suzanne took a step back and crossed her arms over her mid-section. Her stomach was a mess, so were her nerves. No matter what she tried, she couldn't stop her hands from shaking at the idea of meeting his mother, and sisters. His family.

He grasped her upper arms. 'Come now, there's no need to worry yourself sick.'

'I can't help it. I should never have suggested, never should have said, never should have agreed…' What if they learned about her past, how she had no family? That her mother had been a flower in the garden, like Heather.

'That's a lot of nevers,' he said.

It was still hard for her to believe that she of all people, had embarked on something so foolhardy. 'I know.'

He stepped closer while tugging her forward and slid his hands around her shoulders. She leaned in, laying her head against the front of his shoulder before her sensibility told her she shouldn't. By the time that happened, it was too late. His arms had tightened around her and hers had encircled his waist.

The comfort of being held in his arms momentarily took away the fears that had been making her question if she was losing her mind. She'd barely slept last night, but her nerves had leaped to another level upon seeing his mother and sisters arrive in a coach nearly identical to his, as well as another coach full of servants. He'd stopped by this morning to say that a message had arrived, informing him that his mother and sisters would be arriving today.

He'd also said that they would have tea at his house with his family and that they had all been invited to Lady Voss's this evening for dinner.

All of that had filled her with an anxiety she couldn't shake. Especially upon spying the three dark-haired women arriving in the coach. She had truly been on pins and needles before then, and now... She leaned back, looked up at him. 'My mother was a flower in the Flower Garden.'

He frowned slightly. 'Excuse me?'

Had she truly just said that? Just told him the one thing she'd never admitted to anyone? Not even her dearest and best friends. Yet, she had to tell him. He had to know why she couldn't go through with this. 'The Flower Garden was a house of ill repute in Tinpan, that's where my mother worked, where I was born. I never knew who my father was and, when my mother fell ill and died, I was sent to live with Aunt Adelle. Someone had known that my grandmother had been from Virginia and still had a sister there. The town collected the money to send me there. Bishop was Aunt Adelle's last name.'

His hands rubbed her back as he said, 'And it's a very good last name.'

His attempt to make her feel better almost made her smile, but she couldn't. 'Your family won't think so, not when they learn the truth. It'll be a scandal. We have to stop this now.'

He cupped the side of her face with one hand. 'Your last name, your mother's past, your grandmother's past, makes no difference. I consider you a friend, Suzanne. Believe that you and I have become friends and are willing to help each other, despite anything in either of our families' pasts.'

She wanted to be his friend, wanted to help him, but… 'I don't want to make things worse for you.'

'You've already made them better.'

Her heart flipped inside her chest, yet she had to say, 'It'll get worse when people learn who I am.'

'I know who you are. A wonderful, kind and beautiful woman.' He leaned closer and touched his forehead to hers. 'Not to mention charming and an amazing writer.'

She was fully conscious of how their bodies were touching, of the heat of his body, the firmness of it, and of the sensations being evoked inside her. If the truth be told, there couldn't be another man that she'd rather pretend to be engaged to and that made her sigh.

'I'm not going to make you stick to our plan if you don't want to,' he said quietly.

His voice was soft, mesmerising. So were his eyes. Her sigh was broken by her own frustration. 'I want to. I—I just…' She shook her head. 'I've never done anything like this before.' She'd never felt this way before, either.

'I know,' he whispered, while the tip of his nose touched hers. 'I haven't either.'

At that moment, all the feelings and desires that she'd considered wanton erupted into an urge that made her lift her face upwards, to meet his.

The first touch of his lips against hers stole her breath and the second touch emptied her lungs with a soft sigh. Each touch was as gentle as a breeze, a mere brushing. It was as if he was exploring her lips with his and it made her want more.

Much more.

She stretched up on to the balls of her feet and moved her lips to catch his. He made a low, almost hungry, sound as their lips met full on and the pressure between them increased. That happened over and over again, their lips firmly meeting, parting and meeting again.

The unimaginable pleasure that rained down upon her sent her heart racing and the same warm, pulsating need she'd encountered yesterday burst to life deep inside her.

It was a daring, driving need. One that thrilled her as much as it frightened her.

Henry pulled her even closer, tucking her tight against him, and she balled material from his shirt with both hands, holding on tight as the kissing continued. Nothing had ever felt so good.

His lips parted and his tongue slid across her bottom lip. Without her consciously thinking about it, her lips parted and the intimacy of that made her entire body tingle and hum, especially her breasts and the juncture between her legs.

The shocking realisation of that should have made her stop, or at least want to, but it didn't. Instead, she felt a rumbling moan in the back of her throat and joined in a wild game of hide and seek with their tongues that was half teasing, half demanding and overall exciting.

She was breathing fast and hard when he pulled back, looking down at her with a smile in his eyes.

There were dozens of reasons she should be embarrassed, ashamed for behaving so wickedly—for that was surely what Aunt Adelle would have called it—yet Suzanne didn't feel embarrassed, ashamed or even wicked. She felt kissed.

It was a wonderful feeling and she now understood more about some of the things that Clara had said about being married, about being loved by a man.

That was when a shiver rippled over her and she uncurled her fingers, released his shirt and took a step backwards. Henry didn't love her and she didn't love him. Their engagement wasn't real. Would never be real.

What was she doing? Was she turning into her mother? Aunt Adelle had warned that would happen if she wasn't careful.

His hands slipped off her back, but only to find her shoulders, then both of his hands slid down the lengths of her arms before he took hold of her hands.

'Well, now,' he said, 'that was quite believable.'

Her first thought was that it had been quite unbelievable. This was all unbelievable, until something in his tone made her question, 'What do you mean, believable?'

'I mean we are going to have to convince others that our engagement is real. To anyone watching, that kiss would convince them.'

Again, her first, fleeting thought was to agree, until she grasped more of what he'd said. 'Anyone watching?'

She attempted to step back in order to spin about to check for onlookers, but he seemed to read her mind and pulled her forward so quickly she nearly collided with his chest.

His hands were on her back, holding her up against him. 'Don't turn around,' he whispered next to her ear.

'Why not?' Heavens, but being so close to him made thinking so hard. Giving her head a clearing shake, she managed to find a few fading bits of clear thought. 'Who saw us?'

His sigh was fragmented with a slight chuckle. 'Only my sister.'

'Only— Oh, goodnight and God bless!' She sucked in a solid breath of head-clearing air, which also sprouted a flare of anger. 'Only your sister!'

'Yes. Rosemary,' he said. 'You'll like her.' Pausing for a brief moment, he asked, 'How old are you?'

'Twenty-two.' She drew her head back and pushed at his chest to give herself enough wiggle room to see his face. 'Why? How old are you?' Their ages hadn't been something that had come up in their conversations.

'Twenty-seven and I asked because Rosemary is twenty-one and I believe the two of you will get along splendidly.'

'Splendidly?'

She gave his chest a smack with one palm. 'She just saw us kissing and you think we'll get along splendidly?'

'Yes. You and Violet are sure to get along as well.'

'Did she see us, too?'

'I don't know. I only saw Rosemary.'

Suzanne closed her eyes. 'Where?'

'Looking out an upstairs window. Much like you were doing earlier.'

Flustered with herself for thinking that behind the hedge would have been a spot where no one would see them, she huffed out a breath. 'Is that why you kissed me? Because she was watching?'

His gaze caught and held hers as his expression softened. 'No.'

She wanted to ask why, then, had he kissed her, but wasn't certain that she wanted to know the answer. Nor did she want to know why she'd kissed him in return.

Another thought formed. 'Why did you say I'm an amazing writer?'

He grinned. 'Mr Winterbourne sent a message this morning, mentioning that he's impressed by what he's read so far.'

She pressed a hand to the increased beating of her heart. 'He did?'

'He did.'

Henry had done exactly what he'd promised. Therefore, she had to do what she'd promised. She could do it. She could do anything she put her mind to. That's another thing Aunt Adelle had always told her.

She'd already changed her dress today, shortly after his mother had arrived. The peach-coloured one she now wore, with its fitted bodice trimmed in white eyelet, was one of her favourites. 'I baked a rum cake for tea,' she said. 'It's in the warming oven.'

'Well, in that case…' He kissed her forehead and then released her, but kept one hand on her back. 'I'll help you retrieve it. But may I ask did you bake only one?'

She couldn't help but giggle as warmth filled her. 'No, I baked two.'

'My prayers have been answered,' he said, winking at her.

Chapter Ten

Henry's sisters and mother were all very pretty women. Each had dark hair and eyes. Violet and his mother, Margaret, Lady Beaufort, were shorter, with round faces and dainty features. Rosemary was taller, with a slender face and more distinct features which reminded Suzanne of Henry.

Then again, everything reminded her of him.

In fact, she wasn't sure if she was no longer nervous about meeting his family because all three of women had made her feel very welcome, or if it was because she couldn't stop thinking about kissing Henry. She kept checking to see if there was some tell-tale sign in Rosemary's expression to say what she thought about seeing them kissing, or if she'd told Violet or his mother about what she'd seen.

It didn't appear that way, but with Henry sitting next to her on the sofa in his sitting room, she wasn't sure of anything. Not of what his sister thought, who she'd told, or if he would kiss her again.

She couldn't deny that was one of her main thoughts. Him kissing her again.

In her attempts to keep that thought at bay, she told his mother and sisters about Aunt Adelle, Hampton and the trip to England on one of Roger's ships. They told her funny stories about Henry when he was little—to which he said they were exaggerating—and about Beaufort, and Carter and Judd while they ate the rum cake and drank tea.

The cups and plates were empty when Caleb appeared at the door.

'Excuse me,' he said with a bow while addressing Henry's mother, 'the dressmaker has arrived, My Lady.'

'Very well, Caleb,' Lady Beaufort replied. 'Do show her in.' She then said to Henry, 'I'm sure you have things to see to, dear. I requested fittings by Madam Perino to fashion gowns for each of us for the party. We shall be busy for the next hour or more.'

Suzanne stood at the same time Henry did, fully prepared to take her leave.

Henry gave her hand a gentle squeeze. 'I'll see you later.'

'I'll walk out with you,' she said.

'No, dear,' Lady Beaufort said. 'Madam Perino will need your measurements, too.'

'Thank you,' Suzanne replied, 'but I have a gown that I can wear.'

'One created especially for your engagement party?' Lady Beaufort asked.

'Well, no, but—'

'Then Madam Perino will create one for you,' Lady Beaufort said before turning about to face the door as a tall and voluminous woman, whose layered green skirts swished as she sashayed into the room, was followed by three younger women, each carrying a large basket.

Not sure what to say, Suzanne looked at Henry.

He smiled at her, as his sister Rosemary stepped closer.

'I'll take very good care of her, dear Brother,' Rosemary said to Henry.

'Suzanne does not need a nursemaid, merely a friend,' he said.

'I agree,' Rosemary said.

Henry then touched Suzanne's cheek with his lips and whispered, 'Enjoy yourself.'

She didn't have the opportunity to reply before he left her side.

Madam Perino had stopped next to Lady Beaufort. 'Lady Beaufort, I was so pleased to receive your request. I brought along three of my top seamstresses and I assure you, the gowns you choose will be ready in time for the ball.'

Within no time, the tea service dishes were removed and the door securely closed. The younger seamstresses emptied their baskets of material swatches, various lace and button samples, and several sheets of paper with pictures of gowns drawn on them.

Suzanne would have been at a loss without Rosemary and Violet and, despite knowing that she truly didn't need yet another gown, she was quickly drawn into the camaraderie that the sisters created around her.

After seeing to several tasks that he'd been putting off, Henry leaned back in his chair and rested one ankle upon his other knee and stared out the window of his study. Tea had gone remarkably well. Maybe her country wouldn't be at war if Suzanne had set up a meeting between the North and the South and served her Aunt Adelle's butter rum cake. One taste had changed his mother's attitude from stoic to welcoming.

He couldn't remember his mother ever cooking, or baking, but she had wanted to know everything about the cake. Suzanne had shared her Aunt Adelle story, which had endeared her to his sisters completely and his mother hadn't been far behind.

That hadn't surprised him. Suzanne had endeared herself to him, too.

More than endeared.

He couldn't get the kiss they'd shared out of his mind. Or the feel of her body pressed up against his.

He stood and walked to the terrace door and opened it. The hedge that she'd pulled him behind was within his view. Kissing her hadn't been on his mind when he'd seen her waving at him from the window. Even after she'd tugged him behind the hedge, when the idea had formed, his rational mind had told him to remember why he was pretending to be engaged.

His goal was to catch a murderer and kissing her wouldn't advance that goal.

He had self-control and could have applied more of it, but he hadn't. The desire to kiss her, to taste her, had simply been too enticing.

However, the action had caused him to want more. More kisses and embraces between the two of them. That was unusual for him. He'd dedicated his life to caring for his family. The family investments and businesses were profitable again, but he knew how easily things could go awry.

A knock on the inside door shattered his thoughts

and he turned, re-entering the room through the terrace door. 'Come in.'

The door opened slowly and Suzanne barely poked her head around the doorway. 'Sorry for intruding.'

'No need to be sorry.' He crossed the few final steps to the door and held it wide for her to enter the room. 'Come in. Has the dressmaker departed?'

'She's preparing to.' Suzanne stepped into the room. 'I am going home and your mother suggested that I say goodbye.'

He closed the door behind her and gestured to the open terrace door. 'I'll walk you across the gardens.' He took a hold of her elbow. 'Did you decide upon a dress?'

'Yes,' she replied, 'but I must say that I've never been measured in so many ways and places.'

Certain body muscles tightened and he told himself to not image being that measuring tape. The moment he'd seen her in the doorway, the memory of kissing her had become stronger, as had the desire to repeat it. He'd never felt such a strong desire for a woman before and knew it was more than that. It was a desire for one woman. Her. Specifically.

He was going to have to get over that, or figure out a way to deal with it. Quickly. Not only did he need to remain dedicated to his family, he had to remember her desire to return to America. He wondered where she would go upon her return and hoped she wouldn't let her mother's past affect her. She held no responsibility to the past.

'Aunt Adelle taught me how to sew when I arrived at her house and we sewed all of our own clothes,' she said as they walked out of the terrace door. 'We didn't have a sewing machine, but I bet with one like we saw at the Exposition, a person could sew a dress in a quarter of the time than by hand.'

'I'm sure Madame Perino has more than one machine in her shop.'

'Have you seen them? Her machines?'

'I have not,' he replied. 'But all seamstresses have machines of different types.'

'I suspect you're right,' she replied. 'There was a man in Hampton, Mr Carville, who had a machine that sewed heavy canvases for wagons. It was much larger than those we saw at the Exposition.'

'There are many types of sewing machines and new ones are being invented or improved yearly.'

She glanced up at him. 'How do you know that?'

'We have several at our milliner's factory.'

'Oh.' They were almost to her back door when she stopped walking and looked up at him. 'Thank you for walking me home. I can have Hiram drive me to Elaine's this evening so you can travel with your family.'

Henry held his tongue for a moment, weighing his options, before saying, 'I'd prefer that you accompany me.' The things he felt inside were too real. He didn't want them to be real, but they were.

She nodded and he felt a sense of vulnerability in her that he hadn't noticed before. 'I've never had to lie like this before,' she whispered.

He touched the side of her face. 'I haven't either.' A dozen thoughts, including kissing her, flashed through his mind. 'We can end it if you choose.'

She searched his face as her own grimaced slightly before she shook her head. 'No, we have to do this to prove your innocence.'

'I can find another way.' That was true, but his fear

was that the murderer might have already heard about
the engagement, which could put her in danger. Being
engaged to her, he could keep a much closer eye on her.
He briefly questioned if that was an excuse, but let that
idea go.

'No. This is what we've agreed to.' She said no more
as she turned and walked the last few feet to the back
door.

Henry considered following, but didn't, because there
was nothing he could say. This was what they'd agreed
to and, though he regretted involving her in his life, he
had to see it through. To the end.

Instead of returning to the house, he walked to the
stable and saddled Barley himself rather than call for
Caleb, because he wanted no one to know he was leaving.

He had to find a way to put an end to this that didn't
involve Suzanne.

For once, at least at this moment, luck was on his side.
A few streets before the detective's modest home, Henry
espied Adam Henricks walking along the sidewalk.

Adam saw him, too, and the two of them shared nothing more than a brief glance, yet Henry knew the man
would be in the alley behind his house within minutes.

Henry was there, waiting.

Adam Henricks was short, stocky and of an indeter-
minable age for those who didn't know him. Henry had
known Adam for years, due to security issues at some
of the buildings he owned that had attracted thieves at
times. Adam had been a police agent at the time, stopping criminals in the act. It hadn't been until recently
that Scotland Yard had created an investigation divi-

sion to solve crimes of which no perpetrators had been apprehended.

He could tell by Adam's tight expression that the man had news and it wasn't good.

'Another murder?' Henry asked, hoping he was wrong.

'No,' Adam replied. 'Another cufflink. Two days ago, in the spot where the bodies were found. A constable discovered it while walking his beat. The area had been thoroughly searched, so it was left afterwards and deliberately.' Adam took off his squat hat and ran a hand through his flattened dark hair. 'You haven't come up with anyone who might have had them? Or who might be trying to pin these murders on you?'

'No. My mother would be the only person who would have my father's cufflinks in her possession, but I'm sure he was buried with them on his shirt.' His father's cufflinks were unique, commissioned by him and made for him years ago.

'Could someone have had a duplicate set made?'

'I'm not sure, I suppose, I never thought of that.' Trusting the detective, Henry had told Adam about Heather being his half-sister when the detective had come to him with the first cufflink. 'I will look into that.'

'These murders aren't random and whoever is committing them wants all fingers pointing at you.' Adam huffed out a breath of air. 'No one knows about the first cufflink, but I wasn't there when the second one was found. In my opinion, that's why it was put out later, to make sure it arose suspicion.'

Henry balled his hands at his sides. He'd racked his brain, trying to come up with an enemy of his or his father who might now be taking vengeance out on him, but was unable to think of a single name. There had been discontented employees when he'd first taken over for his father, but those issues had been addressed and managers, as well as other employees, had stated that things were far better now. For those he'd had no choice but to let go, he had provided assistance to find other employment and there wasn't one that he could think of who might now want vengeance.

Additionally, other than Heather's mother all those years ago, he knew of no other women his father had been involved with, albeit, one was enough. He just couldn't come up with a motivation for pinning the murders on him.

'Scotland Yard has put several men on to this,' Adam said. 'They are all looking your way. I can't turn them in another direction without something to go on, not without gaining suspicion, which could make things worse.'

'I don't expect you to divert anyone's attention. I just want the real murderer caught.'

Adam nodded. 'You will be called in for questioning. I don't know when, but expect it.'

'I will comply with any and all requests.'

'We need something to turn the attention away from you,' Adam said.

'We need to find the real killer,' Henry replied.

Adam rubbed his chin before asking, 'Is it true that there is an engagement about to be announced?'

Henry doubted that a revelation of the truth about his engagement would help, so he nodded. 'Yes. Miss Suzanne Bishop. An American.'

'I offer my congratulations,' Adam said, 'and hope that the announcement doesn't arouse further suspicions.'

'I considered that,' Henry admitted, 'but chose not to

let some unknown person influence my life.' That was a flat-out lie, but his hands were tied in that respect.

'I commend you on that and assure you that I'm doing everything within my power to find the murderer. I'm doing all I can to find a solid lead.'

'So am I,' Henry acknowledged. 'So am I.'

Suzanne plopped down on the bed and opened the letter that had been delivered while she'd been next door for tea and picking out a dress. It was from the publisher. A single, small envelope.

Henry had said that Mr Winterbourne had been impressed, but had he read more and changed his mind? That could happen.

Or, he could have continued to like it.

She wouldn't know until she read the letter.

She was afraid to. If this didn't work out, she didn't have another plan. She needed a way to make money, enough for a return passage to America. Whether she wanted to or not, that was what Henry was expecting and therefore what she had to do.

After saying a silent prayer, she carefully broke the wax seal on the envelope and took out the single piece of paper.

The handwritten note was signed by Mr Marion Winterbourne at the bottom. She then went back to the top and began reading. The note stated that though the publishing house normally published stories of mystery and intrigue, he found her story of escaping the war very interesting and her writing very professional.

Her heart pounded harder as she continued to read.

Mr Winterbourne went on to say that he would like a few weeks to fully review the story and offer suggestions. If, upon her review of those suggestions, she was interested, an offer of publication might be offered at that time.

Suzanne reread the entire letter a second, then third time, just to be sure every line had sunk in. Then she folded the paper and slid it back inside the envelope. Biting her bottom lip, she glanced left, then right, and then jumped off the bed and squealed with excitement.

She ran to the window, wondering what Henry was doing and if she could go and tell him her news. He was the first person she wanted to tell.

Gradually, almost as if a cloud slowly floated in front of the sun, her excitement faded. Publication would not only mean she had the money to go back to America, it would mean that she would never see Henry again.

She stepped away from the window. Why did that thought make her heart sink? Make her sick to her stomach?

He wasn't like anyone she'd ever known. He was so kind, so caring, and committed to helping others.

He was also the only man she'd ever wanted to kiss, and had kissed, and wanted to do so again.

She plopped down on the bed, afraid of what that might mean.

Furthermore, what did it mean that she'd told him about her mother?

Maybe she should be asking herself what she was going to do about any of that.

Lying down on the bed, that's what she did, asked herself so many questions it made her brain tired, because she couldn't come up with any answers, other than one that frightened her.

She couldn't be falling in love with Henry. That was

impossible. She was far too sensible to let anything like that happen.

Sitting up, she glanced at the clock, then leaped to her feet as panic struck. She had only half an hour before Henry would arrive to escort her to Elaine's!

Thankfully, Elyse, bless her heart, had already pressed the purple gown and had left it draped over the wardrobe door. However, due to several wayward curls that she couldn't get to behave, she was barrelling down the stairs to find Elyse for assistance, when she saw Hiram opening the front door.

Henry walked inside just as she grabbed the handrail newel as she bounded off the last step.

Rocking to keep her balance after coming to an abrupt stop, she held on tighter to the newel and met his gaze.

One brow raised, Henry said, 'We are not in that big of a hurry, are we?'

Suzanne would have sighed if her heart hadn't been racing. He looked overly handsome in his dark green waistcoat and shimmering brown vest over his white shirt. She closed her eyes briefly and swallowed, hoping one or the other would help her gain control of her body and her thoughts, which were remembering how amazing it had been to be pressed up tightly to his tall, hard body. 'I— I—' She swallowed again, and once again told herself that she could not be falling in love with him. 'I was looking for Elyse.'

'I'm right here, miss.'

Suzanne turned about, managing to smile at the servant. 'I need your assistance with my hair.'

'Excuse us, my lord,' Elyse said to Henry, as she led the way into the nearby sitting room for a bit of privacy.

Suzanne followed and sat in the chair while Elyse expertly repositioned a few combs and then nodded. 'Perfect. You look extremely lovely this evening. Perfect for an engagement dinner.'

A flash of guilt struck Suzanne due to the closeness that had formed between her and Elyse, and Hiram for that fact. She had told them about the engagement, had to, for they were sure to hear, but it felt as if she was tricking them.

Tricking everyone.

Including herself.

'The Earl of Beaufort is handsome, intelligent and kind, you couldn't have chosen a more wonderful man,' Elyse said. 'I'm very happy for you.'

'Thank you,' Suzanne said, trying hard to sound sincere. Henry was all of those things, but she hadn't *chosen* him. Nor had he chosen her. They'd simply needed something from each other. 'I don't want to keep him waiting.'

'No, of course not,' Elyse said. 'Your hair looks perfect now.'

'Thank you, very much.' She rose to her feet and straighten her shoulders. 'I shall see you later.'

With a cheeky grin, Elyse said, 'We are sure to have some busy days coming up.'

Chapter Eleven

Busy didn't begin to describe the days that followed the evening meal at Lady Voss's house. Every day there was something to do, somewhere to be.

Between dress fittings, outings with Henry's mother and sisters, planning meetings at Lady Voss's and gatherings that had no real meaning, but she had to be in attendance, Suzanne felt run ragged. She didn't have time to worry about returning to America, other than late at night, like now. Long after Henry had walked her across the gardens. That was the only time she really saw him. At least it was the only time they were alone, and that was the most vexing part. There was no time to ask him if he'd learned any more clues or information.

She sensed that he had, because he was often busy with *errands* while she was occupied with what she considered frivolous things. Seriously, did it truly matter what the dance cards looked like? Not to her. Nor did she care how many bouquets of flowers were placed where, nor what songs the musicians played first. And, trying on a dress while it was only pinned together was painful.

Thank goodness that wouldn't need to happen again.

Her new blue gown would be delivered tomorrow, which truly was gorgeous with layers of white lace, multiple blue bows that held up different layers of the skirt and a row of tiny pearl buttons down the back. Clara and Annabelle would both arrive tomorrow also, along with their husbands, and the engagement ball would take place the following night.

Suzanne was nervous about that—her friends arriving. She walked to the window of her bedroom. Would she be able to keep up the pretence in front of her friends? Both Annabelle and Clara knew her well and that meant they knew her feelings on marriage. Her plan had always been to follow Aunt Adelle's advice about living the life she wanted, not one a man wanted for her. Some had called Aunt Adelle an old maid. Aunt Adelle had called those people jealous.

Others she'd called stupid.

Not necessarily stupid. Aunt Adelle had been more colourful than that. She would have said something along the lines of, *don't mind them, they don't know their head from a hole in the ground.* Or *don't mind her, some people read books, she just eats the pages.*

For the most part, Suzanne had always grasped her meanings and had agreed with many of them. She'd never had to depend on someone else, nor had she ever had expectations set upon her to marry and become a wife and mother. Just the opposite, in fact, and she certainly had never been forced to follow social rules like she had to now. There were so many rules when it came to the engagement party that her head swam just thinking about them.

Her saving grace was Henry. He'd told her not to worry about any of it.

It was odd how she hadn't worried about those rules before, but now, when people would be thinking that she would become his wife, she was worried.

She wanted him proven innocent, wanted the real murderer caught.

She owed him that. He'd been very excited about the letter she'd received from Mr Winterbourne and offered to instruct him to speed up the process. Of course she'd refused, explained that if her story was published, it would be on its own merit.

Staring out the window, at the dark and quiet back gardens, she told herself that there was one thing that she did know for sure. That she should be happy that there hadn't been another opportunity for Henry to kiss her.

She wasn't happy though. Probably because if they'd been alone long enough for him to kiss her, they would have been alone long enough for him to tell her if he'd learned anything new recently about the murders or murderer, or if he'd met with his friend from Scotland Yard again.

Her heart did a fast somersault as something outside caught her attention. She leaned closer to the window. She was certain she'd seen movement near the hedge. Was it Henry? Who else could it be? It had been several hours since he'd walked her home.

Staring at the point where she'd thought she'd seen movement, she held her breath while waiting to see if anything moved again.

The air gushed out with excitement when she saw movement. Someone was behind the hedge. She could see a slight shadow that was most certainly a person. She stared longer, waiting to see if they moved.

They didn't. Just stood in the darkness of the hedge.

It had to be Henry.

Her brows tugged above her eyes. Was he sneaking out and hadn't told her about it? Did he believe having his mother and sisters staying with him was enough of an alibi?

She scanned the few windows of his house that she could see, but there wasn't a light on in any of them. A quick glance at the clock showed it was after midnight, well after. Nearly one o'clock in the morning and another look out the window said the shadow had not moved.

Maybe he was sneaking back home and was looking to see if she was still awake to tell her about his excursion.

Torn, because she was only wearing her sleeping gown and knew there wasn't time to get dressed, she questioned what to do. In two shakes of a dog's tail later, with her black cloak covering her nightgown and wearing her house slippers, she hurried from her room.

The third stair creaked beneath her foot and she paused for a moment, listened for any sounds coming from above before moving downwards again.

Glad that the servants' quarters were on the third floor, she hurried to the bottom of the stairs, then ran down the hall to the kitchen and to the back door. The kcy was hanging on the hook next to the door and she snatched it, quietly unlocked the door and pushed it open.

A silence that was broken only by the odd sounds of insects and the soft breeze blowing through the leaves greeted her. Slowly, and while scanning the back garden, she stepped out of the door and pulled it closed behind her.

She couldn't see the shadow from here, but knew exactly where she had seen it. Near the end of the hedge, on Henry's side of the bushes. Her heartbeat echoed in her ears as she stepped down the landing steps and on to the grass.

From there, she could see his entire house. The light in his study was on and she took that to confirm it was him near the edge of the hedge.

She couldn't see if anyone was inside his study, just a glow of lamplight behind the thin curtains, but the door was ajar. As quietly as possible, she hurried forward, towards the hedge. His carriage house was further back, behind his house, past the hedge, and she wondered if he'd met his detective friend again tonight.

Maybe that was who the shadow had been, his friend, waiting for Henry.

Either way, she had to know.

A horse nickered just as she reached the hedge and she dropped down, knees bent, to make sure the hedge hid her, and pushed aside some branches to peek through the hedge, trying to see if the shadow had moved closer to the carriage house.

She wasn't scared. Sneaking in and out of army camps had cured her from being afraid of things that go bump in the night. The only thing she'd been afraid of back then had been getting caught.

The horse nickered again and, though she couldn't see anyone, she stayed still, listening as the silence settled.

A muffled snap or thud, some sort of small sound, came from behind her and she eased upwards to turn around, sure that Henry was approaching.

Before she was all the way upright, a stench hit her and, deep down in the pit of her stomach, fear exploded.

It wasn't Henry. She was sure of that, even before something was thrown over her head.

Henry pushed the terrace door that he'd left cracked open to let in the cool night air all the way open. He wasn't sure what had made him walk to the door, but the first place he looked was next door, up towards the window of Suzanne's bedroom. Her light was still on, as it had been every night lately. He had no idea what she was doing until the wee hours of the morning, but couldn't sleep until her light went out.

Even then, sleep didn't come easily. His lips pursed at the thoughts that had become more invasive lately. They all included Suzanne. Nothing seemed to clear his head. It was to the point that even walking her home in the evening was difficult, because it wasn't just the kiss he remembered, it was the passion of which she'd returned his kiss that he couldn't get out of his mind.

One of the horses nickered and he stepped out on to the terrace. There was only a quarter-moon tonight, just enough light to cast faint shadows.

A horse nickered again. He moved to the edge of the terrace, and stood there, listening for anything else.

What sounded like a muffled yelp made every hair on his arms stand up straight and he leaped off the terrace, running across the garden. Thuds, thumps and hmphs sounded from the other side of the hedge. Instinct alone made him shout, 'Suzanne!'

'Hen— Ugg!'

The way his name was cut short and the grunt sound fuelled his speed.

He rounded the hedge. Saw someone running, but

also a body on the ground. 'Suzanne!' Fear encompassed him as he ran to where she lay on the ground.

No! No! She couldn't be hurt.

'Suzanne! Suzanne!'

She moved, pushing up on her hands and knees as he dropped down beside her.

He grabbed her shoulders, carefully, not wanting to cause injury to injury. 'Where does it hurt?'

'I'm fine!' She pushed at his chest with both hands, hard. 'Go! Stop him!'

His concern was her first, but as she scrambled to her feet, he knew she was right and he leaped to his feet, taking chase to where he'd last seen the man.

The sounds of horse hooves and wheels churning echoed in the air by the time he rounded the end of the hedge and he barely caught sight of a single, galloping horse pulling a cabriolet before it disappeared into the darkness.

Flustered, because he knew there was no way he'd catch them, Henry let out a curse, then turned around to return to Suzanne and complete a full assessment to confirm that she wasn't hurt.

'Dagnabbit!' she growled and slapped her thigh with one hand. 'I almost had him!'

'You almost had him?' Henry asked, not sure if he was more stunned or angry. She shouldn't have almost had anyone! Should have been upstairs in her bedroom.

'Yes! I thought it was you, or perhaps your detective friend, but he sneaked up behind me and put this over my head.' She held up a long, black, silk scarf. 'He tried to get it around my neck, but—'

'You're bleeding!' Henry grabbed her hand to examine it more closely in the moonlight. Blood covered the back of it.

'No, I'm not. That was his blood. I hit him in the nose.'

Now anger, shock and amazement battled inside him. He needed to know everything, but one thing was the most important. 'Are you hurt anywhere?' he asked, while examining her hand for an injury. 'Anywhere at all?'

'No. I'm fine.'

There was no cut on her hand and the relief that was now flooding his system was stronger than anything else. He didn't know if he should shake her or hug her. Telling her she should never have left the house was on the tip of his tongue, but this was Suzanne and she'd argue that point to high water.

He chose instead to hug her and pulled her close, kissing the top of her head and holding her tightly against him until some of his frustration eased. Then, still needing to make sure she wasn't injured, he turned them both around to walk towards the carriage house. 'Let's get you cleaned up. Make sure you are all right.'

'I'm fine. Just mad that he got away. I had him down on the ground!'

'You had him on the ground?' Henry shook his head. She would see it that way and not the other way around. As in the he—whoever he was—had her down on the ground.

'You don't think we woke anyone, do you?'

He glanced at the houses, both of them, and not seeing any additional lights on, he said, 'I don't think so. Start at the beginning, tell me everything.'

She sighed. 'I saw a figure out my window and thought it was you, or your detective friend, so I came out. One of the horses made a noise and I ducked down behind the hedge and then, while I was standing up, he came up behind me. I got hold of the scarf before it tightened around my neck and we fought over it, fell to the ground. That's when I hit him in the face with my elbow and then punched him when he lost his hold on me. I tried to catch hold of his legs, but he got away.'

Henry was doing his best to keep the mixture of fear, anger and frustration out of his voice as he asked, 'Did you see his face?'

'No. He had a hood that covered the top half of his face. But he stunk. Smelled like a saloon.' She shrugged. 'Like stale cigar smoke, men who haven't bathed and whisky. I had a student whose father owned a saloon and wasn't overly concerned if his son made it to school in the morning, so I went there serval times and brought his son to school.'

He didn't doubt that she had done that. She cared more about everyone else than she did herself. Tonight was more proof. Proof he hadn't needed.

They had arrived at the carriage house and, upon entering, he lit a lantern. 'Sit here,' he said, gesturing to a short stool in the corner near the water barrel. 'I'll get a rag to wash your hand.'

She sat and brushed some sprigs of grass off her black cloak. 'I was trying to get hold of his leg when I heard you shout. Had you seen me?'

He'd found a rag, dipped it in the water barrel and ring it out while saying, 'No, I just heard muffled thuds.' Her name had been his first thought, that's why he'd shouted it.

'I tried to answer, but he kicked me.'

'Kicked you where?' When he found this man, he'd

make sure he got what he deserved. He would find him. He'd rip the world apart until he did.

'I don't really know. My arm mainly. Nothing hurts. It just knocked the air out of me for a moment.' She let out a growl. 'I was so close to getting that scarf around his legs. He was worried about his nose bleeding and...' She sighed and looked up at him with sorrow on her face. 'I'm sorry. I should have had him.'

'No, you shouldn't have,' he said while washing her hand and noting there weren't any scratches or scrapes.

'Please don't tell me that I should have stayed inside,' she said. 'We don't know what he was here to do.'

Henry had a damn good idea, but held his tongue on that point. However, he did say, 'I don't like the idea of you being in such danger.'

'I don't like the idea of you being in danger, either.'

He rinsed the rag and hung it up to dry on a nail. 'I wasn't in danger.'

'You don't know that,' she said. 'He could have been here to break into your house. He was on your side of the hedge when I first saw him.'

He shook his head. 'He wasn't after me.' Knowing she would need more information before believing him, he continued, 'Another cufflink has been found. Left after the last body was found, but in the same spot. Whoever this is doesn't want me dead. They want me imprisoned.'

Her lips formed a tight line as she stared at him. 'Why?'

'I don't know.'

'Have you asked your mother if any of your father's cufflinks are missing?'

'No. That information hasn't been released yet.' He still believed that the fewer people who knew that detail, the better chance he had of actually finding the culprit. Somehow, that person was connected to his family. Bart was highly suspect in his mind, but he couldn't be pulling this off from Beaufort. Furthermore, his mother would never have allowed his cousin access to his father's cufflinks. She'd never trusted Bart, even as a child.

'You need to talk to your mother.' Her expression softened. 'Ask her about the cufflinks.'

The fear that had gripped him earlier had morphed into anger that she'd been so close to being seriously injured. 'I need to solve this before anyone else gets hurt,' he said. 'It's my duty.'

'Duty?'

'Yes. As the man of the house, it's my duty to take care of it. To take care of everyone. Just like I did the businesses and everything else since my father died. I can't involve my mother, or anyone else, and I sure as hell shouldn't have involved you.'

'You didn't involve me,' she said. 'I did that all on my own and I'm the one who came up with the plan to help you.'

'Which I should never have agreed to!'

She stared at him for a stilled moment, which was long enough for regret to form.

'I'm sorry, I shouldn't have snapped like that. I just…' He shook his head. 'I just don't want anyone else to get hurt.'

'Neither do I, including you.' She laid a hand on his arm. 'It's not your duty to do it all alone. Nor is it your duty to take care of everyone. Everything.'

'Yes, it is. It comes with the title.' He'd never aired his frustration to anyone and was an ass for doing so to her.

'It's not your duty to take care of me,' she said, quietly,

but firmly. 'That's my duty. Though I may be a woman, I'm not helpless. Neither is your mother or your sisters.'

'I know you're not helpless.' He knew that better than anyone else. 'But what if I want to take care of you?' For that was the truth. He wanted to make sure she was taken care of for the rest of her life. She deserved to be taken care of, to be cherished.

Her eyes scanned his face for a moment. 'What if I want to take care of you?' she asked. 'Because that was our agreement. A partnership, where you help me and I help you. You did your part and now it's my turn to do mine.'

'My part was too simple. Your writing is amazing.' As long as he was admitting things, he added, 'I've read your story.' The things she went through had been harrowing and an even deeper sense of respect for her had formed after he'd spent a day at the publishing house doing nothing but reading her manuscript.

'When?'

'While you were attending dress fittings and ball-planning sessions.' He took hold of her hand. 'It's a gripping story of strength and courage, one that will be published.' He could guarantee that. Winterbourne had fully agreed that her writing was spectacular.

She shook her head. 'Not until you're proven innocent. A deal's a deal.' A grin formed then. 'But thank you. I'm glad you liked it.'

'I did very much and I'm looking forward to buying the first copy.'

She let out a light laugh. 'Well, then, we'd best catch the real murderer quickly, don't you think?'

He wasn't totally sure how she could so easily control things, but she could. It must be that charm, because she could flip things around and have him eating out of her hand in an instant. Her writing was just like her. Charming. Captivating. Enchanting.

As much as he didn't want it to be true, he knew that he wasn't immune to her charm in any way.

Giving him a look that sent his heart careening inside his chest, she asked, 'What else were you doing while I was being poked with pins and tying bows on dance cards?'

There was no use trying to change the subject. She'd get it out of him. He'd been telling her things that he'd never told anyone since the first night they'd met. 'I was called into Scotland Yard, questioned about the nights all three women were murdered, and though I was at balls on those nights, the suspicion that I still could have had time to complete the deeds is there.'

'I'll tell them that you were with me.'

He had no doubt that she could convince every man at Scotland Yard of that. 'That's not necessary.' He leaned against the water barrel. 'When Heather died, I was sure it was because she was my half-sister, but now I believe it's more about me and she was simply the first victim. I told you how I sold some assets after my father had his stroke and reinvested them in order to strengthen other investments, long-standing businesses, and now I am wondering if I acquired an enemy in doing so.' There wasn't anyone he could think of, but there must be someone. A discontented past manager or employee.

'Do you have any idea who?'

'No, but after tonight, I think they'll show up again.'

She stood up. 'We have to tell your friend, or Scotland Yard what happened tonight.'

His frustration returned. 'We don't have any proof that anything happened tonight.'

'We both saw him.'

'And we are faking an engagement. They figure that out and they won't believe anything we say.'

Other than the air she huffed out, they both remained silent, staring at each other.

He had no idea what to do, what to suggest they do. She'd already endeared herself to his family, and the Vosses were going to extreme measures to host their engagement ball. He hated the danger he'd put her in. Hated it more than he'd ever hated anything.

'It's late,' she said. 'We both need to go to bed.'

He shook his head. 'You aren't safe alone.'

'I'm not alone,' she said. 'Hiram and—'

'No one woke up, tonight. They would be out here checking if they'd heard anything.'

'That doesn't mean—'

'Hiram is getting on in age,' he said, lightly touching her shoulder. 'Someone could overpower him easily. I don't want anyone injured.'

Or worse and the idea of what could have happened to her tonight shattered a part of him. A part he hadn't known had existed. He touched the side of her face, then slid his fingers into her hair, all the while being mesmerised by those blue eyes.

Every last bit of self-discipline dissolved, leaving no option but to kiss her. Softly at first, but then passion erupted between them and the kiss deepened. The fear of her being hurt, the confusion of what was happening in his life, all disappeared, because there was no room for anything except him and her. Them.

He very well could be surrendering to the one thing

he shouldn't, but at this moment, there was nothing more that he could ever want than her in his arms. She felt so right there, so perfect, and he took full advantage of the moment.

Yet, he knew it had to end. Slowly, regretfully, he pulled away, then tucked her up against him and held her close until he had the wherewithal for clear thinking to return.

When his thoughts fully returned, he stepped back, holding on to her shoulders. There was only one solution that he could think of. 'I want you to go to Beaufort. You'll be safe there until the murderer is caught.'

She stared up at him, shaking her head. 'I'm not going anywhere. It doesn't matter that no one heard anything tonight. Whoever that was won't come back tonight. Drew and Annabelle will arrive tomorrow, so then I really won't be alone.'

That was true and, when Drew and Annabelle left, he'd make sure that she went to Beaufort with his family. He took hold of her hand and blew out the light. He could imagine her response, but still said, 'That is correct, but you will spend the rest of tonight at my house.'

'I can't,' she whispered. 'Imagine the gossip that will create.'

'No one will know. I'll walk you home at sunrise. Or I will stay at your house and leave at sunrise. Those are your choices. Choose one. Your place or mine.'

She stopped walking and pulled her hand out of his, clearly not pleased with his demand. Neither was he, but he was dead set about monitoring her every move until morning. Afterwards, as well. He'd figure out a way to make that happen, too.

Suzanne now fully understood exactly what Aunt

Adelle had been referring to each and every time she said that men needed to rule everything. Duty. That's what Henry had called it. She called it hogwash and considered telling him that, but arguing never got a person anywhere.

Other than a moment ago, when arguing had ended up with him kissing her. To the point that she hadn't been able to think clearly.

She could now and wouldn't be told what her choices were, especially when neither choice was something that she wanted. She did not need to be taken care of.

Therefore, with her head held high, she walked to the carriage house door. 'Fine. If you want to sleep on the sofa in the sitting room, go ahead. I'm going to my bed.'

The desire to tell him that he hadn't won, not even a slight battle, was so desirable that she clamped her lips tight together to make sure that not a single word slipped out. That would happen later, if he tried to tell her what to do again. Like going to stay at Beaufort. She couldn't do that. They had a murderer to catch. That had to have been who had been in the garden tonight and she was sure he'd been after Henry, not her. He'd been on Henry's side of the hedge.

Henry was being stubborn and obstinate, demanding that he got his way. In other words, he was exactly how Aunt Adelle had described men.

He was a man all right and, after tonight, she was even more worried about falling in love with him. Especially after he'd complimented her on her writing. Knowing he liked it had been like having a wish come true. For whatever reason, his opinion seemed to matter more to her than anyone else's.

Of course, she couldn't let him know that.

At the house, she lit no lamps, merely locked the door behind them, hung the key on the hook and started down the hallway. 'You know where the sitting room is,' she said as they arrived at the staircase and the sitting room was merely around the corner. 'Goodnight.'

If she wasn't so miffed, she might have offered him a pillow and blanket, but he was going to extremes by insisting that she couldn't be alone tonight. She'd lived without a man overseeing her for her entire life.

Once in her room, she blew out the light and climbed into bed, determined not to think about him downstairs on a much too short sofa, with no pillow or blanket.

But she did think about that and her mind kept floating back to kissing him, too. She didn't regret kissing him. How could she? It was... She sighed. Kissing him was beyond amazing. It was as though everything in the world was right. Perfect.

But it wasn't. Nothing about any of this was right or perfect.

She had finally fallen asleep and was still mad at Henry when she woke up. Before last night, he hadn't been controlling or overbearing, he'd been kind and understanding, and agreeable. She'd seen him being unyielding with his cousin, but not towards her.

Thankfully, there were no fittings or gatherings that she was committed to attending today, but after dressing, and eating breakfast, and insisting upon helping Elyse get everything ready for Annabelle's arrival—which included only a small amount of dusting because Elyse was so efficient, everything was already in order—she found herself with nothing to do, except think about

Henry, and that caused her to question if she was being too stubborn about being angry with him.

Shortly before noon, she was heralded downstairs to greet a visitor. Seeing Rosemary in the sitting room surprised her. She'd expected it to be Henry and told herself that she was not disappointed that it wasn't him. 'Did I forget an appointment?' she asked.

Rosemary's smile grew. 'No, not at all. We've been so busy the past few days, I feel as if we haven't had a chance to talk privately and, with Judd arriving today, we may not have another opportunity. He and I will stay at his family's town house, I hadn't wanted to stay there alone. Mother and Violet will join us for supper there this evening. I do hope I'm not intruding.'

'No, not at all.' Suzanne sat down in the adjacent chair. 'I have not completed a single significant task today.'

'Neither have I,' Rosemary said, with a laugh. 'And it feels good. Mother and Violet are visiting the Exposition and I have no idea where Henry is, but he's never been one to sit idle. As I'm sure you know.'

There were many things that she didn't know about Henry, but Suzanne knew that he was not one to be idle. Yet, she didn't agree or disagree, because she was still working at being angry with him and didn't want that to come through to his sister. That wouldn't be fair.

'I'm sure you also know how overprotective he can be at times, too,' Rosemary said. 'He just can't help it. It comes from being the eldest, and the only male. When our father had his stroke, Henry had to deal with so many things, including our mother. She kept thinking that Father would get better and she fought against

Henry, telling him that he was taking away our father's will to live.

'I understand that he was her husband and she was fearful of losing him to death, but we all knew he wasn't going to get better and the business decisions he did make, made things harder for Henry. It's sad to say and I'm only saying it because I trust you, but it was a blessing when our father died. For him and for the rest of the family. Henry was able to salvage the family fortune, but it wasn't easy on him.'

Her attempts to still be angry were waning greatly. 'I'm so sorry for your family's loss and difficulties,' Suzanne said. 'Henry takes his duty seriously.'

'Thank you, and, yes, he does. I wish there had been more that I could have done to help him, but he thinks he has to take care of everyone, all on his own. He has such a good heart. He's always wanted everyone to be treated just and fairly, no matter who they are.'

'I can see that,' Suzanne admitted.

'I just am so happy that he's found you. He deserves his own life, his own happiness. I was afraid that he'd never realise that and I wanted you to know that, despite his faults, for we all have those, he is an exceptional man, who will do anything, everything, for those he loves, and you two are certainly in love.'

Suzanne shifted in her seat at how that made her feel uncomfortable. What she felt for Henry was unlike anything she'd experienced before, but Aunt Adelle had always said love for a man was a weakness. She didn't want to be weak, didn't want to give up control of her own life.

'There truly is nothing like being in love.' Rosemary's expression grew thoughtful. 'A few years ago, I thought

I was in love with a village boy, Reggie Evert. Hamburg is a small town near Beaufort and Reggie's father owns the inn there. My parents were both aghast at the idea of me marrying beneath myself, but Henry merely said that a man shouldn't be judged because of who his father was and that owning an inn was a respectable business, one that was needed in Hamburg.'

'What happened between you and Reggie?' Suzanne asked, choosing to focus on that, because she knew nothing about having a father, but knew plenty about being judged for who her mother had been. Aunt Adelle had said that no one could ever know the truth, because they would hate her for it. No one had known, until she'd told Henry. He hadn't judged her. He'd hadn't judged her mother, either, but that had been because of his half-sister. Wasn't it?

'We discovered that we weren't in love and weren't right for each other.' She shrugged. 'We are still friends and the funny thing about it is that Judd and I used to be friends. I never imagined marrying him. Then, one day his horse became lame and he stopped at Beaufort. We were married six months later and I know one thing for certain. Henry was right. It doesn't matter who a man's father was, it matters how good a man's heart is.'

'You are probably right,' Suzanne said, feeling at a loss for words, yet also compelled to say something.

'I am right and Henry has a good heart. So does Judd. There are times he can drive me crazy at how he thinks he needs to take care of me.' Rosemary pressed a hand to her chest. 'But I know it's just because he loves me and wants to keep me safe.' She waved a hand. 'Henry's the same way, so I know you know what I mean.'

Rosemary clearly knew nothing about her and Henry

and their fake engagement, however, they must be doing a good job of pretending for his sister to be so convinced that they were in love.

Suzanne couldn't say that made her happy, but it made her believe one thing.

The true test would happen later today, when Annabelle and Clara arrived.

Chapter Twelve

By mid-afternoon, both Annabelle and Clara, each looking lovelier than ever, had arrived and all three of them had confined themselves to Suzanne's bedroom to see her engagement ball gown and to gossip.

Both of her friends had numerous questions about how she and Henry had gone from being neighbours to an engaged couple and Suzanne was proud of herself for coming up with answers that were as close to the truth as possible.

'I'm just so happy, I'm giddy,' Annabelle said, giving Suzanne yet another hug. 'All three of us, here in England, forever! I can't think of anything that could be better than that.'

With her long black hair and shimmering blue eyes, Annabelle had always been a beauty, and still was, but it was Clara who Suzanne really noticed a change in since she'd last seen her. Clara's brown hair was thick and full and she had the longest eyelashes imaginable around her brown eyes, but there was something different about her today that kept Suzanne glancing her way.

It wasn't just her dress, which was a soft pink colour, though it did look lovely on her.

'Can you imagine what Betty Ann Sinclair would say if she knew that we were royalty?' Clara asked with a giggle. 'A duchess, marchioness and a countess.'

'Oh, heaven forbid!' Annabelle exclaimed. 'She would pull our hair out, that's what she'd do.'

Suzanne joined in with the other two and giggled, even while knowing that she wouldn't ever be a countess, nor would she be in England forever. However, Betty Ann Sinclair had been the meanest and snootiest girl in school. Her father had owned the mercantile and Betty Ann had always had the finest clothes and toys, and rubbed people's noses in that as though they were puppies peeing in the house. Betty Ann had never grown out of that, either. Even as an adult, she'd been snooty and mean. Betty Ann's entire family were a few of those who had been spared during the attack, their home and business survived, and the last time Suzanne had been in town, the mercantile was charging ten times the price for simple, needed items, with no empathy for those who couldn't afford such prices.

'Remember when she washed her hair with lye because she wanted to look like you and her hair fell out in clumps?' Clara asked.

'Yes,' Suzanne replied. Betty Ann had light-coloured hair that wasn't brown or blonde and had tried to lighten the colour herself. 'I'll never forget it. She blamed me, told everyone that I'd told her to do it. Aunt Adelle had been fit to be tied when her mother had shown up at our house, screeching like a cat with a knot in its tail.'

'Oh, I remember your aunt saying that,' Annabelle said. 'She was a feisty old lady.'

'Yes, she was,' Clara said, giving Suzanne's hand a squeeze. 'We all loved her, but I'm not ashamed to say that I'm glad you aren't taking her advice. Being married is the best. The absolute best. I've never been so happy. Ever.'

That's when Suzanne realised what was making Clara look so pretty. She was literally glowing with happiness. Everything about her had a shine to it like Suzanne had never seen before. 'I can tell,' she said. 'I'm very happy for you.'

'And we are so happy for you.' Annabelle clapped her hands together. 'This is all so wonderful! Drew and Roger have known Henry for years. It's as though best friends all married best friends.'

'We aren't married yet,' Suzanne said, hoping to tone down the excitement. Both Clara and Annabelle would be so disappointed when they learned the truth. 'This is only our engagement party.'

'Only?' Clara laughed. 'You are already excited about your wedding night, aren't you?'

Suzanne felt her face and swallowed, hard, twice before saying, 'No, that's not what I meant.'

The other two were giggling like school girls all over again.

'There is nothing like the moments shared between husband and wife in the marital bed,' Clara said, glowing even brighter.

'Amen to that,' Annabelle added. 'The passion and pleasure are truly like nothing you can imagine, Suzanne.' Annabelle flopped on to the bed on her back and, with her yellow dress flowing out around her, stared at the ceiling. 'It's indescribable. And afterwards, it's like you're floating on air.'

'There are times when Roger looks at me and I just melt,' Clara said with a sigh.

'There are times when Drew looks at me and I drag him into the bedroom,' Annabelle said, giggling. 'Because I'll die for want if I don't.'

Clara laughed. 'There is that, too.'

Suzanne busied herself by rearranging papers on her desk, not wanting to hear any more or to see the way their eyes lit up as they talked. The perfunctory acts that Aunt Adelle had described had sounded uncouth and, as her aunt had described them, wicked.

'When is the wedding?' Clara asked. 'Soon, I hope. Roger and I are leaving in a few weeks.'

'Leaving for where?' Annabelle asked.

'The tropics,' Clara said, sounding as smitten as when talking about other things. 'He's taking me sailing on one of his ships so I can eat bananas.'

Suzanne turned to face her friend. 'Sailing?'

Annabelle sat up and flipped her legs over the edge of the bed. 'Bananas?'

'Yes, sailing,' Clara said. 'And bananas are a fruit that are quite delicious, I'm told.'

'You almost died the last time you were on a ship,' Suzanne reminded Clara. Upon arriving in England, Clara had been so sick, she'd spent days in bed.

'Because I hadn't eaten properly for months before boarding the ship,' Clara said. 'That won't happen again. Roger will make sure of it. He takes very good care of me and Abigail. You know that.'

Suzanne had seen that. Roger had been the one to sit with Clara the first night of her illness, spooning water into her mouth, and he'd continued to see to her care afterwards. Not to mention all of the other things he'd provided for all of them.

'When is the wedding?' Clara asked again.

'We haven't decided yet,' Suzanne said, turning back to the desk.

A friend appeared on each side of her, both staring at her.

Suzanne looked from one to the other, then plopped down on the chair and pressed a hand to her forehead. This was so hard.

'Oh, dear,' Clara said, kneeling down beside her. 'Suzanne, what is it? What's wrong?'

Suzanne had known lying to them would be difficult. These were her two best friends, had been for ever and always would be. She felt a loyalty to them, to tell them the truth, but she felt a loyalty to Henry, too. An allegiance to help him prove his innocence and that had to come before her friends. It not only had to, she wanted it to. The loyalty she felt towards him was strong. Stronger than to anyone else.

Knowing they would see through a lie, she chose a very viable truth. 'What you two described about the marital bed is nothing like what Aunt Adelle warned me about.'

'Suzanne,' Annabelle said softly. 'She warned you because she didn't know herself. She didn't like men. She thought they were cruel and evil. She told all of us that. How a man had stolen her sister. Claimed he was why she never got to see your grandmother again. More than once. But you aren't your aunt or your grandmother. You are you and this is about you.'

'It is,' Clara said. 'All about you. And Henry.'

Both friends were kneeling beside her, patting her

back and arm, because they cared. They truly did. And what they said about Aunt Adelle was true, but it was all so confusing.

'What does it feel like when he kisses you?' Annabelle asked. 'Do you get butterflies in your stomach?'

Suzanne closed her eyes and pinched her lips together. Just thinking about kissing Henry made her heart beat faster. 'Yes, and kissing him takes my breath away,' she said quietly. 'Makes my heart beat faster and I can't think of anything else except for him. Us. I feel an invisible connection to him that is uncanny. Special. And I don't want to stop. Stop kissing him.'

'That's exactly what it should feel like,' Annabelle whispered. 'And it only gets better. Trust me.'

'But…' Suzanne swallowed. 'The other things I feel are…wicked.'

'A wonderful, daring kind of wicked?' Annabelle asked.

'Yes,' Suzanne admitted.

'There's nothing wrong with that,' Annabelle said. 'It means you're normal, enjoying life and sharing your love with the man of your dreams.'

Suzanne stifled a sigh. They both loved their husbands. She and Henry were merely pretending and it would never be more than that. He expected her to go back to America. She had no one but herself to blame for starting this conversation and needed to find a way to end it. 'Aunt Adelle would say only a she-devil had thoughts like that.'

'Then it's a good thing that Aunt Adelle isn't here,' Clara said. 'But you are. You are in England, on an amazing adventure. That's what you've called it since the beginning. I didn't agree with you then, but you were right. It has been an adventure. One I never would have dreamed of. Yet, here we are, all three of us, and the one thing that I know for a fact is that yesterdays don't matter. It's today and tomorrow that count.'

Suzanne pressed a hand to her chest. They had all lost their homes, but Clara had lost her husband, yet, despite that, had found a way to move forward, find love again. Suzanne was very proud of her for that and refused to spoil any of the happiness Clara had found. Or Annabelle's. In that sense, she could remain loyal to her friends. 'You're right,' she said. 'It's today and tomorrow that count.'

'That it is,' Clara said.

They all three hugged. And laughed. Being happy for them was easy and that happiness was what she'd use to get through the days while they were here.

Clara let out an exaggerated sigh. 'How is it that these English noblemen stole our hearts so fully, so quickly?'

'I don't know,' Annabelle said. 'But I'm glad they did.'

'Me, too,' Clara replied.

They were both looking at her and, out of necessity, Suzanne said, 'Me, three.'

'What is it about a southern accent that cuts through a man's defences like a warm knife through butter?' Drew asked before taking a swig of his drink.

'I don't know,' Henry replied, finding a lot of truth in what Drew had just said.

'I don't either,' Roger replied, holding up one finger. 'What I do know is that I worship the ground my wife walks on.'

They were all three in Henry's study. Their wives,

along with Suzanne, were at Drew's house, where they all would eat an evening meal together in an hour or so. The women had insisted. The men had agreed. He'd known Roger and Drew for years, yet today felt a stronger kinship with them.

'I also know,' Roger continued, pacing the floor like an actor on stage. His coal-black hair, thick sideburns and vivid green eyes gave him the appearance of an actor, too, 'that I, Roger Hardgroves, the Marquess of Clairmount, once London's most eligible bachelor, am now a happily married man. Will wonders never cease?'

'You truly missed your calling, old man,' Drew said, his brown eyes laughing, even though his tone was dry. 'You should have inherited an opera house rather than shipping companies.'

'Henry owns one of those, don't you?' Roger asked, using his glass to point across the room at him.

Henry shook his head while swallowing a sip of whisky. 'I own the building, not the production company.' However, he himself had become a good actor of late, even if he was the only one who knew that. Keeping things platonic with Suzanne, while also pretending to be engaged to her, took a hell of a lot of acting. He'd forgotten that last night, in the stable, and shouldn't have given in to his desires and kissed her again, but he had.

'You own half the buildings in London,' Roger declared.

'Not half, but a goodly sum,' Henry replied. Then, because he truly needed to focus his mind on something, he asked Drew, 'How's the coal-mining business these days?'

The three of them spent a considerable amount of time discussing businesses, Parliament, and other gentlemen subjects. Both Drew and Roger knew of the issues he'd faced while his father's illness had progressed and then, after his father had died, with his inheritance, including the businesses that had fallen into disarray under his uncle's watch. Stories of despicable work environments had filled the newspapers and the milliner's factory had been singled out in more than one article. Some had accused him of squandering the family fortune when he'd first started to clean things up and he'd sought Drew's advice more than once during that time.

He also knew the two men would have heard about the murders and the rumours now circulating and figured he might as well be the one to bring it up. 'I didn't kill any of those women,' he said when there was a lull in conversation.

'I never thought for a moment that you had,' Drew replied.

'Nor I,' Roger supplied.

'Someone is attempting to pin them on me,' Henry said. 'I haven't figured out who, or why, or how to clear my name.'

'You will,' Drew said. 'Just like you cleaned up all your family's business holdings.'

'Which was no easy task,' Roger said. 'My inheritance issues were a breeze compared to what you went through.' Roger nodded at Drew. 'You, too.'

'Because until you met Clara, you never took anything seriously,' Drew said.

Roger nodded and shrugged. 'That could possibly be true.' Holding up a hand, he then said, 'None the less, if there is anything we can do to help, Henry, old chap, just ask. We'll be there.'

'Indeed. Anything,' Drew reiterated.

'Thank you, I appreciate that. Scotland Yard has men on it, but they have very little to go on.' Henry set his empty glass on the table. 'I am worried about Suzanne. Her safety. There was a man in the gardens last night. I don't know who. I've informed Scotland Yard, but I'm concerned that he will return.'

'Rightfully so,' Drew said. 'Did you get a good look at him? Any idea who it could have been?'

'No. It was too dark, but I've asked Caleb to keep watch tonight.'

'My groom from Mansfield is here with us,' Drew said. 'I'll have him keep watch, too.'

'Thank you,' Henry replied. 'I've suggested that Suzanne go to Beaufort after the engagement party.'

'But she refuses to go,' Drew said, with a grimace. 'She's a friend of Annabelle's, so that makes total sense.'

'Here, too,' Roger supplied. 'Those three women have more in common than their accents.'

'Yes, they do,' Drew said. 'They don't like being told what to do. In all fairness, I don't believe that anyone does, even when it's in their best interest. But if you can find a way for Suzanne to believe that going to Beaufort is her idea—and it might take some finessing—she'll go.'

'I agree with Drew,' Roger said. 'I can't even begin to describe how hard it was to convince Clara of things, but she eventually agreed with me.'

Henry took what both men said into consideration, for it made perfect sense. Even the part about it taking some finessing to convince Suzanne it was her idea. He was more than willing to try anything, because there was no way he'd let her stay alone at Drew's house again. Last night was too close to her being hurt, or worse. He could not, would not, let that happen again. Ever.

'When are you returning to Mansfield?' Henry asked Drew.

'Within a few days,' Drew said. 'It's a busy time at the mine right now, but I want to visit some exhibits at the Exposition. Why?'

'Because,' Henry said, 'I'm thinking that Beaufort is on the way to Mansfield, and perhaps the Duchess would like to see where her friend will be living.'

Drew nodded. 'She might at that, if she were to be invited by said friend.'

Henry was rubbing his chin, thinking this might just be a way to get Suzanne there. 'I know Beaufort is the opposite direction from Clairmount, but...' he said to Roger.

'But we could take the long way home,' Roger said. 'Those three like to spend time together. Furthermore, anything to keep any of our women safe, I'm in all the way.'

For the first time in a long while, Henry felt as if he might just be accomplishing something.

Drew slapped his thighs and then stood. 'Well, gentlemen, on that note, shall we progress next door for the evening meal?'

Chapter Thirteen

Several things crossed Henry's mind when he entered the sitting room in Drew's house. The very room where Suzanne had informed him that he could sleep on the sofa last night. He hadn't slept there. He'd spent the entire night outside, watching on the off chance that the assailant would choose to return and making sure that Suzanne wouldn't decide upon another night-time excursion into the grounds. Neither had happened. At sunrise, he'd informed Hiram he'd seen a prowler in the middle of the night and requested him to keep an eye out. Then he'd gone home, where he'd told Caleb the same thing.

The first thing he noticed while walking into the room was how lovely Suzanne looked. Her gown was pale green and fitted her curves perfectly. Her hair was neatly styled, while allowing several blonde curls to frame her face in a carefree way. That was also when he noted the apprehension in her eyes, for they had not seen each other since she'd bid him goodnight and marched up the stairs in the wee hours of the morning.

The next thing he took note of was the way the other two women rose from their chairs to greet their husbands with welcoming looks. Neither woman tried to hide their adoration, nor did they shy away from walking to meet their husbands with loving embraces.

He walked past both couples, to where Suzanne had risen from her seat on the sofa. Perhaps he'd become such a good actor, because he truly didn't need any unusual abilities to be attracted to her. That came quite naturally.

Taking her hand, he considered kissing the back of it, but in that moment, felt a sense of envy at how Drew and Roger had been able to greet their wives. He and Suzanne would never have that. All they would have would be a few weeks of pretending to be engaged. He would have to accept that as enough and leaned in and kissed her cheek. 'How are you?'

'Fine. You?'

'Fine.' They were talking quietly and he continued, 'No ill effects from last night? No bruising or soreness?'

'No. None. Just disappointment, as you know.'

'I've informed Scotland Yard and told Caleb and Hiram that there was a prowler on the property last night. They will be keeping a close watch out.'

She'd been scanning his face as he'd spoken and a hint of a smile flashed on her lips. 'Thank you.'

He leaned closer again, pressed his forehead to hers. 'I apologise for upsetting you last night. I just wanted— no, I needed to know that you'd be safe.'

She moved her face enough to softly press her lips against his cheek, before she whispered near his ear, 'I know and I'm sorry for not understanding your concerns. I'm not used to that. Unlike some women, I've lived my entire life taking care of myself. And others. My students and my aunt, then Clara and Abigail.'

'You are the most amazing woman I've ever known.' The words were out before he'd had time to process them, to stop them, but he wouldn't take them back even if he could, for they were the truth. Her manuscript had told him all that and more and he'd failed to take that into consideration.

She leaned back, looked up at him with those blue eyes that sucked the breath right out of his lungs. What he wouldn't give to be in private with her right now. Motives behind that thought twisted in his mind, until they forced him to admit that it was a good thing that they weren't alone. She had suggested and agreed to this engagement with no ulterior motives. He needed to remember that at all times. Even when his desires attempted to override his sensibilities.

'Shall we sit?' he asked.

Her cheeks flushed as she nodded.

He held her hand as she sat and then watched as she arranged her wide skirt, giving him plenty of space next to her.

He sat and, within minutes, the six of them were talking, laughing, and enjoying the evening in ways he'd never experienced. Suzanne's laughter was enchanting and warmed him inside like nothing ever had. He could spend his entire life listening to it, feeling how it encompassed him with an essence of happiness that he hadn't felt in a very long time.

The gaiety continued through the evening meal and afterwards, until the hour grew late. When Clara and Roger announced their leave, Henry voiced his as well. He had some serious thinking to do.

After thanking the hosts, he kissed Suzanne's cheek. 'I shall see you tomorrow.'

He sensed a hesitancy before she nodded. 'Goodnight.'

Was she questioning their agreement to go through with all this? He certainly was. Tonight, he'd seen how happy married couples could be. The dedication and commitment the other couples displayed couldn't be missed. The truth was that he could never have that. He had family commitments that would last a lifetime.

The other truth was that he'd never wanted marriage. Not after what his father had done, creating a child out of wedlock. His current infatuation with Suzanne was just that, an infatuation that would fade. Actually, it would end when she returned to America. Her writing was extraordinary and was sure to provide financially for herself, which was what she'd wanted. The only reason she'd agreed to this sham. 'Goodnight,' he replied and left.

He'd only been home a few minutes when his mother and Violet arrived home from joining Rosemary and Judd for the evening meal. Violet wished him a goodnight and proceeded upstairs, while his mother nodded towards his study.

That wasn't surprising. He was sure she'd heard about the rumours and had expected her to question him about them before now. Granted, she'd been busy since her arrival, but she'd been about town enough to hear the latest gossip. He was far more concerned about Suzanne's safety than what his mother might have heard.

As she took a seat in one of the armed chairs, he closed the door. 'Would you care for something to drink?'

'No, thank you.'

'How is Judd?'

'Fine.' She smoothed her skirt over her knees. 'You are becoming more and more like your father, Henry.'

He crossed the room and took a seat opposite her. 'From your tone, I sense that doesn't please you.' It didn't please him, either. If not for the insight of how his father had turned his attention so easily to another woman, he would be free to consider a real engagement to Suzanne. Free to believe that some day he could have a marriage like those he'd witnessed tonight.

No, he wouldn't be free to do that, because he still had his family. Those who depended upon him. He couldn't afford to take his focus off that. He'd inherited the earldom for that very reason. To be responsible for all. His desires had to come last, or not at all. He couldn't fail them and needed to get his infatuation with Suzanne under control and focus on finding the murderer, because that, too, was for his family. The entire family's reputation was in his hands.

'Your father used to attempt to keep secrets from me, too.' She folded her arms across her chest. 'Did you think I wouldn't hear the rumours?'

'No. I assumed you would.'

'Did you not think it would be better coming from you than some ninny at the Exposition?'

'They are rumours, Mother, and hold no truth.'

'I know they hold no truth,' she said. 'You are not an evil man. Just the opposite and that's what angers me. Your father would stop at nothing when it came to helping others, but when it came to himself, he would do nothing.'

Despite his own frustration, he said, 'I'm not doing nothing, Mother. I've been working with Scotland Yard.'

'What were you thinking?' she asked. 'Dragging Suzanne into this with an engagement now?'

'I agree, the timing may not be ideal.'

'Ideal?' Eyebrows raised, she gave him the same stare she'd used during his childhood when she'd expected him to change his behaviour immediately.

'Her safety is the most important thing to me,' he said, not because she expected him to respond. It was the truth, plain and simple.

'As it should be,' she replied. 'Why is your name being associated with the deaths of those unfortunate women?'

He considered asking her about the cufflinks, but there was too much danger in anyone knowing about them. It would come out eventually, but even Scotland Yard was keeping that under wraps, believing, like him, that a cufflink showing up after the body had been found was too suspect. 'I can only assume because Heather was the first woman murdered.'

'You were trying to help her, not hurt her.'

'I was, but perhaps you weren't the only one upset by that.'

She bristled, but it was the flash of something darker in her expression that made the hair on the back of his neck rise.

'Would you happen to know anything about that?' he asked.

'Of course not.' She cleared her throat. 'I am merely concerned about you and Suzanne. I would hate for her to think she's marrying into a scandalous family.'

'Of course, you would hate that.'

'I will not argue the importance of a family's reputation again,' she said.

They had already done that when he'd taken over for his father, when he'd put property up for sale and, of course, when he'd requested the barrister to legally see to Heather's inheritance.

She stood. 'It's late.'

He rose from his chair and crossed the room, opened the door for her. 'Goodnight, Mother.'

'Goodnight.'

She strode out of the room and he questioned if he should have forced her into an argument about the family's reputation. She knew something that he didn't. Something that had to do with Heather.

Or perhaps he should have told her that Suzanne wouldn't be marrying into a scandalous family because she wouldn't be marrying him. The damn engagement was a hoax that he never should have embarked upon. The fact he had was as much of a mystery as the murders. He'd never done anything so foolhardy, nor had he ever let his emotions have so much control over him. For they did have control over him. Every part of him desired Suzanne in a way he'd never encountered.

He should put an end to the engagement, now, before it went any further, for it truly wasn't needed to catch the murderer or prove his innocence. The rumours were out—claiming to be engaged wasn't going to stop them. But, ending the engagement could make society look at Suzanne in an unkind light. He couldn't let that happen. She was an innocent when it came to the aristocratic society and how damaging their hypocrisy could be. She'd been raised differently, had lived differently, and he could fully understand her desire to return to America.

That couldn't happen until the war had ended—until then, it was his duty to protect her. Protect her from society and from himself.

* * *

Suzanne stared at her refection in the mirror. The blue gown was gorgeous, her hair styled to perfection with not a single strand out of place and she barely recognised herself. No one who knew her back home would have recognised her either. Not even Aunt Adelle.

Besides telling her that she was tall for a woman, Aunt Adelle had said that getting her blonde curls to behave was like herding rabbits. Back home, she'd taken care of that by keeping it braided and wound into a knot at the nap of her neck. Here, she'd given the curls rein, securing them in place with combs and pins. She didn't do that by herself—Elyse was very skilled at fashioning hair.

She had become used to that, to having someone fix her hair and do so many other things that she used to do all by herself.

She'd also become used to wearing gowns. Lovely gowns rather than the simple dresses she'd worn back home.

She touched the gorgeous necklace around her neck, the dazzling earrings hanging from each ear, and looked at the ring on her finger.

All of these things were on the outside. Inside she hadn't changed.

Or had she?

She hadn't wanted to think so, but reality was that she had changed. Not until talking with Annabelle and Clara about kissing Henry, and other things, had she realised just how much she had changed. In many ways. She'd never felt the things that Henry made her feel, but she and Henry weren't in love, weren't engaged for real, so what she felt was wicked, like Aunt Adelle had said.

She was sure of that. Last night, today, she'd tried to justify other things she'd done since arriving here, but there was no justification.

Was she doing all of this because she wanted what Clara and Annabelle had? A husband. A future. Love.

She couldn't believe that. Those were not things she'd dreamed of acquiring.

Was that more proof that she had changed, or was she still seeking justification for acting so out of character since the moment she first saw Henry out the window? That's when it had all started. Her first day here, she'd seen him mounting his white horse and thought of an aged old fable of a knight on a white horse saving a damsel in distress. That had been before she'd known who he was, or that he'd owned the publishing house.

'Knock, knock,' Annabelle said while pushing open the door. 'Henry has arrived.'

Suzanne didn't turn from the mirror, too many thoughts were hanging too heavily to let them go. 'How long did it take you to change? To accept this life as normal?'

Annabelle walked up behind her, looking at her in the mirror. 'I don't think I changed,' she said.

'You're a duchess,' Suzanne said.

'Yes, I am and I'm proud of that. I'm proud to be married to Drew. My *life* changed when I met him, but I'm still *me*.' Annabelle squeezed Suzanne's shoulders. 'And you are still you.'

'Am I?' Suzanne shook her head. Back home she would have never suggested a pretend engagement. She would never have got used to having people wait on her or to wearing fancy gowns and going to balls as though she was some kind of royal. 'Life is so different here.'

'Yes, it is, but it's a wonderful different.'

Suzanne turned around, blinking at the tears forming in the back of her eyes. 'I need to go home, Annabelle. Back to America. I know who I am there. Here...' She swallowed hard. 'It's all pretend.'

Concern filled Annabelle's face as she reached out, touching her arm softly. 'That doesn't sound like the Suzanne I know.'

'Because I'm no longer me.' Suzanne waved a hand around the room. 'None of this is me.' Gesturing to the desk, she continued, 'Even that. Writing. I would never have sought out a publisher back home.'

'Because you would have been too busy teaching,' Annabelle said. 'Now you have a major publishing house ready to publish your book. A book you put your heart and soul into.'

That was the problem. Had she sold her soul for that? Both Clara and Annabelle had asked about her story upon arrival and she'd shown them the letter from Mr Winterbourne, but hadn't told them about Henry's part in getting the publisher to read her manuscript. She couldn't tell them that, because then she'd have to tell them about the engagement, how it was fake, a partnership between her and Henry.

She didn't want them to know that, just like she'd never told them that she was a child born out of wedlock and that her mother had been a flower in the Flower Garden.

She'd never wanted anyone to know about that, yet she'd told Henry. He'd said that he didn't matter, but that was because of Heather. Not everyone would be as understanding as him.

He was...he was one in a million and she couldn't

stop any of this until the real murderer was caught. For Henry's sake.

Annabelle touched her arm. 'You're just nervous, rightfully so. You're about to become a countess and a published author. That's a big change from being a school teacher in Hampton.'

Suzanne drew in a deep breath and let it out, gaining clarity in the process. Once her agreement with Henry was fulfilled, she'd have all the time in the world to dwell on what she'd done. Alone. In America. Though the thought nearly gutted her, she forced herself to smile and sound normal. 'You're right.' She turned to the mirror and fluffed the curls hanging over her forehead and then laid a hand on the sapphire necklace. 'I just had a moment of silly thoughts. Forgive me. I'm fine now.'

'There's nothing to forgive,' Annabelle said, smiling brightly. 'If you can't talk to your friends, who can you talk to?'

'Right again.' Suzanne turned away from the mirror and hooked an arm through Annabelle's, 'Time to go. The men are waiting for us.'

Chapter Fourteen

The Viscount Voss's house was lovely in its own right and all of the decorations not only enhanced the beauty of the home, they created an effervescent atmosphere. Laughter and joyful conversation mingled with the ever-flowing notes from the musicians gave even more life and gaiety to the fanfare and Suzanne couldn't deny that she was drawn into it all. This might not be her, but it was an adventure and she had always loved adventure.

The actual announcement of their engagement was a simple occurrence that happened early in the evening and required nothing difficult from her. She didn't need to pretend that she adored Henry, because he was adorable. Lovable. The pretend Suzanne knew all of that and that's who she was tonight.

The pretend Suzanne, excited to become a pretend countess. What could be more of an adventure than that?

After the announcement and a round of congratulatory speeches, the two of them took to the dance floor. Suzanne had known dancing with Henry would be amazing and that, too, proved true. She didn't need to worry about her toes being stepped on, or where his eyes wandered. His gaze was locked on hers as he expertly led her around the dance floor, making her feel as if her feet weren't even touching the floor.

Impeccably dressed in his dark suit, Henry was in perfect form. Tall, handsome and so endearing, it would have been impossible to attempt to hide that he moved her. Butterflies fluttered in her stomach, her heart thudded with enthusiasm and the warmth that enveloped her was as exciting as it was comforting. Tonight, she was accepting those things and more. If some people chose to think that she'd sought to marry a titled man like so many others, so be it. Nothing would alter her state of mind.

This was all part of her agreement and she wouldn't disappoint him. Or herself. Tonight wasn't about drawing out the murderer, it was about convincing all members of the *ton* that Henry Vogal, the Earl of Beaufort, was incapable of performing the dastardly deeds that rumours suggested.

'You are a skilled dancer,' Henry said.

She grinned. 'I was just thinking the same thing about you.'

'Were you?'

'Yes.' Teasing, because she was feeling so carefree, she added, 'I must be reading your mind.'

'Well, then, were you also thinking that you are the most beautiful woman here tonight?'

Laughing, she shook her head. 'No, why would I think that?'

'You would be if you were reading my mind.'

He had tilted his head, bringing it closer to her, and there was a genuine tenderness in his eyes. She told herself that he was pretending just as much as she was, but that didn't stop her from feeling mesmerised. The pressure of his hand near her hip increased and his fingers gently caressed her side. The warmth caused her breath to catch, then release with a shuddering sigh.

She attempted to break the spell she felt herself falling into by looking away, scanning the crowd.

Annabelle and Drew floated by, their gazes locked, their focus on no one but each other, confirming yet again the love they shared.

Not far behind them were Roger and Clara. Roger's hand was in the small of Clara's back, holding her closer to him than some might consider appropriate, but neither Roger nor Clara cared. That was evident by the way they, too, only had eyes for each other.

'Everyone appears to be having a good time,' Henry said.

'They do,' she agreed, turning her gaze back to him. For whatever reason, at that moment, she wanted him to know one solid truth. 'I'll never regret this, Henry. Until the day I die, I'll be glad that I met you during my time in England.'

'I'll be glad for ever that I met you, too.' He brought his face even closer. 'You've changed my life.'

His lips barely brushed the skin of her forehead, but the touch was enough to make her knees feel weak.

With a slight chuckle, his hand slid to her back and pulled her closer, allowing her to depend more on him than on her own legs to keep her moving across the floor. 'We can't have you twisting an ankle,' he said softly. 'The night is still young.'

Closing her eyes, she breathed in his amazing, wonderful scent and let herself focus on nothing but him, because this, too, dancing with him, was something she'd never regret, or forget. Long after she left England and returned to America, she would still think of him, remember him.

Love him. For that's what you did with friends. You loved them.

Henry kept the smile on his face throughout the night, while dancing, seeking cool air on the terrace and sharing the meal or a refreshment. Suzanne was at his side the entire time, but that wasn't why he had to remind himself to smile. It was because of what she'd said: *'... during my time in England'*. Those few words kept echoing over and over again and, each time that happened, it was as though a knife sank a bit deeper into his chest.

He knew that her ultimate goal was to return to America. Her homeland. There was nothing contradictory about that. What was clashing inside him was how he didn't want that to happen. Actually, it wasn't necessarily her going to America, it was that he didn't want to be separated from her. Not ever.

She had changed his life. Changed him.

The truth was more powerful than that.

She'd made him fall in love. With her. He wasn't totally sure how she'd done that, or even when, but he was in love with her. As impossible as that should be, it had happened, despite him claiming that he'd never allow himself to do that.

There wasn't anything he could do about it, either. Except learn to live with it.

He didn't doubt that he could do that, it was the second part of being in love with her that would be the challenge. He'd have to not act upon that love. She had a life to return to without any strings attached.

He would be more than a string. He'd be a noose around her neck. Just last night she'd told him how she was used to taking care of herself, and others. That was the truth. She'd sneaked into army camps for food so Clara and Abigail wouldn't go hungry, because she cared so much. Not for herself, but for others.

She had a heart of gold.

That had been made clear when they'd arrived at the Vosses' earlier. As soon as Abigail had seen Suzanne, the little girl had let out a squeal and run towards her, arms out. Suzanne had knelt down and scooped up the child, hugging her tightly.

That, her caring and loving heart, was one more reason why he couldn't ever confess his love to her. She'd feel obligated to him and obligation was not what he wanted. He had enough of that when it came to his family and he would never want her to feel as if she had to take on those obligations. He knew that weight, that burden, and wouldn't ever want to impose it upon another.

That wouldn't be fair. She deserved the life that she wanted, that of returning to America, and that left only one fair thing for him to do.

To never let her know how he felt.

Furthermore, this love that he was feeling for her might not last. He was his father's son, after all.

To provide her with a permanent place in his arms, his family, his life, and then lose interest, turn away from her, would be far more unfair than to let her return to America.

The tension that coursed through his body grew as the night proceeded. Growing accustomed to having Suzanne at his side, looking into her eyes, hearing her laughter, was tormenting. All of that made the desires inside him battle with his intelligence.

'Are you tired?' she asked as they once again left the dance floor.

Despite the mental exhaustion that the battle inside him was causing, he shook his head. 'No, but I am concerned that you will wear yourself out. You've barely sat down since we arrived.'

She leaned against him, whispered, 'I'll tell you a secret.'

'What's that?' he whispered in return.

'My feet went from hurting to numb some time ago.'

They were at the edge of the dance floor and he stopped, looked down at her. 'They did?'

She was smiling while nodding, but the tiny knot between her brows told him that she was being completely honest.

Without a word of explanation, or warning, he shifted his stance, caught her around the back with one hand and behind the knees with his other hand and scooped her off the floor.

'What are you doing?' she asked.

'Getting you off your feet.' He strode for the doorway, nodding at the people stepping aside to give him room.

'Goodnight and God bless,' she hissed near his ear, while wrapping her arms around his neck. 'You are going to create a scandal.'

That might be true and he didn't care, because what he saw in her eyes wasn't horror or humility. It was amusement and delight. 'The scandal would be you not being able to walk for weeks,' he said.

'That's hardly the case.'

'Are you sure?'

'Yes, I'm sure.' She laughed. 'You, my lord, are imprudent.'

He kissed her temple. 'Something else we have in common, my dear.'

They exited the room with a large portion of the crowd left behind laughing and applauding.

'You're sweeping her off her feet again, I see,' Roger said from where he and Clara stood in the hallway.

'Stop,' Clara said, slapping his arm. 'They are simply in love.'

'I made the mistake of saying my feet hurt,' Suzanne said, shaking her head at him.

Henry grinned and did nothing more than lift a brow, then chuckled at the rise of colour in her cheeks.

'My feet hurt, too,' Clara said. 'We were on our way to the sitting room to rest for a bit.'

'Yes, we were,' Roger said, then, not ever one to be bested, he scooped his wife into his arms. 'We'll lead the way.'

Both women laughed as the four of them proceeded down the hallway. In the sitting room, Henry walked to the sofa, set her down on the cushion, then sat beside her and twisted her about so her legs were draped over his thighs. She declared that was improper, but made no effort to move as she let out a long sigh.

'Better?' he asked.

'It feels heavenly to be off them.'

He reached beneath the hem of her skirt. 'Would you like me to take your shoes off?'

She twisted her ankles and tugged her feet back up under the hem of her skirt. 'Don't you dare!'

He chuckled. 'I dare, but I won't if you don't want me to.'

'I don't,' she said softly.

He touched the tip of her nose. 'Then we will just sit here and rest.'

'Thank you.'

Drew and his wife had also entered the room and Rosemary and Judd weren't far behind. Before long, the room was nearly as crowded as the ball room had been.

While the crowd had been growing, Suzanne had removed her feet from his lap, but they remained seated side by side as the conversation flowed. Henry participated in several conversations, but for the most part, he observed. Watched the other couples, many married, communicating with one another with little more than looks and slight touches, yet showed the entire room how connected they were to one another.

He felt stuck, like an outsider looking in through a window, wondering if he was destined to live a life without truly living it. Fate, his fate, had set things up that way, and wishing things could be different was a useless act.

Suzanne's fingers curled around his hand as she whispered, 'Henry?'

It was amazing how hearing her say his name warmed him deep inside, as if his very soul was touched by nothing more than the sound of her voice.

'People are leaving,' she continued. 'We should go and thank them for coming.'

He agreed and led her to the front door, where they spent what felt like hours, thanking people for coming and accepting congratulations.

Long after the first guests had left, he and Suzanne climbed into his coach for the ride home.

Covering a yawn with one hand, she said, 'If all the

balls we attend last until this late, I will have my days and nights mixed up.'

He lifted his arm, wrapped it around her shoulders and pulled her closer to his side so she could rest her head on the front of his shoulder. 'We won't have to stay this late at any other ball.'

'We might. You don't know how long it will take you some nights.'

That had been part of the bargain, for him to leave the balls and search for the murderer while she covered for him. That seemed like ages ago and renewed the frustration inside him. He had to find the murderer, but he would not put her danger. Not now or ever.

One more reason he could never have a normal life, one that included a wife—her. There was a reason that someone was attempting to pin him as a murderer and that could happen again in the future.

With her cheek pressed against his shoulder, she was looking at him, eyelids heavy and lips curled in a gentle smile. Despite all he knew, he could only think that the opportunity that presented itself would not happen again.

They would soon arrive home and go their separate ways.

He wasn't ready for the night to end and brushed the side of her face with a knuckle as he leaned closer. Her smile grew slowly and she licked her lips.

The next moment, as their mouths connected, he let the touch, the taste of her, consume him. She cuddled closer, and when her lips parted, he deepened the kiss and fully lost himself in the passion that exploded between them.

He closed out the outside world and the inside one. Closed out the battles of sense and sensibilities, and focused on nothing but her. She was sweet, passionate and, at this moment, his. He took all she had to give and gave in return.

When their lips parted, to gasp for air, he took note of the silence. The still silence. Although he was unsure how long the coach had been stopped, he took the time to give her one final soft kiss before saying, 'We're home.'

Her lids fluttered opened, her eyes staring at him blankly for a moment, before she gasped, 'How long have we been here?'

'We just arrived,' he claimed, although he doubted that. 'I'll walk you to the door.'

Climbing out, he told the waiting Caleb to take the coach around the back, that he'd walk home. Then, after delivering Suzanne to the house door, where Hiram greeted them, he waited until the door was closed and he heard the click of the lock before he returned home.

There he went up to his room, undressed and climbed into bed, where he contemplated the irony of being engaged to a woman he could never marry. The irony of how he wished he wasn't who he was, so that he'd have the freedom to love.

It was mid-morning when he awoke and his first thoughts went to Suzanne. So did his second and third ones. He grinned, thinking about her getting her days and nights mixed up, and hoped she was still sleeping while he got dressed and proceeded downstairs.

Seated in the dining room and while accepting a cup of tea from Caleb, he was told that his mother and Violet had already left for Beaufort.

'When?' he asked.

'At sunrise, sir,' Caleb replied.

Henry searched his mind for when he'd last seen his mother at the ball and couldn't remember seeing her after the engagement announcement, nor recall her saying anything about returning home so soon. The last time they'd spoken was the night before last, when he'd mentioned someone else not wanting Heather to receive money. 'Pack a bag for me and prepare the coach. Both you and Anna will be accompanying me.'

Having always been an early riser, Suzanne found it impossible to sleep once the sun was up. Today, however, she had slept longer than ever before, but had made it downstairs in time to breakfast with Annabelle before she and Drew left to visit the Exposition.

They had been gone only a short time when Hiram informed her that the Earl would like to speak to her.

Her heart skipped a beat, for she had been sitting at the table, sipping a second cup of tea and thinking how last night had been the best night of her life. Her nerves then got the best of her and she reached up to smooth back her hair. It was still in the braid she'd plaited it into before crawling into bed last night.

Thankful she'd put on a day dress before coming downstairs, she asked Hiram to show Henry into the dining room.

A moment later, when he appeared in the doorway, her heart skipped more than a beat. It leaped into her throat because the idea of kissing him took control of her thoughts. Standing next to the table, she forced her voice to sound natural. 'Good morning.'

He gave a slight bow. 'Good morning, I hope you slept well.'

'I did, thank you. I hope the same for you.' She was

still gathering her wits and her hand shook as she waved at the table. 'Would you care for a cup of tea?'

'No, thank you,' he declined while approaching. 'I've come to speak with you.'

The seriousness of his expression gave her a case of nerves that had nothing to do with her appearance. 'Of course. What is it?'

He ran a hand through his thick, dark hair. 'I'm not going to tell you what to do, nor am I going to attempt to convince you that it's your idea, I'm simply going to tell you the truth.'

Not exactly sure what he was about to say, it took her a moment to find her voice. 'All right.'

'I'm leaving for Beaufort shortly and I would like you to come with me because I need to know that you are safe.'

Suzanne stared at him for a brief moment, before saying, 'I'll need to pack a few things.'

The relief on his face was evident. 'Thank you. I would like to leave as soon as possible.'

She wanted to ask why they were going, why he was so agitated, but the urgency she sensed held her from saying anything other than, 'I'll be ready in half an hour.'

He caught her arm, slid his hand down over her wrist and wrapped his fingers around hers. 'Are you not going to ask why?'

She saw a vulnerability that she hadn't seen in him before, but recognised it because she'd seen it in others. Accepting help, accepting that someone might care enough to want to help, was difficult for some people and he was one of those people. He felt it was his duty to take care of everyone, without aid from anyone else.

The fact that he'd agreed to her help hadn't struck her until right now. 'No.'

He glanced away, then looked back at her. 'My mother knows something and I must find out what that is. She didn't say anything, I saw it in her expression when I mentioned Heather's death the other night. The fact she left early this morning without telling anyone worries me.'

Suzanne was so filled with compassion that she didn't dare speak. If she did, something might come out of her mouth that she hadn't dared consider, let alone admit. Stretching on her toes, she kissed his cheek, turned and left the room in a hurry.

Chapter Fifteen

Hours later, Suzanne watched the green, lush countryside roll past the coach window. Across from her, Anna's attention was on the needle and thread that she was pushing and pulling through a square of white cloth, making neat stiches for the hem of a handkerchief. Like Elyse, Anna's hands were never idle and she'd brought along a basket of sewing to keep her busy during the trip.

Suzanne had been surprised to see Anna waiting inside the coach, but shouldn't have been. It would have been inappropriate for her and Henry to travel alone.

They wouldn't have been completely alone. Caleb was driving the coach.

Furthermore, Henry wasn't inside the coach. He was riding his horse. She caught glimpses of him every now and again. It would have been faster for him to travel alone. He would be, if not for her.

She could have been left behind and could have told him so, assured him that she would take every precaution to stay safe, but hadn't. He wouldn't have agreed. She hadn't wanted to remain behind, either. There was no hesitation inside her in admitting that.

Where the hesitation lay was in admitting how deeply she'd come to feel for Henry. In ways she'd never thought she'd ever feel for a man.

It wasn't just the sensations she felt when he kissed her, or the butterflies when he looked her at. There was a special affliction deep inside her that accompanied several other sentiments and they were all connected to him. Pride, honour, affection, adoration, enchantment, and more. They all moulded together to form one thing.

Love.

And not the love for a friend that she'd admitted before.

She loved him the way a woman loves a man.

She'd believed herself immune to that. She had loved Aunt Adelle and loved Annabelle, Clara and Abigail. That love, though, was different. As was the love she'd felt for her students and her home.

The love she felt for Henry had become all consuming. It had been growing for some time. Ever since she'd thought him a knight in a fable. Ignoring her feelings hadn't made them go away. In some ways that had made them grow more, forcing her to notice them.

What she'd claimed had been pretending had been real and had allowed her love to grow more, and put her in the predicament she found herself in now. A woman destined to live the rest of her life with a heart so full of love that she couldn't share, it would be broken when it was time for their pretend engagement to end.

Tears stung the back of her eyes, and she closed her lids, keeping them inside. She had to do that. Just like so many other secrets. Not just those of her birth or her mother. Aunt Adelle had told her that if she fell in love with a man, he would take her away, leave Aunt Adelle alone, just like what had happened to her grandmother.

She had promised that would never happen, that she wouldn't leave her and that she wouldn't fall in love with a man.

Aunt Adelle was gone, so it wasn't as if she was breaking that promise, but what about the other ones she'd made? The ones she'd made to herself. She was already slowly breaking them. She'd vowed to never depend upon a man, yet, she had depended upon Henry to get Mr Winterbourne to read her manuscript.

He just seemed to break every rule she'd put in place about men. What if he kept doing that? Would she become a woman who wasn't even allowed to think for herself? Aunt Adelle had pointed those women out, but she'd also seen them while teaching. Women who had to ask permission from their husbands for nearly everything. She could never do that.

She leaned her head against the side of the coach, sighing. She had survived the war in America by hiding out in a cellar and would survive this, too. Instead of a root cellar, she'd continue to hide inside herself. Until the time came that she would once again leave a country. A country that she'd come to love. Where there were people whom she loved.

'Miss Suzanne.'

Suzanne heard the words, felt the gentle touch on her shoulder, but it was a moment before she could pull her eyes open.

'We will soon arrive at Beaufort Castle,' Anna said, gesturing to the window. 'You can see it in the distance.'

Blinking aside the aftermath of sleep, Suzanne also

rubbed her temple at the sleep-induced fog that must still be hampering her hearing. 'Castle?'

'Yes, miss. Beaufort Castle.'

Still feeling foggy headed, Suzanne pushed the curtain further aside to poke her head out the window. The structure was still a distance away, but she could see stone turrets, towers and castellations. 'Goodnight and God bless,' she whispered, 'it is a castle.'

She then blinked harder, several times, because while sleeping, she'd been dreaming about a knight on a white horse who had saved her and then taken her to a castle.

'Excuse me, miss?' Anna asked.

'Nothing,' Suzanne replied, eyes still stuck on the massive structure that seemed to be growing up out of the ground as the carriage rolled closer. For a child born out of wedlock, to a woman of ill repute, to pretend she belonged among the likes of aristocrats in London was one thing, but to pretend she belonged in a castle took that tale into fable territory.

'Beaufort Castle was a stronghold during the English Civil War between the Roundheads and the Cavaliers over two centuries ago,' Anna said. 'The Vogals have held residency in the castle since the time the Crown bestowed it on Sir Charles Vogal, the King's Chief Engineer, after he'd defended the property against five thousand troops.'

Suzanne glanced at the woman, saw the pride on her face.

Anna's chin lifted a bit higher. 'Forgive my boasting. Generations of my family have been honoured to serve the Vogals.'

'Nothing to forgive,' Suzanne replied as her gaze went out the window again. 'Thank you for the history, it's very interesting.' She knew a cavalier was another word for knight.

'Oh, it is, miss.' Anna then continued with other historical titbits concerning her family, their employment in the castle, and, of course, the gallant and noble Vogal men who had been knights.

The first signs of dusk, a mere hint of dullness to the sky that had been bright blue all day, were appearing when the coach rolled passed what Suzanne considered a medieval gatehouse, complete with stone-mullioned windows and battlements circling the top of the round building, before they passed beneath a stone archway and into a large courtyard.

A stone wall covered with ivy in places encircled the courtyard that included a large manicured grass area as well as several flower beds and tall, leafy trees. No wonder Henry had claimed she'd be safe here. This place was a fortress.

Gravel crackled beneath the wheels of the coach as it rolled to a stop.

Henry opened the door and held out a hand to her. 'Welcome to Beaufort.'

The mere sight of him tossed her heart into a fit and the touch of his hand didn't help in getting it back under control. Once on the ground, she stared at the intimidating building, took in dozens of stone-mullioned windows where multiple panes of glass were reflecting the last rays of the day's sunlight, arched wooden doorways with huge triangular hinges and, of course, the stone parapets running the length and breadth of the top of the building with notched areas where guards had once protected the property from enemies.

Then she turned, looking at the elaborate square-cut

stones that had been precisely laid together to create the impressive arched entranceway that they'd passed beneath.

'Is something amiss?' Henry asked.

She shrugged, attempting to appear perplexed as she said, 'I don't seem to recall a drawbridge or crossing the moat.'

Amusement flashed in his eyes. 'Ah, yes, about that. Unfortunately, the moat had to be filled in after the dragon died.'

'Why would that be?' she asked, playing along with him.

'Castles only needed moats to house dragons, did they not?'

She frowned, trying to recall anything she'd ever read about moats and dragons, but it was hard because she was still focused on a knight in shining armour. 'I'm not sure.'

Henry laughed. 'Nor I, but if anyone would know, it would be Anna. She knows the history of Beaufort better than any family member and, as I can assume, has been singing her praises of the time when Beaufort was a castle.'

'It still is a castle.'

'No, merely built to resemble the original one in places.'

'Built by whom?'

'Generations of my family. This is the spot where the original castle stood, however, it was very large and impossible to maintain with so few people living here. Rather than let it fall to ruins, one of my great-great-great-grandfathers had it dismantled and the stones were not only used to build this much smaller structure, but most of the buildings in the town of Hamburg that is a few miles away from here. Some stones were hauled to London, used to build buildings there.'

'Some of which your family still owns?' she asked. His mother had pointed out several buildings that the family owned while they been travelling to and from dress fittings and party-planning gatherings.

'Yes.' He took hold of her elbow. 'This way.'

As Suzanne pivoted back towards the house, her footsteps stalled. A line of people stood in front of the arched, double door at the top of the steps. 'Who are they?'

'Household staff,' Henry replied, 'waiting for your introduction.'

Henry had never expected to feel the amount of pride that he did while introducing Suzanne as the future Countess of Beaufort. Like many other things that he'd never expected since he'd met her, that pride was revealing yet another factor about himself that he would need to accept. He would never be the same. The man he used to be was gone. Suzanne would remain in his heart and mind, long after she'd returned to America.

'Suzanne, dear, welcome,' his mother said, walking out of the doorway where she'd waited as he'd introduced Suzanne to the staff. 'I have a room in the north wing ready for you and Lavender has been assigned to see to all of your needs.'

As a young maid stepped forward and curtsied to Suzanne, Violet walked to Suzanne's side. 'I'm so happy you are here. I will show you the way.'

Henry placed a tiny kiss on Suzanne's temple while giving her hand a gentle squeeze before he released it.

She walked beside Violet into the house, but shot a glance over her shoulder that bounced between him and his mother.

'I expected your arrival,' Mother said, turning about and walking inside.

He chose to hold off saying anything until they were in private.

She chose the sitting room again and he scanned the room from the doorway. For what, he wasn't entirely sure, but would discover whatever secrets she was keeping before they left the room.

He entered the room, closed the double doors and stood there while waiting for his mother to be seated.

She walked to the buffet instead. 'Would you care for a refreshment after your travels?'

'No,' he nearly barked, unable to keep the frustration out of his voice.

'Very well.' She waved to the furniture. 'Have a seat.'

'I've been riding all day. I think I'll stand.'

'Suit yourself.' She smoothed her skirt before sitting in her chair and then arranged the skirt around her feet before she met his gaze with one just as straightforward. 'We will get straight to business. Heather was not your father's daughter.'

Any hopes he'd had of learning the truth flew out the window like a proverbial bird. 'Mother, at least give me the decency of—'

'No,' she snapped harshly. 'You give me the decency of listening, of hearing the truth despite what you have already conceived as such.'

Holding back his anger out of respect, he gave a nod.

'Heather was not your father's daughter.' She closed her eyes, pinched her lips together and gave her head a slight shake before saying, 'I'm breaking a solemn vow of silence, but your innocence means more to me than a vow I made to your father years ago. I know he would agree. Heather was your cousin.'

He pursed his lips, drew in a deep breath. 'My cousin, you say?' He hadn't expected her to try to shift blame.

'Yes.' She sighed as if what she was saying caused great pain. 'I know you believe I'm a liar right now, but I do ask you to remember that I have never lied to you in the past. We have disagreed about a few things, some of little importance and some of great importance that have affected our family, our legacy and financial security.'

That hit a nerve and he moved closer where she sat. 'Nothing I have done has affected our family, legacy or financial security negatively.'

'I did not say that it had. I said that we have disagreed and I grant you the privilege of knowing that I was wrong and you were right pertaining to some of those past disagreements. I do hope that is not fruitless of me.'

He rested a hand on the top of the chair back beside him and gave her a nod that he respected her acknowledgement, even though it grated on his nerves to give her the satisfaction that flashed on her face.

'As your parent, your mother, I've prided myself on the man you've become, even before you became that man, because I saw so much of your father in you. He, too, took great pride in you, in knowing his son would continue to uphold the reputations of generations of Vogals, of Earls of Beaufort.'

Growing impatient, he said, 'Father told me that Heather—'

'Was a Beaufort,' she interrupted. 'He never said that

he was her father. Even as incapacitated as the stroke had made him physically, he had his mind, Henry.'

That was true. His father had been greatly frustrated that his body would not do what his mind tried to make it do. Even speaking had been difficult. Non-existent at first, and he'd worked hard to gain back the small amount that he'd had.

'Do you deny that?' she asked.

'No, I do not deny that Father's mind was still sharp.'

'Thank you.' She blinked several times, as if her eyes stung. 'I came to this house, this family, as a young bride from a family where scandals were prevalent. My grandfather's gambling debts had greatly depleted the family coffers, and though my father wasn't a gambler, his poor management of the meagre funds left to him had almost put the entire family in the poor house by the time your father agreed to marry me.

'It was the generosity of your father that prevented that from happening to my family and I'm proud to say that my brother, your Uncle Foxworth, took what small inheritance he had received when our father died and built it into the small fortune that once again supports the entire family.'

None of that was new to him. Although his mother rarely spoke of her family's past, he had learned of the mismanagements that had occurred.

'Your father and I were honest and direct with each other in all aspects of our lives. Right from the start. He knew I'd married him to save my family and I knew he'd married me to produce an heir. You.' She smiled softly for a moment. 'Edward had attempted to keep secrets from me at first, but we soon agreed that there was no room for that in our marriage. His secrets had never been of any magnitude, small things, mainly so I wouldn't worry, but I'd told him that I worried more when I didn't know things than when I did.'

Henry nodded, letting her know that he was still listening.

'Heather had never been a secret that he kept from me. We both knew of the affair that your uncle, Emmet, had embroiled himself in with a young girl from the village. Even though Emmet would never have inherited the earldom, she was not a suitable match.'

Henry bristled inside. His mother and father had always been adamant that those from nobility should only marry others from nobility. She had not said anything to him yet, but if she attempted to declare that Suzanne was not a suitable match for him, there would be a disagreement between them. A stronger one than ever before.

'Edward insisted that Emmet end the affair and provided the young woman the finances to move away. Emmet hadn't been the only young man she'd had relationships with and Emmet was forever fighting for her sole attention. Your father was afraid Emmet would end up in a duel over her and we were all grateful that she accepted the money and left.

'However, a couple of years later, when the marriage between Emmet and Minerva had been arranged, Edward had suspicions that the affair may not have ended. He questioned Emmet, who swore it had.' She sighed. 'It hadn't. Shortly before Emmet and Minerva's wedding, the woman threatened to reveal she'd had Edward's child. A girl.'

Henry rubbed a hand through his hair. What she said could be true, but why wouldn't his father have mentioned any of it to him? 'Why wasn't I told any of this? Father agreed that Heather should receive finances from us.'

'Yes, he did, because he never blamed the child.'

'You did,' he said, sounding accusatory even to his own ears.

'I didn't blame anyone, especially an innocent child, but I was very concerned about the scandal her receiving an inheritance could cause. You were already fighting to get businesses and property back in order from Emmet's bouts of mismanagement. Emmet had died months before and your father was on his death bed. For you to provide a large sum of money to a woman in Whitechapel would have had consequences. Some were already claiming you were squandering the family fortune by selling the properties that you had. That is why I told you that if you had to do it, to do it quietly, but you insisted upon hiring a barrister.'

'Because I didn't want Heather cheated out of it.' Tension was making his head throb. Fairness had been his goal. 'Instead, my actions cheated her out of her life,' he admitted.

'You can't take that on to your shoulders,' she said.

'She was my responsibility, just as the rest of the family is.'

'That may be true, but family shouldn't be a burden, dear. They should be a support.'

He shook his head. Not in disagreement, but in believing differently. However, the crux of the issue at hand had him asking, 'Did Aunt Minerva or Bart know about Heather? Know Emmet was her father?'

'As far as I know, your father, myself, and Emmet, beside Heather's mother, were the only people who knew about any of this. When the woman threatened to come forward in the past, Emmet was petrified that Minerva might learn the truth. Your father told him that he'd take care of it. He met with the woman and agreed to pay her a yearly sum until Heather was of age, as long as the woman kept quiet.'

'Heather's mother died when she was ten,' Henry supplied.

'Yes, she did. Afterwards, your father paid for Heather to reside at a girls' school. She ran away from there and, though your father attempted to find her, we never heard another thing about her, until you saw her in Whitechapel.'

Heather hadn't mentioned a school, but they'd only spoken twice. He turned the conversation back to his earlier question. 'Do you think that Aunt Minerva could have learned about Heather and had something to do with her death?'

'I don't believe Emmet would have ever told her, nor do I believe that Minerva is capable of murder. Her entire live has been devoted to spoiling Bart.'

'But you feel there's a connection there. I saw it on your face the other night.'

'I admit, she is who I thought of and, when she didn't attend your party, well—' She shrugged. 'It's the only explanation if you truly feel that Heather's murder wasn't random.'

'I know it wasn't random, Mother,' he said slowly. 'One of Father's cufflinks was discovered by her body.'

Chapter Sixteen

Suzanne quickly discovered that Beaufort Castle wasn't as large or intimidating as her first impression had implied. It was sizeable, being three storeys tall, and the largest house she'd been in, including those in London. The house itself was actually built in a large square with towers at all four corners and a massive enclosed courtyard in the centre that could be accessed from numerous rooms on the ground floor. The second floor, which consisted mainly of bedrooms with cavernous fireplaces and thick rugs covering oak flooring, had balconies overlooking the courtyard and the third floor, which Violet had not included in the tour, was designated for storage and living quarters for the numerous staff.

One family did not need this number of servants, Suzanne was sure of that, but Anna had claimed that the family lineage of staff members went back as far as the Vogal family line and Violet had confirmed that by stating that any child born at Beaufort could remain at Beaufort their entire life.

Each edge of the house had been given the names of north, south, east and west wings. The long hallways of each wing ran along the outside walls, where the numerous windows filled them with light and provided views of the front, sides and back gardens. The rooms all had windows, besides doors, that led to the courtyard that boasted flower and herb gardens, as well hedges and several seating areas.

In the corner tower of the house where the south wing met the east wing was a large library that had a wooden ceiling and spiral staircase that led to another library on the second floor, and was connected to a conservatory that put Suzanne in mind of Clara because Roger's house had a large glass growing room that Clara loved.

The conservatory room was an octagon-shaped room that extended into the courtyard from the library, with a large and ornate glass domed ceiling. Besides many potted plants there were chairs and chaises-lounges to sit on and read or simply enjoy the sun shining in through the glass walls and ceiling.

'This has always been my favourite room,' Violet said. 'I will miss it immensely when I marry Carter and move into his estate.'

'I can see why,' Suzanne said, running a finger along the top of a glass mosaic table. She'd tried her best to be interested in seeing each and every room, for they were beautiful, elegant and unique, but her mind was on Henry, as always. However, right now, she desperately wanted to know about what he and his mother were discussing. She hoped that he asked about the cufflinks. She was looking for answers as strongly as he. Proving his innocence was of the utmost importance.

Once that happened, she could determine her life. Determine what she was going to do about her feelings towards him. She was so confused about that. Not only how she'd allowed it to happen, but what it meant for her future.

'As Mother says,' Violet said, 'I'll be so busy being a wife that I won't have time to miss living here.'

'I'm sure that's true,' Suzanne said absently, because her mind was imagining the things and people she would miss when she left England.

'Is that how you feel?' Violet asked. 'So excited to be married to Henry that you don't have time to worry about America? I can't imagine being that far away from home.'

Petite, with big brown eyes and dark hair, Violet was as kind-hearted as she was inquisitive, Suzanne had noted that in London and knew her questions were genuine, not probing.

'I don't find myself with time to worry about much,' Suzanne lied. Flat out lied, because worrying was what she'd been doing more than anything else. Which was not like her. Leastwise, it hadn't been in the past. One more way she'd changed. 'I'd imagined that we'd run across Henry by now. I believe we've circled the house on the second and first floors.'

Violet giggled. 'Almost. I'm sure they are in Mother's sitting room. I'll show you the music room and then take you to him.' While leading their way from the conservatory to the library, Violet asked, 'Do you play the piano?'

'No, but I love the sound of it.' Suzanne sighed, thinking about how lovely the music at the Exposition sounded. She'd never forget going there with Henry. 'Henry said you play the piano.'

'I do, both Rosemary and I had lessons for years. Henry plays the harp and the violin.'

'He does?'

Violet's eyes shimmered. 'Yes, Mother made~ lessons, too. He hated it.'

'Thank you for that bit of information,' Suzanne ~ teasingly. 'He seems to have forgotten to mention it, ~ don't worry, it'll be our secret.'

Violet giggled. 'Thank you.'

The music room was impressive. Suzanne had never seen a harp. It was not only huge, it was gorgeous. She couldn't help but touch the golden wires running from stop to bottom and being touched by the ping of delicate sound.

'You'll have to ask Henry to play it,' Violet said. 'He is really good.'

Suzanne nodded, yet knew she would never ask him to play the harp. Her heart was already going to be broken when she left here, she didn't need to destroy everything about herself with more memories. 'Where is the piano?' she asked, moving away from the harp.

'It is in Mother's sitting room because she likes for us to play for guests.' Violet had moved to the door 'This way.'

Henry was in the hallway when Suzanne followed Violet out of the room. Her heart not only skipped several beats, she couldn't help but smile, because that's what he was doing, smiling, with his head tilted to one side.

Violet laughed. 'I do think our secret is already out, Suzanne. He knows I told you.'

Henry shifted his gaze to his sister and gave her a mock scowl. 'Of course you did, you little imp.'

'I'll go see how long before supper is served,' Violet said, with laughter floating in her wake.

'She lied,' Henry said. 'I don't know how to play any musical instruments.'

...e his best efforts, Suzanne was certain that he
...t pull off a lie if his life depended on it. 'I may
...to ask you to prove that,' she said.

He stepped closer, touched her arm with a single finger. 'Did you get the entire tour?'

'Yes, I did.'

'Even the courtyard?'

'Yes.' She then shook her head. 'I've stepped in it from several rooms and viewed it from many balconies.'

He grasped her hand and tugged her into the music room. 'I'll show you a favourite spot of mine.'

They crossed the room and exited through a single glass door. The terrace was made of either polished stone or tile, she wasn't sure which, but the heels of her shoes echoed off it as they crossed the platform and down the few steps on to a stone and gravel pathway.

She'd been silent until then, but couldn't hold back a question any longer. 'What did you discover?'

'I will tell you all I know, once we arrive.'

'Arrive where?'

'You'll see.'

Dusk had fallen, giving everything a shadowy haze around the last bits of golden light left from the sun. The pathway curved around various shrubs and bushes and Suzanne didn't need to know as much about plants as Clara knew in order to know that a single weed could not be seen.

When they walked beneath an arched arbour that was covered with honeysuckle, she slowed her steps to look up and all around her. 'I didn't notice this from any of the rooms.'

'That's because you didn't know where to look. I'll have to show you.'

It was more than one arbour, it was a series of them and the vines overhead and on both sides made it appear as if they were walking in a tunnel. It was darker beneath the vines, but not dark, more like a secretive shade that made her want to whisper.

'When I was little, my father told the gardener to not trim the honeysuckle,' Henry said.

'Why?'

'Because then the vines covered the entrance, all the way to the ground.'

'So no one would walk inside?' she asked, thinking that didn't seem right, for it was enchanting and the smell of the honeysuckle flowers was captivating.

'So only I could,' he said. 'I told my sisters that trolls lived in here and they'd steer clear of it, giving me my own private space.'

She giggled. 'Now I don't feel bad that Violet told me you that can play the harp and the violin.'

'I told you she lied,' he said.

Suzanne laughed. 'I don't think so.'

They had arrived at the back of the arbour, where there was a small stone bench at the end of the pathway. Henry wiped the seating area with his hand before gesturing for her to sit.

Looking around, she could see how a small boy would love hiding out in a place like this. 'Your father must have been a caring man.'

'He was,' Henry said. 'I managed to forget that for a time.'

She could hear the regret, the sadness, in his tone and laid a hand on his thigh. 'Because he was ill for so long?'

'No, because I was stubborn, determined to believe that what I thought had to be the truth. The only truth.'

'Pertaining to what?'

'That Heather was my sister,' he said.

Suzanne's breath caught. 'She wasn't?'

'No. She was my cousin. My father's younger brother, Emmet, Bart's father, was Heather's father.' He laid his hand atop hers as he proceeded to tell her about an affair his mother had just told him about.

Listening, she covered his hand with her other one, understanding how difficult it had to have been for him to believe the truth at first, but was also proud of how he was open minded enough to admit he'd been mistaken. That was not easy for people.

'Do you think your Aunt Minerva had something to do with Heather's death?'

'I know she does.' His voice had turned harsh. He noticed that, too, and touched the side of her face. 'I'm sorry, I didn't mean to sound so bitter.'

'It's understandable,' she offered.

'My mother informed me that there were three sets of cufflinks with the Beaufort insignia,' he said.

'Three? Who has them?'

'My father had two other sets made. He gave one set to my uncle Emmet when he married Minerva, and the second set, he had made for me. I was only a child then and his plan had been to give them to me on my wedding day.'

Taking in a long breath because she knew when he did get married, it wouldn't be to her, she asked, 'Does your mother still have that set?'

'Yes. No, actually, I have them.' He reached into his pocket and pulled out a box containing the set of gold cufflinks. 'She just gave them to me. My father was buried with his set, so that leaves my uncle's set.'

'As the set found by the bodies,' she finished.

'Yes.'

Nothing had changed, she was still sitting in the enchanted tunnel with him, yet a shiver rippled over her.

Henry's arm went around her, drew her close. 'Don't fear. You're safe here.'

She didn't fight the desire to be close to him, as close as possible. They were alone, with no need to pretend they were in love. She knew that and she also knew that she wasn't pretending. Wrapping her arms around his waist, she rested the side of her face against his shoulder. 'I'm not scared,' she whispered. 'I'm just…mad. Mad that your aunt would want you to be blamed for murder.' For that was the conclusion. His own family was behind it all.

Henry tightened his hold around her, kissed the top of her head. He was angry, too. Angry at himself for believing that his father had taken a lover, had had a child out of wedlock. He'd been wrong, so wrong, yet he'd forged ahead with those beliefs, for no other reason except for his own foolish stubbornness. He'd never even considered other aspects, other possibilities.

Now, those other possibilities, at least one of them, made perfect sense.

'If I were to be incarcerated for murder, and sent to my death for those deeds prior to having any heirs, the earldom would pass down to the next male relative,' he told her.

She lifted her head. 'Bart?'

He nodded. 'Bart.'

A frown formed between her eyes. 'Why wouldn't they have just killed you instead of Heather?' Her eyes

...dened and she jolted backwards. 'I didn't mean for it ɔ sound like that! That they should just have killed you, I just—just— Oh, goodnight and God bless. But I can say some stupid things at times. The stupidest, foolish...'

Laughing, he pulled her up against him again and, rather than kissing the top of her head, he kissed her lips. Just enough to stop her from berating herself. One, fast kiss was hardly enough, but he knew he had to stop while he could. 'My mother and I wondered the same thing. All we can surmise is that having me murdered would have been too suspect. All fingers would have pointed at them first.'

He pushed the heavy air out of his chest. 'I think they panicked when fingers didn't point at me after Heather's death and they had to try again. And again.'

She nodded, then asked, 'How are we going to prove it was your aunt?'

'I've sent a messenger to London, requesting that my contact at the Yard, Adam Hendricks, pay a visit to Beaufort. Until then, we wait.' That wasn't completely a tale. He had sent for Adam Henricks, but he wasn't waiting for anything. He was going to speak to his aunt first thing in the morning. He just didn't want Suzanne to know, because, like in London, she might decide to follow him.

He gave the end of her nose a fast peck. 'Let us go. It must be about time to eat, I'm starving.'

It had grown dark while they'd been sitting there, but he'd sneaked in and out of this hiding spot so many times in his life, he didn't need light to know his way out. Taking her hand, they rose and he walked behind the bench.

'Where are we going?' she asked. 'The entrance is the other way.'

'I know. This is my secret way out.' Reaching through the vines, he found the door handle. He then separated the vines wide enough for them to step through and into the opened doorway.

'Where are we?' she asked.

'The tower of the north and east corner,' he replied. 'It's the upper hall. The room where various activities take place. Balls, weddings, funerals.'

'Violet showed me this room, I just can't see it now. It's too dark.'

It was dark in the room with the curtains pulled against any moonlight that was starting to penetrate the night sky, but they wouldn't be in the room long enough to light a lamp. 'I know the way.' Holding her hand, he guided her through the room and into the hallway, where the yellow glow of the lit lamps made her look as pretty as ever. He plucked a single green leaf from her blonde hair.

She looked up at him, smiling, and took the leaf.

He tried to think of something besides kissing her, but his mind refused to be detoured. It had a specific destination in sight. Her name was barely a whisper as he bent down, pressing his lips to hers.

What sounded like a hum of pleasure emitted from her as her lips moved beneath his, encouraging him to continue. She wasn't a practiced kisser, simply a natural one. He loved how her every move was of need and want and how she didn't hold back on that.

He pulled her closer, so their torsos were aligned, touching, and parted her lips with his tongue. She arched her back, pressing parts of her more firmly against him. Neither of them held anything back as the kissing grew more passionate. He could only imagine what an amazing delight she would be in bed.

His imagination continued down other unimaginable routes.

To her becoming his countess.

To having children with her, sons, the Seventh Earl of Beaufort, and daughters, girls who would look just like her.

To living with her for the rest of his life.

To loving her for ever.

None of that seemed unimaginable, it seemed possible, real.

Henry ended the kiss with several small ones, then held her close, hugging her until his breathing returned to normal and, during those few minutes, he knew one thing for certain—she'd woven a web around him so tight, he'd never break free.

Then, because this had been a day of reckoning for him, he fully admitted something else. He had set a lot of boundaries around himself due to misconceptions. Things he'd believed had been true, yet hadn't been. He now knew the visits he'd accompanied his father on had been to provide Heather's mother with payments. That also explained why his father had told him to look at all the street urchins. All the children who, through no fault of their own, were fatherless.

His father had told him that a real man would never do that and Henry had sworn then that he was a real man and would never do that.

His father had also told him that family came first, before businesses or investments, and Henry had promised he would always think of his family first.

His thought-filled trance was broken by Suzanne shifting her stance and looking up at him.

He smiled down at her, touched her cheek. The time would come, soon, where he could reveal how he felt, what he wanted, to her and let her decide, without the pressure of their pretend engagement, if she was interested in possibly becoming a countess for real. It was a new idea for him, but while giving him the cufflinks, his mother had made some comments that stuck with him. His family was shrinking and growing at the same time. His sisters would soon both be married and be under their husbands' families, leaving just him and his mother, unless, of course, Suzanne would change her mind about returning to America.

He hadn't discussed any of that with his mother, of course, but it was consuming his mind.

'What are you thinking so hard about?' she asked quietly.

Withholding the truth from her was tough, but he had to wait until after the murderer was found, because he didn't want anything to impinge on her decision. 'That I'm starving,' he replied.

He was, just not for food.

'Then, let's go to the dining room,' she said.

He released her and teasingly asked, 'Do you know where it's at?'

'Yes. The layout of your castle is quite simple, even though it is also exquisite.'

Holding hands, they walked down the hallway. 'It's simply a house,' he said. 'It's the people inside that make it a home.'

'Or a castle,' she said.

Chapter Seventeen

After a sleepless night, Henry chose to skip breakfast and to not wait for Adam Hendricks to arrive from London. He was ready to get his life back on track—actually, he was ready to get it on another track, one where it included things that he wanted. However, that couldn't happen until the truth was out.

He saddled Barley and rode cross country to his aunt's house. He'd pondered so many things throughout the night that he shouldn't have had any thoughts left. Yet he did. Half of his riding time was spent thinking about Suzanne and the life they could have together and the other half was spent wondering what he should do with Aunt Minerva. She wouldn't be arrested, for he was convinced that she had hired whoever had killed Heather and the other two women and he doubted she'd be punished for that.

By the law.

He, however, had the power to see she paid for her deeds.

Upon arrival Henry turned his horse over to the groom and when the butler answered the door to the house,

Henry greeted him with a nod and walked straight to the dining room, where Minerva was sitting with a single boiled egg in a silver holder in front of her.

Her hand shook as she put down her fork and that was enough to know she was as guilty as he imagined.

'Good morning, Minerva,' he said, strolling to the table.

'Henry.' She lifted her chin higher. 'I was not aware you were in the area.'

'Yes, you were,' he said, taking a seat at the table. 'You've had someone tracking my every move for weeks. Months.'

She pursed her lips and folded her hands in her lap. 'I'd have no reason to do that.'

'No, you wouldn't, yet you have.' He poured himself a cup of tea from the place setting that had been put out for Bart, who was still sleeping no doubt. 'Forgive me if I'm wrong, but your family is still in Scotland, is it not?'

The smile she attempted to hold on her face was tight and empty. 'Yes. Why would you need to know that?'

'Because that is where you will soon be, along with your son, expelled from Beaufort and stripped from any family connections.'

Her eyes turned cold and cruel, filled with hate.

'Or, if you prefer, the two of you can spend the rest of your years in Newgate.' He took a sip of the tea, finding it much too weak for his taste, and set the cup down, pushing it away. 'It's up to you.'

Her neck turned bright red. 'Exactly what are you insinuating?'

'Insinuating?' He shook his head. 'I'm here to give you a choice. Scotland or Newgate. You see, I know you hired a man to kill those women. The first being my cousin, your husband's daughter, and when I wasn't arrested for that murder, even though you had your henchman leave a cufflink with the Beaufort insignia with the body, you were so angry, you hired him to kill again. And again.'

The colour drained from her face. 'I did no such thing.'

He released an exaggerated sigh. 'Very well.' Pushing away from the table, he rose. 'You've made your choice.'

She leaped to her feet. 'I've made no choice.'

'Had you admitted the truth, I would have dealt with this personally—now it will be left in the hands of a judge and jury. For both you and your son.'

'You are just like your father!' she spat. 'Thinking you are so high and mighty! Looking down on everyone else! You won't get away with this!'

'No, Minerva, you won't get away with this.' He shook his head. 'It's a sad day when a mother sends her own son to prison. Her only son. Only child. Such a waste.'

'Bartholomew did nothing wrong!'

Following his instincts, Henry said, 'He delivered the second cufflink to London. His father's cufflink. One would have thought that he'd want to keep those as family heirlooms.'

Her screech echoed off the walls. 'Emmet deserved more than a set of cufflinks! My son deserves more! Bartholomew should be the Earl of Beaufort!'

Suzanne walked along the hallway of the ground floor, following a sound that she knew well and one that made her smile. Lavender, who was as adept at fixing hair as Elyse, had told her that the children of the staff were playing in the gardens and, because she wanted to see them, that's where Suzanne was headed.

Henry had left before breakfast this morning. She was certain he'd gone to see his aunt. That worried her. So did not knowing how long he'd be gone and she needed something to get her mind off him. That was not an easy feat. No matter what she was doing, she found herself thinking about him.

That certainly had been the case last night. The kiss they'd shared in the hallway had kept her up until exhaustion had taken over. She had no future here and shouldn't keep pretending as if she did. Their bargain would end now that he knew who was responsible for the murders.

The war was not over in America and she wasn't sure where she should go, but knew it wouldn't be back to London. Living next door to Henry would be too hard.

Living without him anywhere was going to be very difficult.

When had life become so complicated? So complex?

Or was it just love that was so complicated and complex?

Either way, she had things that she needed to figure out.

She found a door that led to the outside slightly ajar. As she pulled it open, an old familiar warmth spread through her. Teaching had been wonderful and she missed many aspects about it.

The half-dozen children—two girls and four boys, all between five and ten years old, she would guess—were playing a game of tag in the thick green grass. An older girl, perhaps sixteen or so considering how her brown hair was pinned up, was reading a book in the shade of a tree a short distance away from the children, but noticing Suzanne, the girl quickly set down the book and called the children to her side.

Suzanne walked to the tree. 'Is recess over?'

'I apologise, my lady,' the young girl said with a curtsy. 'I will take the children upstairs.'

'Whatever for?' Suzanne asked.

The girl curtsied again. 'So they will not disturb you, my lady.'

'They are not disturbing me,' Suzanne replied. 'Just the opposite. I disturbed their game and did not mean to.'

'You sound funny,' one of the boys said, looking up at her.

'Spencer,' the older girl hissed.

Suzanne knelt down and looked the boy square in his big brown eyes. 'Hello, Spencer. My name is Suzanne.'

He glanced at the older girl before saying, 'Hello, my lady.'

'You are right, Spencer,' Suzanne said. 'I do sound funny to you and others here in England. You sound different to me, too. We get used to hearing words said one way and, when we hear them said another way, we think they sound different, or funny.'

He nodded.

'I like hearing how different people sound,' she said, including the other children in sweeping gaze. 'I also like playing tag!' She tapped Spencer on the shoulder. 'You're it!'

She took off running at a slow pace as giggles and squeals filled the air again as the children joined in on a lively game until everyone had a turn at being tagged and tagging others. Then she called them all close, including the older girl, and asked them to join hands, then taught them a sing-along song about three blind mice as they all held hands and walked in a circle.

When the song ended, the child begged for another song and she started singing about a London bridge.

Cheering, they all joined in.

After several other songs, she'd learned all of their names and encouraged them to have a foot race to the tree where the older girl, whose name was Kathryn, had left her book.

'Would you care to read to them, my lady?' Kathryn asked.

Suzanne settled herself on the ground, leaving the chair open. 'I think I'd like to listen, thank you.'

Kathryn's cheeks turned red as she sat in the chair and her voice declared her nervousness as she began reading from the book.

The book was a collection of short stories for children, one that Suzanne had never heard of, and she enjoyed listening to Kathryn read not one, but two short stories, before putting the book down.

'You are doing a wonderful job of teaching, Kathryn,' Suzanne said.

'Thank you, my lady.' Kathryn's brown eyes sparkled as she continued, 'It is my hope to become a governess when one is needed here at Beaufort.'

'Why just at Beaufort?' Suzanne asked. 'You could be a governess or a teach at a school, anywhere, not just here.'

'My family has always worked here,' Kathryn said, as if that explained everything, before she added, 'and there are no schools nearby.'

'No schools? What about Hamburg? Isn't there a school there?'

'No, my lady.'

Suzanne planted that in the back of her mind because the children were growing restless. Turning to them, she said, 'I have another game.'

Their attention locked in on her. 'It's called a scavenger hunt. Everyone needs to find something that is green, something that is white, something brown, and something of another colour. Any colour you choose. Red, blue, orange, black, yellow or pink or purple, whatever you decide.' Waving a hand at the surroundings, she added, 'You can't go past the garden, or past the stables.'

As the children took off running, she told Kathryn, 'I was a teacher in America and, while I'm here, I can give you some ideas of fun things for the children to do that also teaches them without them realising it's a lesson. Children learn by doing as much as by listening.'

'Oh, my lady.' Kathryn then shook her head. 'I couldn't expect that of you.'

'You aren't expecting it, I'm offering it.' She hooked her arm with Kathryn's. 'Come, let's join them. Each thing they find, we'll explain what it is and what it does.'

Kathryn frowned. 'What if it's just a blade of green grass?'

'Grass? Oh, my, there are so many things to teach about grass. It feeds animals, birds use it make their nests, it keeps the dirt from blowing away, it needs sun and rain to grow and it goes dormant in the winter, resting so it's ready to grow again in the spring. Those are just a few things that you can discuss about grass. You can look up grass in a book and read all about the varieties and many, many other things.'

'I never thought of that,' Kathryn said. 'Of something so simple being such a learning lesson.'

Suzanne nodded, no longer thinking about grass. Everything was more complex than it appeared. Most of all life and love.

The sounds of laughter had drawn her attention back to the children and the next hour was filled with exploration and learning that was as much fun for Suzanne as it was for the children. However, twice, she'd seen someone in the woods behind the garden.

After months of scanning to make sure there were no soldiers anywhere near before she'd made a single move back home, she'd easily picked out the man, even though he kept himself well hidden. It could be a woodsman or gardener, for she certainly didn't know all of the servants, but her stomach told her it wasn't. Whoever was out there wasn't working, they were watching.

It could just be her, because this entire time Henry had still been on her mind. His aunt might be behind the murders, but there was still the man who'd attacked her in London. Not comfortable because she was wondering if that man had followed them, she gathered the children and said they would take the items that they had found inside.

At the door, she instructed Kathryn to take the children upstairs to their study room and lay out all their finds on a table and label them. 'I'll be up to see them shortly,' she said. 'I need to take care of something.'

She remained at the door, watching for any movement through a tiny crack. Her breath caught when a man emerged, then crouched down, scanning his surroundings as he scurried to the garden, to be hidden by the tall fence.

Scenarios raced through her head. No matter how

many people she found to help her, if they took chase, he would run into the woods and they'd lose him. She needed to set a trap for him, a snare.

To do so, she also needed bait.

Henry strode in through the front door of Beaufort, less than satisfied and more than flustered. Minerva had finally admitted to hiring a henchman, yet claimed she didn't know his whereabouts.

He now knew a name, Robert Dupree, but had little else to go on and that was what Henry needed. More to go on to find this man. Bart, who had been hauled out of his bed and downstairs, had admitted that he had given Dupree the cufflink and that Dupree had been the one who had attacked Suzanne.

Both Minerva and Bart were being confined to their home and would continue to be until the murderer was caught. Only then, Henry had told them, would he consider having them expelled and stripped of family ties rather than imprisoned.

A servant girl who barely paused long enough to curtsy to him before rushing down the hallway was Henry's first indication that something wasn't right.

His second one was seeing James, the long-standing and aged butler, running towards him from another direction. 'So glad you've returned, my lord.'

'What's happened?'

'Miss Suzanne has ordered all doors to the inside courtyard be locked,' James said.

Ordered? Suzanne had never ordered anyone to do anything in her life. Henry was sure of that. 'Why?'

'I'm not sure, sir, but they should all be locked by now.'

Every nerve in his body began to zip and sizzle beneath his skin. 'Where's Suzanne?'

'I'm not sure, my lord.'

'Henry!'

He spun at the sound of his mother's voice. 'What the hell is going on here?'

'I don't know,' his mother said, clearly agitated. 'Suzanne was outside with the children, and brought them all inside, sent them upstairs and told a maid to have all the doors lo—'

'I heard that much!' he interrupted. 'Where's Suzanne?'

'That's what I'm trying to discover!' His mother gestured to a maid beside her. 'This is Marlo, the maid Suzanne told to have the doors locked.'

Henry recognised the maid as the one who had run past him a few moments ago. 'Tell me what happened,' he told her. 'Everything.'

'Miss Suzanne had been outside with the children,' the maid started explaining, 'then brought them inside and sent them upstairs with Kathryn. I was mopping the hallway and she waved me over, told me to make sure that no one was in the inside courtyard and to have all the doors locked to it, except for the upper hall and the dining room. She told me to keep people out of those rooms and to hurry. She appeared to be very worried. It frightened me.'

'Worried?' He was worried. None of this made sense.

'Yes, sir, she kept looking out into the back gardens.'

The maid was clearly shaken, and Henry fought to stay calm enough to make sense of what was happening. 'Where did you last see her?'

'She stepped outside, into the gardens, my lord, and I ran to the kitchen for help in locking the doors.'

'Henry?' his mother asked.

'Suzanne wouldn't do this for no reason,' he said aloud, racking his brain for explanations. 'Mother, make sure the children and women are safe. Gather them in one room and keep them there.' He then turned to James. 'I want all the men in the east hallway.' That was where the dining room and hall were located and that's where he ran to.

The dining room was the first room he entered. It was empty. He shot back out the door and was halfway down the hallway towards the upper hall when the door to that room opened and Suzanne rushed out.

Henry's entire being felt relief, but only briefly, because she was running towards him, shouting.

'He's here!' she shouted. 'We have to get to the dining room!'

Henry caught her arms, brought her to a stop. 'What's happening? Who's here?'

'The man from London! The murderer! He's here!'

'Where?'

She twisted in his hold. 'In the courtyard! We have to lock the dining room door to keep him in there!'

Still not fully understanding everything, except for her urgency, he released her and ran with her into the dining room.

'Where's the key?' she asked as they arrived at the glass-paned door. 'We have to lock it.'

James and Caleb, along with other male servants, ran into the room behind them.

Once again, Henry grasped her upper arms. 'We'll lock it. Just tell me what happened. Tell me everything!'

'I wasn't sure what to do, but knew I had to set a snare. Trap him.' She was breathing hard and pressed a hand to her throat. 'I saw him in the woods when I was outside with the children. I sent them upstairs with Kathryn and stood outside until I was sure he saw me. Then I came inside, but left the door open, and made sure he saw me come in here, the dining room, and then out this door.'

Henry looked out through the glass panes in the door, searching for movement. Between the tall hedges, the conservatory and vines growing up the sides of the building and arbours, there were plenty of places for a man to hide.

'He's still out there,' Suzanne said. 'Looking for me. I used the arbour to sneak into the upper hall. I couldn't find a key to lock that door, but I shoved a lounge chair up against it.' She laid a hand on his arm. 'I know it's him. He still smells like a saloon.'

Henry scanned her, for what he wasn't sure, she looked untouched, but the fear inside him of knowing how close she'd been to the murderer—again was turning into rage. He would annihilate Dupree once he got his hands on him.

He turned to the men in the room. Barked, 'James, make damn sure every courtyard door is locked. Including the upper hall. Caleb, make sure the women are safe, that no one is near the courtyard, not near a door or balcony. Samuel, send a messenger for the constable in Hamburg.' He then addressed the three gardeners in the room. 'Come with me and keep in mind that we don't know what weapons this man has, but he's killed before.'

As the men began moving, he turned back to Suzanne. 'Be careful,' she whispered. 'Please, be careful.'

Because there was nothing he could think to say right

now, he kissed her. A fast, hard kiss. Releasing her, he said, 'You stay here. Right here.'

She nodded.

He opened the door and entered the courtyard.

Fully aware that Dupree could have a gun, he directed the men behind him each in a separate direction, told them to stay low, as hidden as possible, and to leave no leaf unturned. Certain Dupree was still looking for Suzanne near the arbour, that's the direction Henry moved, shouldering his way through hedges as needed.

Near the arbour, he heard rustling, knew the man was on the other side of the vines, searching for Suzanne, fully prepared to kill her.

Not on his watch!

Without even telling his body to move, Henry crashed through the vines. All he saw was the man's back and he grasped the material on Dupree's shoulders, hoisted and threw the man on to the ground.

Scrambling backwards and trying to get up at the same time, Dupree pulled a gun from his pocket.

Fuelled by fury, Henry kicked the pistol from the man's hand and grabbed him by the material of his coat again, lifted him and slammed him into an arbour post. The sound of wood splintering mingled with the man's shouts.

The blood was pounding too loudly in Henry's ears to decipher what the man said, but it didn't matter. He wasn't done with him. This man had killed three times and had almost made Suzanne his fourth.

Henry leaped forward, hoisting Dupree off the ground again with one hand, then threw a punch with his other at the man's face. Dupree wailed and blood splattered, but Henry wasn't finished.

He threw another punch, and another, until the man's sobs filled him with such disgust that Henry threw Dupree against another arbour post.

As the man slithered to the ground, he begged, 'Don't kill me, my lord. Please, don't kill me.'

Thinking about all the harm this man had caused, the lives he'd ended, Henry could have justified the man's death, but not by his hands. 'Death,' he growled, 'would be too good for you.'

He grabbed the man by the collar and dragged him out from beneath the arbour, where the gardeners were arriving one by one.

'Get some rope. Tie him up,' he said, releasing his hold and letting Dupree fall on to the ground. 'Lock him in the stables until the authorities arrive.' As he started to walk away, his mind had cleared enough to add, 'There's a gun back there that needs to be collected.' Then he straightened his coat and walked away.

Chapter Eighteen

The moment Suzanne saw Henry walking along the pathway, she turned the key in the lock of the door, threw it open and ran into the courtyard. She had been happy to see him in the hallway earlier, but right now, she was beyond elated. Beyond thankful that he was unharmed.

At least he looked unharmed. She had to know for certain and ran straight to him, searching his person for tell-tale signs of injury as she rushed closer. When he held his arms out at his sides, she leaped the last few feet, landing in his arms and wrapping hers around his neck.

His solid, amazing body, the strength of his arms around her, it was all like shelter in a storm. The events that had happened since she'd seen the man in the woods were washing over her, making her shiver. So many things could have gone wrong. So many people could have been hurt.

Henry's arms tightened around hers and she clung tighter to him, telling herself those events were over. She no longer had anything to fear. It took time for all that to settle, for all that to become clear.

Releasing a cleansing sigh, she lifted her head, looking up at him.

He grinned. A wonderful smile that came easily and then he kissed her.

She kissed him in return before saying, 'You are all right.'

It was a statement, not a question.

He nodded. 'I'm fine. You?'

'Yes, I'm fine, too.'

Shaking his head, he cupped one side of her face. 'That was a very dangerous thing for you to do.'

His statement wasn't unexpected, but he was wrong. 'It would have been more dangerous for me to have asked someone to chase him. He would have disappeared into the woods. Still be out there. I had to set a trap. Confine him so he could be caught. He was the killer, wasn't he?'

He closed his eyes and shook his head, but then nodded, and she knew he understood that she was right.

With yet another grin, he leaned his forehead against hers. 'I've said it before, but will say it again—you are an amazing woman. The most amazing woman I've ever known.'

She accepted that, because he was the most amazing man she'd ever known. No matter where she ended up in life, another man would never compare to him.

With that thought, another one emerged. 'It's over.'

He hugged her again. 'Yes, it's over.'

She wanted to remain in his arms, but couldn't, because it was over. Coming up with the first excuse that popped into her head, she said, 'I need to go check on the children.'

'They are upstairs,' he said, as his arms slipped away. 'I know.'

'Thank you,' he said. 'Thank you for keeping everyone safe. No one else could have done what you did.'

'Yes, they could have.' She turned and walked away, feeling as if a part of her was being left behind.

The women and children were in the study room on the third floor, including Lady Beaufort, who was speaking to James, the butler, when Suzanne entered the room. He was most likely explaining what had happened. Suzanne crossed the room and immediately joined in on the exploration of the treasures the children had found earlier.

'Look, my lady,' Spencer said, holding up a black, white and blue feather. 'This feather is from a jay. That's what the book says. And it says they like acorns and I found an acorn, too!'

'That's amazing,' Suzanne replied, kneeling down to examine his feather.

'The book says that jays hide acorns in the ground and come back later to find them.'

'That is what it says,' she agreed, looking at the book on the table. 'It also says that the acorns they forget where they hid grow into oak trees.'

'It does?' he asked.

'It does.' Suzanne stepped back so the rest of the children could move closer to see the picture of the bird, the feather and the acorn, and read what it said.

Lady Beaufort stepped up beside her. 'This was quite ingenious of you,' Lady Beaufort said. 'The children were so engrossed in their findings that they didn't know about the commotion going on downstairs.'

Although she hadn't planned it that way when she'd set the children on their scavenger hunt, Suzanne was glad the children hadn't been alarmed.

'I'm very impressed with you, Suzanne,' Lady Beaufort said.

Not sure how to accept that compliment, she reminded Lady Beaufort, 'I mentioned that I was a school teacher in America.' She had told Lady Beaufort that the first day they'd met. One of the few things she'd told them about her past.

'I don't mean just this,' Lady Beaufort said, 'though, you certainly have expertise when it comes to children. I don't just mean what you did today, either. Trapping that evil man in the courtyard was dangerous, but also clever. I would never have thought of that.'

'I was afraid that if we chased him, we'd lose him in the woods,' she explained.

'That was a real possibility and I'm so grateful that he's been caught.'

'I am, too,' Suzanne said.

'I was worried that Henry would never find a proper woman to marry, he just didn't seem to have an interest in that.' Lady Beaufort sighed. 'And now all this hulla-baloo with Minerva and Bart—I sincerely hope it doesn't make you question your decision to marry him. I assure you, our family is not filled with scandals. The Vogal family's pedigree is quite untarnished.'

Suzanne's stomach churned harder than it had while being pursued by the murderer.

'Henry will see this mess is cleaned up with the least amount of disgrace as possible, therefore, as his mother, I beg you to be considerate in knowing this was a single act and highly unlikely to cause any issues with your marriage.'

The lump in her throat was nearly too large to swallow around. 'Of course,' Suzanne replied.

'Thank you, dear.' Lady Beaufort patted her arm. 'I'm relieved. A broken engagement has been known to cause a scandal, although they are bearable ones. It is very true that love conquers all.'

'My lady,' Spencer said. 'Come and look, I found another picture of a jay.'

'Excuse me,' Suzanne said to Lady Beaufort, and moved back to the table, squeezing her trembling hands tight together. A broken engagement scandal would be nothing compared to the one that would occur if the daughter of a prostitute married an earl. The Vogal family's pedigree would be tarnished beyond repair by that.

Henry was tired. Adam Henricks had arrived shortly after the officer from Hamburg and the entire day had been dedicated to dealing with Dupree, Minerva and Bart. He'd been right about his aunt and cousin not being charged, even though Dupree had confessed to everything, including being hired to kill Heather and, when that hadn't resulted in what Minerva had wanted, the other women. Including Suzanne.

The thought of that, of how close she'd come to being hurt, or worse, ignited his fury all over again.

There seemed to be no good answer as to what to do with Minerva and Bart. He would never trust them and didn't want them near his family. Scotland didn't seem to be far enough away, but he couldn't simply put them on a ship and have them deposited on some foreign land.

For now, they would be imprisoned in their home and Dupree in the stables, under guard by the local constable, until a prison wagon arrived from London to transport him to Newgate.

With all the anger and frustration, there was also gratefulness inside him because Suzanne was safe. Unharmed. He hated knowing that she'd been in harm's way because of him. That was not something he could ever forget, nor was it something that she could ever forget.

That brought up even more emotions.

He moved to the window of the second-floor library, staring out over courtyard, where the gardeners had spent the afternoon repairing the arbours that had been damaged. If there was a way for this all to be worked out, he couldn't think of it. He accepted all the blame, but that wouldn't be enough to ease her fears.

She was fearful.

He'd seen it on her face this evening, while eating supper.

The strong, clever, beautiful southern belle that he'd fallen in love with had been merely a shell of herself. She'd kept it hidden from others as they'd eaten and conversed throughout the dinner hours, but he'd seen it. He'd felt it each and every time she'd looked at him.

He'd felt her tremble when he'd kissed her cheek before she'd retired to her bedroom for the night. She wasn't asleep. Lamplight shone behind the balcony door and it was open, letting night air filter inside.

Flustered, he turned from the window. There had to be something he could say, do, to ease her fears.

He set his glass down on the table and strode out of the room.

There was a question in every step he took, making him think about things he wasn't sure he wanted to accept. He had at one time. Her going back to America was what he'd agreed to and he would have to abide to that agreement.

At her door, he paused only long enough to convince himself that knocking was the right thing.

It felt like hours, but probably hadn't been more than

seconds before the door opened. She took a slight step backwards upon seeing him, then reached down and tightened the belt of the dressing gown that was tied around her waist.

'I just wanted to check on you,' he said. 'And to apologise.'

Her hair was hanging loose, in long spirals that reached past her elbows, and nearly hid her face as, head bowed, she asked, 'Apologise for what?'

He glanced up and down the hallway. 'May I come in? Speak to you in private? Or we can go to another room. The library, perhaps.'

She shook her head, then nodded while stepping backwards and pulling the door all the way open for him to enter.

He took hold of the edge of the door and closed it behind him. The bedroom was like the others in the house, with a platform bed, a dressing area near the wardrobe and a sitting area near the fireplace. There was also a table and two chairs near the balcony door, which had to have been where she'd been sitting because there was a lit lamp, paper and an inkwell sitting atop the table.

'You were put in a precarious position today,' he started. 'I apologise for that. It was never my intention for you to be in harm's way.'

'I know that, Henry. I know you would never intentionally put anyone in harm's way.'

She was so forgiving. So loving and caring. Her response proved how much character she had. More than him. She came by her character naturally, his was inherited. Everything about him was inherited. 'Beside apologising, I came here to say thank you. Because of you, your quick thinking and actions, no one at Beaufort was injured today. They could have been.'

With a half-smile, she shook her head. 'You already thanked me and I merely led him into a trap. You captured him. You are the one who prevented anyone from being injured.'

Drawn to her like a moth to light, he stepped closer. 'My mother can't stop singing your praises, nor can others, and I agree with them.' He reached for her hand, but she pulled it away and stepped back, out of his reach.

Clearing her throat, she said, 'About that, Henry.' Turning, she moved even further away, then turned her back to him. 'Now that it's all over, the mystery solved, we need to discuss breaking our engagement. I—I've been thinking that I will go and stay with Annabelle, at Mansfield, until I can return to America.'

He balled his hands into fists to combat the pain that shot through him. His mind was blank, as shrouded in pain as the rest of him, leaving him with no verbal response, so he remained silent.

'We don't have to announce the broken engagement right away,' she said, walking across the room. 'We can wait until news of Mr Dupree's arrest calms, or maybe it would be better to announce it now and it'll get lost in the news about Mr Dupree.'

Despite the way his pounding heart was causing an echoing thunder in his ears, he heard the tremble in her voice.

'Whichever you think is best,' she continued. 'I don't want to cause a scandal.'

'A broken engagement could cause a scandal,' he said. It was an excuse, but he had to say something. Anything.

'A bearable one,' she said, stopping in the balcony doorway.

'Bearable for whom?' he asked.

'Society. You. Your family.'

He had to see her face. Strode across the room and gently grasped her shoulder, turning her about. The tears trickling down her cheeks disturbed him. He wiped them aside with his thumbs. 'Don't cry. We can figure this out.'

'I'm sorry,' she whispered. 'So, so sorry.'

He encircled her shoulders, pulled her close and rocked her as she melted against him. She was holding back tears, he could tell by the way her shoulders shook, the way she sniffled and gulped.

Wordlessly, he held her, rubbed her back, kissed the top of her head, as they stood there with a cooling breeze encircling them.

After she'd gone still, quiet, for some time, he whispered, 'There now.'

She eased her arms from around his waist and pressed her palms on his chest, as if needing to in order to lift her head.

Her eyes were still red and dull. As dull as they'd been earlier this evening, while eating supper. 'Suzanne—'

She shook her head.

Not knowing what else to do, he lowered his face. Kissed her. Her response was instant, but only lasted a brief moment before she pushed on his chest and pulled her lips away from his.

'I can't do this, Henry.'

'All right, I understand and apologise, I—'

'No, you don't understand, I'm not talking about kissing you, I'm talking about—' She gasped and turned away, moved away from him. 'Being engaged to you.'

Her back was to him again, but he saw her pick something off the table. She turned, then handed a piece of paper to him.

He didn't want to take it, but did, and noticed it wasn't just a piece of a paper. It was a cheque.

From his publishing house.

For a sizeable amount. More than enough for her to return to America.

Nodding, he said, 'Congratulations.'

Suzanne had considered just leaving. Asking Caleb to take her to Annabelle's country home. She had the money to go anywhere. The letter from Mr Winterbourne, along with a very sizeable cheque, had been delivered during the afternoon commotion. She had been sent away as a child, sent to her aunt, and both she and Clara had been saved by the ship's captain, but this time, it would be her decision to leave. Her choice. But she had to know one thing before she left.

'Did you tell Mr Winterbourne that he had to buy my story?'

'No. I did not.' Henry reached around her and set the cheque on the table. 'Your manuscript sold on its own merit.'

She believed him and wasn't overly sure if that had been what she'd wanted to hear. 'Well, then, we both got the results we wanted.'

That sounded so cold, so uncaring, even to her.

He nodded. Then shook his head. 'The war in America hasn't ended.'

'I know. I'll stay with Annabelle until that happens.'

'There is no reason why you can't stay here.'

'Yes, there is.' She drew in a deep breath to combat the pain of her heart breaking in two. 'If I remained here, we would have to continue the pretence.'

'And you don't want that.'

'We don't want that,' she said. 'We agreed to the stipulations.'

He nodded. 'Yes, we did, but what if one of us changed our mind?'

She didn't want him to have changed his mind. That would have made this easier, because it truly was the hardest thing she'd ever done. The most painful thing. 'It won't matter. I can't remain here. I have no pedigree.'

'Damn it,' he muttered. 'I don't care about a pedigree. Don't care about—'

'I do,' she interrupted, head held high. 'I care.' That was the ultimate truth. She cared too much about him. He would argue that, so she continued, 'I am who I am and that will never change. I hope you will allow Caleb to transport me to Mansfield.'

He stood stock still, looking past her, not at her. 'Of course.'

'Thank you.'

He took a step forward towards her and, afraid that she would lose her resolve, she turned around and walked to the door. Opened it.

On the way out the door, he gave her a slight nod.

She balled her hands into fists to keep from reaching out and touching him.

It felt as if the very life was being sucked out of her by a merciless force that was willing to leave nothing behind. She closed the door behind him, then crossed her arms, hugging herself against the agony. Did it hurt worse because a moment ago she'd known the utmost comfort of being in his arms? A feeling she'd never know again.

She had to swallow against a gasp caused by a new, stabbing bout of anguish of knowing she would never be held by him again. Never be kissed or comforted, or even smiled at by his overly handsome face.

Her knees, her entire body, gave out. She landed on the floor and didn't attempt to try to get up. There was no use. No use attempting to stop the sobbing or the tears, they were in control. Consuming every part of her body.

Her only saving grace was knowing that she was saving Henry from pain in the future. From a scandal that could ruin him.

When the pain eased enough, she rose and moved to the wardrobe to pack. She'd be ready whenever Caleb wanted to leave.

She also continued to tell herself that this was how things had to end. Even if her mother hadn't been a flower in the Flower Garden, she couldn't marry Henry. She had no defences against him. All she had to do was lay eyes on him and her insides melted. He made her want things she'd never imagined wanting. He'd changed her and she didn't want to be changed.

At some point during the night, when exhaustion had taken over, she'd climbed into the bed and laid there until the sun began peeking in the windows. She might have slept, or not. It didn't matter.

She rose, dressed, fixed her hair and left the room before Lavender had a chance to knock on the door.

Slowly, she made her way along the hallway, heading for the stairway that would take her to the kitchen on the lower floor, hoping that would be where she would find Caleb. The sooner they left, the fewer people she'd have to say goodbye to. Which was cowardly. She knew. That wasn't like her, but it was for the best.

Something, perhaps the flight of an early morning bird, caught her eye as she walked past a window and she paused, looked through the glass. There was no bird, but Henry was outside, strolling across the yard towards the stables. His stride was purposeful, as usual. He carried himself in such a gallant, noble way. Would she ever stop missing him?

Probably not.

Her gaze shifted towards the stables and an odd sensation rippled along her spine. Something wasn't right. Something… Dupree!

She pounded on the window. 'Henry!' Then she ran, knowing he couldn't hear her shouting through the window. Nor could he see that Dupree was sneaking towards him.

She raced to the stairway, shouting for help, and repeated her shouts as she flew down the steps. Her heart was racing. Dupree had a gun! She had to get to Henry before he got closer to the stables. Had to. He couldn't get hurt. Wouldn't get hurt! Not on her watch!

Henry felt as if it was his duty to protect and take care of people. It was her duty, too. Had been for years. She'd taken care of Aunt Adelle, then the school children and Clara. That's why she was afraid of loving Henry, because there would be no one to take care of, but she was wrong. He needed someone to take care of him.

She could do that. Would do that!

James was running down the hallway when she leaped off the bottom step. 'Get help! Get a gun! Dupree has escaped! He has a gun!' she shouted, while running to the outside door.

Throwing it open, she shouted, 'Henry!'

Her heart was pounding and her mind spinning. She had to reach him, knock him to the ground, before Dupree could shoot him! He was stronger than her and would simply catch her if she tried to shove him to the ground. She quickly surmised that she'd have to dive and grab him around the thighs or knees, force him to the fall to the ground with her.

Chapter Nineteen

Henry's entire body had felt weighted down all night. He was chained to his life. Chained by responsibilities that he couldn't forgo. Would never be able to forgo. He had pondered a dozen ways he could try to convince Suzanne to remain in England, but he hadn't been able to convince himself to do any of them. It wouldn't be fair to her and it wouldn't be fair to his family for him to up and leave, follow her to America.

Ultimately, he'd determined that there was no way for him to have what he wanted while still remaining true to his title, to the responsibilities that he'd inherited.

He had never imagined that he would ever have a broken heart, but knew that he did. Would for the rest of his life and that there was nothing he could do about.

However, he could make sure that Suzanne had the life she wanted. This morning, he determined that he'd see Dupree loaded in the prison wagon that was due to arrive within a few hours, then take her to Mansfield himself. Not so he could attempt to change her mind, but in order to show her that he was willing to help her in any way he could. For ever.

At the sound of Suzanne shouting his name, he turned, saw her barrelling towards him and waving her arms as though her skirts were on fire.

Something was wrong and he moved, ran towards her. She was only a few feet away when, arms out, she dived forward and, even though he reached down to grab her, she caught him around the thighs and hit him with her full weight, which wasn't much more than seven stone, but it still off-balanced him.

He grasped her upper arms, pulled her upright and held her tight as they fell, making sure his body would cushion hers when they hit the ground.

A mere second before he landed on his back, a gunshot echoed through the air. Holding her tight to his chest, he rolled off his back and covered her body with his.

Other gunshots rang out, so did shouts and a thundering of footsteps. Men, armed, ran past towards the stables.

'We need to talk,' Suzanne said.

He looked down at her, lying beneath him. Stunned, yet unsurprised those were the first words out of her mouth.

'Dupree escaped,' she said.

He'd surmised that and also saw that the men who'd run past were quickly gaining on Dupree as he ran for the woods.

'I saw him from the window upstairs,' she said.

He knew one other thing. This woman had a penchant for putting herself in danger. He was destined to worry about her the rest of his life. Therefore, he would do that with her at his side, not halfway around the world.

She wiggled beneath him, attempting to push him off her. 'We need to catch him!'

'He is being apprehended,' Henry said and, although his obligations told him that he should go and help Henricks and the others who had Dupree on the ground, he chose to kiss her instead.

Not just a fast kiss of thankfulness, but a deep, all-consuming kiss that filled his soul, confirming that no obligation was greater than the love he felt for her.

Her passionate response filled him with validation that he was making the right choice. He ended the kiss, smiled at her, then kissed the tip of her nose before saying, 'We need to talk.'

He rose to his feet, lifted her off the ground and joined her in gazing towards the stables, where Dupree was being escorted to. The guard who had been watching the prisoner through the night was led outside, holding his head.

Grateful that all had ended without further injuries, he tightened his hold around her shoulders and turned her towards the house.

'Shouldn't you go see what happened?' she asked.

'No.'

'But—'

'Others will see to Dupree and the guard,' he interrupted.

She glanced up at him with a slight frown, yet said no more.

His mother, and others, were outside the door. 'All is being taken care of,' he said. 'Please excuse us.'

In silence, he led Suzanne down the hallway, with his study being their final destination. His mind was a racetrack of thoughts of how he would convince her they belonged together. None of the challenges he'd faced in the past was as important as this one.

No one would ever be as important as her.

In the room, he closed the door behind them, took hold of both of her hands and went straight to the point. 'I've been very cautious my entire life. Swore I would never let my emotions override my obligations. Thought nothing or no one could ever change my beliefs, yet you did that in one act.'

'What one act?' she asked.

'Leaping off a balcony. My life changed the moment I watched you do that.' He squeezed her hands. 'I understand you want to return to America, you want to find out more about your family. I will help you do that. All I ask is that you allow me to do that while being at your side. With you, each step of the way. For ever.'

'Because you want to protect me?'

He knew his answer would bare his soul in a way it had never been bared before, yet he was willing to allow that. 'Because I love you.'

She closed her eyes.

She'd become a light in his life that had never been there before, as well as a friend and confidant. 'With that love comes my protection, my dedication, none of which will ever falter.'

She lifted her lids, looked at him. 'Returning to America had never been my goal. I wanted to sell my story in order to have an income, so I wouldn't be dependent upon anyone. Then I met you and became afraid.'

His heart constricted at knowing the dangers he'd put her in. 'I apologise for everything. Dupree, the murders, involving you and—'

'No, none of that scared me.' She shrugged one shoulder. 'I was fearful that you'd be hurt, but that's not what I was afraid of. You changed my life, too. I was very set in my ways and thought I knew what I wanted. You showed me there was more to life than what I'd known in the past.'

Biting her lips, she nodded, before continuing, 'My aunt had her own reasons for mistrusting men and, due to lack of experience, I agreed to believe in some of her reasonings, until I met you. You didn't conform to those beliefs and that scared me. I found myself being two people. The one who was pretending that all I was doing was helping you and the one who had fallen in love with you.'

An unsurpassable amount of joy encompassed him. He pulled her closer, then cupped her face with both hands. 'I love you, deeply, wholly, and vow to spend the rest of my life making sure you'll never be afraid again.'

She shook her head. 'That would be an impossible vow.'

Convinced of his own abilities, he asked, 'How?'

A slow smile grew on her face. 'Because I'm petrified of spiders and you can't rid the world of spiders.'

He kissed her forehead. 'I can squish every single one I come across.'

She laid her hands on his shoulders. 'I will love you for that, but the truth is, my greatest fear is of never being held in your arms, of never feeling my heart go aflutter when you look at me. When I saw Dupree sneaking through the stables, with that gun in his hand and you unaware, I knew that I didn't want to live my life without you.'

'I don't want to live my life without you.' To prove it, he kissed her. A sweet, gentle kiss that said he would cherish her for as long as he lived.

* * *

By the time their lips parted, Suzanne was filled with such wonder, she couldn't imagine how she'd ever considered being parted from this man. He was a force to be reckoned with. He'd broken down her defences, her misconstrued beliefs, with nothing but kindness. Others had seen that kindness as a weakness and would soon learn how wrong they'd been.

She was ready, willing, to spend the rest of her life at his side, taking care of him when circumstances arose and being protected by him when she faced obstacles, but that couldn't happen until she did one more thing. Not only for him, but for herself.

He'd spent his entire life being responsible for others, with little care or concern for himself. She couldn't allow for that to happen once more. Lifting her head from where it laid against the front of his shoulder, she smiled up at him. 'I would like nothing more than to stay in this room with you, alone, but there are issues that you need to see to and there are things that I need to see to.'

'What do you need to see to?'

'Well, for one thing, I have trunks to unpack.' That was true, but not the task she needed to complete. 'And you need to see how the guard is faring and that Dupree is secure until the prison wagon arrives.'

When he hesitated, she stretched up and kissed his lips. 'I will never stand in the way of your duties.'

He sighed, rubbing her cheek. 'I love you.'

'I know,' she replied, because she did know and that made her feel complete in a way she never had. Stepping back, she hooked an arm through his.

'I'll see to things as quickly as possible,' he said as they walked towards the door.

'I know you will.' So would she.

A short distance down the hallway, they parted, because she saw his mother in the sitting room. The very person she needed to speak to. Henry kissed her cheek before he walked away and she entered the room.

'Hello, dear,' Lady Beaufort greeted from where she was seated in a lovely chair. 'Do come in. A fresh pot of tea has just arrived. I needed it after such an unsettling morning. I'll be so glad when this is all over.'

Suzanne gestured towards the door. 'Do you mind?' she asked, questioning if she could close it for privacy.

'No, not at all,' Lady Beaufort replied, already pouring tea into a second cup. 'Forgive me, I'm still in my dressing gown. Awaking to shouting and gunshots set my nerves atwitter. The first pot went cold before I was able to drink a cupful.'

'We can talk later if you prefer,' Suzanne said, with her hand still on the door.

'No, now is fine. I was hoping we'd have a chance to talk in private. Close the door and come, sit.'

Suzanne closed the door and crossed the room.

'As you know,' Lady Beaufort said. 'Violet is getting married next spring, so I was thinking that a winter wedding would be lovely. Around the New Year? What do you think?'

Suzanne seated herself on the sofa, accepted the cup of tea and took a sip before she set the cup and saucer on the table. 'I have something I would like to tell you.'

Lady Beaufort set her cup on the table. 'It sounds serious.'

'It is. There is something you need to know.' Suzanne took a deep breath. 'I love your son, but I can't marry him without your blessing.'

'You have it, dear.'

Suzanne shook her head. 'I was raised by my great-aunt in Virginia. I'd been sent to live with her when I was seven, after my mother died. I have no idea if I have any other relatives, because my mother worked in a house of ill repute. I have no idea who my father was, nor do I know if she did. Henry knows this.' She had to blink as a single tear formed—her actions might indeed ruin the very thing she wanted, but she had to be truthful. Upfront. 'But I've never shared it with anyone else.'

Lady Beaufort rose from her chair and Suzanne braced herself for whatever the woman might do. Call for Henry. Tell her to leave. There were other options as well.

The one she didn't expect was for Lady Beaufort to sit down next to her.

'My grandfather was a gambler and a bounder, and my father wasn't far behind him. My family's reputation was far from stellar. My hopes of a suitable marriage were limited, then Edward Vogal appear. I claimed he came out of nowhere in my hour of need. In reality, he'd heard my father had some property for sale. I fell in love with him nearly on the spot. We were married within months, with him vowing to provide my family the funds to keep us out of the poor house, and I promised to give him an heir.' She folded her hands together. 'And prayed to the Almighty to fulfil that promise.'

Suzanne smiled, but held her tongue, waiting for more.

'That prayer was fulfilled and we had an amazing life together. Truly amazing, and now I have something just as vital to pray for.' Lady Beaufort took a hold of Suzanne's hands, held them tight. 'Your forgiveness. I imagine you came to me with this information, told me something that there was no need to share, because your past holds no importance to your future. To your happiness with Henry. I apologise for my comments about scandals. That is the reason you wanted me know.'

Suzanne nodded. 'Yes. I do not want to disgrace the family in anyway.'

'The fact you are sitting here, talking to me, is proof of that, and, besides apologising for installing fear where none needed to lie, let me assure you that as much as my son loves you, so follows his family. You are already considered family and with that comes our love and protection. My son has chosen an extraordinary woman as his wife. Anyone who would ever attempt to say otherwise would face the wrath of the entire family.'

'I appreciate that,' Suzanne said, for she truly did, but still had hesitation. 'Someone, somewhere, might know of my true parentage. Might discover where I'm from.'

Lady Beaufort's face took on a glow. 'Wouldn't that be wonderful? For if that were to happen, it would be out of love. There would be no other reason.'

It took a moment for that to settle, because that had never been a possibility in her mind. It made sense, though, there would be no other reason for someone to seek her out.

'Now, what do you think about a winter wedding?' Lady Beaufort asked.

Suzanne attempted to hold her smile to a proper proportion, but her happiness won out. 'It sounds lovely, but I would need to talk to Henry.'

Lady Beaufort giggled. 'Darling, he'll agree to anything you want. He is just like his father. Now, let's drink this tea before it grows cold, shall we?'

They drank the tea while conversing about several subjects, all of which left Suzanne feeling even more confident in the choice she had made. For it had been a choice to remain here, with Henry.

He was busy for most of the day, with people coming and going, leaving Suzanne little more than glimpses of him and a brief encounter during the noon meal. But even those simple snippets of time filled her with joy.

She spent time unpacking, sharing teaching ideas with Kathryn, and a few hours demonstrating those lessons. She did love children and liked the idea of being able to assist Kathryn in seeing to their studies on a regular basis. However, her main reason was so the children wouldn't see the prison wagon from the window. There were some things that children shouldn't witness.

It was shortly after that occurred that Henry found her in the children's study room. He motioned for her from where he stood in the doorway.

Kathryn was reading to the children and Suzanne gave her a brief wave as she crossed the room.

'Would you join me for a walk?' he asked quietly.

'Of course,' she agreed and stepped out of the room.

He closed the door and took hold of her hand. The familiarity of his touch, the warmth of his hand, reached her heart and that was even more confirmation that at his side was where she belonged. They walked in a comfortable silence down the hall, into the library, and then down the spiral staircase and out into the conservatory.

Sunlight filled the room and he stopped, turned and pulled her into an embrace. 'Finally, I have you where I want you.'

She looped her arms around his neck. 'In the conservatory.'

'In my arms,' he said, as his lips met hers.

As usual, she melted into his embrace, into the kiss, and would have gone on kissing him, but had a few things to tell him. Even though what Lady Beaufort had said, might be true, she'd still made a decision.

Ending the kiss, she looked up at him. 'I've decided to not accept Mr Winterbourne's offer.'

Of all the things she could have said at that moment, Henry doubted one would have surprised him more. 'Why?'

She lowered her arms from around his neck. 'A few reasons, actually. I'd started keeping my journal after the fire, after I'd lost everything, because I wanted to remember things that wouldn't have mattered to anyone but me. The train set I told you about, and Aunt Adelle's favourite chair, that I'd reupholstered twice for her, little things like that.

'By the time the soldiers ransacked and burned Clara's barn, it had become a habit to write everything down each night. Clara thought it would be wonderful for Abigail to some day read about the farm her first husband had purchased for them. As time went on, we talked more about my journal becoming a story that others might want to read. Then, while on the ship, I knew we'd need money and thought selling my story could be a way to obtain it.'

Having read the manuscript, he knew how good it was and, from the cheque Winterbourne had sent, he wasn't the only one who had been impressed. 'It's an amazing story. Harrowing and inspiring at the same time. I don't understand why you wouldn't want it published.'

'Wouldn't it seem suspect?'

Not following her, he asked, 'Wouldn't what seem suspect?'

'The wife of the owner of the publishing house having a book published?'

He traced the side of her face with one finger. 'No. I have no say in who gets published and who doesn't.'

'Some people might think otherwise.'

'I don't care what some people might think.'

She stepped back, then walked to a plant, touching one of its leaves. 'There is another reason.'

He walked up behind her, rubbed her upper arms. 'What?'

'What if someone in America read the book and knew about my past. My parentage?'

Henry turned her about and lifted her chin to meet her gaze. 'The only way that would happen is if they were trying to find you.'

Her eyes widened. 'Did you talk to your mother?'

'No. I've been trying to get people out of the way all day so I could find you. Just you.' A twinge deep inside made him ask, 'Why?'

She sighed. 'Because I told her. I told her who my mother was, because I had to. She's your mother and I had to be honest about who you were marrying and that's what she said.'

He pulled her close, hugged her. 'Because it's the truth. A child has no control over who they are born to.'

She looked up at him and a smile almost touched her lips. 'It could still cause a scandal.'

'Breathing wrong can cause a scandal to some.' He

leaned his forehead against hers. 'So could marrying an American, but like Drew and Roger, I would rather cause a scandal by marrying an extraordinary woman, than not cause one and be a miserable old codger for the rest of my life.'

She grinned. 'You will never be a miserable old codger.'

'I won't, because I'm going to marry you.' He hugged her tight again. 'I never thought I could love someone. Never thought that I'd find a woman that I knew I would love for ever. Who would become such a part of me that I know I couldn't live without her.'

She searched his face with a frown. 'You never thought you could love someone? Why?'

The truth was no longer hidden, it was right there, inside him, and it made perfect sense. 'Because I never thought I'd be worthy enough for them to love me in return.'

'Worthy? You are an earl.'

'That's a title. An inherited title that means nothing when it comes to being worthy of someone's love. Love has to be earned and I'd never had to earn anything, because I'd already inherited everything I needed. Until I met you. You made me want to be worthy of your love.'

She was still frowning. It had taken him time to figure it all out, too. 'I'd always known what was expected of me and set into doing those things, taking care of the finances, the holdings, the family, but I'd never known what I wanted. Not until this beautiful woman moved in next door. She not only caught my attention, she amazed me. She'd lived through hell and back, yet lived as if she'd never been hurt. She wasn't afraid of anything and, even though I didn't know it at first, I finally figured out that I wanted to live like that too.'

Her cheeks had taken on a blush.

'That is the honest truth,' he whispered.

A full smile filled her face and she snuggled in closer, laid her head on his chest. 'You, my lord, reminded me of a knight in shining armour the first time I saw you out of the window and I must admit that I wondered what it would be like to be swept off my feet and carried off to a distant castle.'

He threw his head back in laughter, never so happy to be exactly who he was, then he scooped her up into his arms. 'Your wish is my command.'

She caught him around the neck with both arms, laughing, and then kissed him with such passion he wished they were already married.

'If that is the case,' she said as the kiss ended, 'I don't want to wait until December to get married.'

He froze momentarily, wondering if she'd read his mind. Which, knowing her, could be a possibility. 'December?'

Chapter Twenty

Suzanne felt her cheeks growing flush again. Good-night and God bless, but this man made her feel things that were downright wicked.

Correct that. The swirling heat that had risen up inside her, the fascinating sensations of her breasts tingling and the juncture between her legs stinging, were not wicked. They were amazing. As amazing as him.

Letting out a sigh, she nodded, 'Yes, December.' That would be an eternity to wait. 'You mother has suggested a winter wedding.'

'My mother has no control over when we wed.' Then with a laugh, he said, 'Checkmate.'

'Checkmate?'

'I told you we had the upper hand. We both knew how this game was going to end when we started it.'

She laughed, remembering when he had said that. Pressing a palm to the side of his face, she whispered, 'I love you.' She would never tire of repeating that.

'I love you.' He kissed her softly, swiftly. 'So very much.' Then, he set her on her feet and grasped her hand. 'Let's go and tell my mother to contact the vicar. Plan a wedding for as soon as possible.'

She hugged his arm. 'Don't you need to go to Scotland?' Lady Beaufort had told her that he was going to take Minerva and Bart to Minerva's family.

'No. I sent a messenger for Minerva's brother to come and get her today. Enough time has been wasted on them. I, we, have much better things to do with our time.'

She leaned her head against his upper arm as they walked. 'I shouldn't be so selfish, but I am. I don't want to be apart from you.'

'I don't want to be separated from you,' he said.

'Ever,' she said.

'Not for any amount of time,' he said, looking at her in such a way her insides were swirling all over again.

'Day or night,' she whispered.

He looked down at her, as if trying to read her mind. She bit her bottom lip as her thoughts grew even more wild, more wicked, and watched his grin grow.

The thrill that shot through her was incredible and made her laugh at how daring she felt. Stretching on to the balls of her feet, she whispered, 'Starting tonight.'

He lifted a brow. 'Tonight?'

She nodded.

'You're certain?' he asked with a low voice.

'I've never been more certain in my life. I love you, Henry.' The happiness bubbling inside her made her laugh. 'I love saying that.'

'I love hearing you say that.' He pulled her towards the doorway. 'I'll order supper be served early.'

She giggled. 'How early?'

A few hours later, Suzanne's heart quickened at the soft knock on her door. Lavender had left a short time ago and had no reason to return. There was no reason for anyone to be knocking on her door, other than Henry. Her soon-to-be bridegroom.

Her entire being tingled with excitement.

The door opened and he walked into the room, with the sleeves of his white shirt rolled up to the elbows and several buttons undone. He didn't say a word, just closed the door, locked it and walked to her.

Suzanne's breath caught as his lips brushed over hers in a soft, delicate touch that was laced with promise. She slid her hands up his forearms and upper arms before letting them rest on his firm, bulky shoulders as his kiss grew more demanding.

Her entire body was alive, pulsating, tingling, filling with warmth. She welcomed each sensation, welcomed the heady desire he brought to life.

He lifted his head, looking down at her. 'You are still certain?'

'Yes,' she said, hearing the conviction in her own voice. 'I'll always be certain where you are concerned.'

Smiling, he softly traced the line of her chin with his knuckle. 'You once told me that you'd never regret meeting me during your time in England.'

She nodded, already melting due to the way he was looking at her. That was what love looked like. The shimmer in his eyes. The smile on his face.

'I will take you to America as soon as the war is over,' he said. 'Take you to Virginia, Missouri, and anywhere else you want to go.'

'There is nowhere that I want to go. Everything I want, will ever want or need, is right here.' Her heart was so full that there wasn't room for past worries. They were gone for ever. Forgotten. 'This is where our future lies and that is all that matters.'

He kissed her and she gave herself over to him completely. Not caring about anything but the connection between them. The love between them.

Like when they'd danced, she let him lead, knowing he knew things she didn't. He was the teacher now, she the student. Along with consuming kisses and soft caresses, he led her to the bed, stopping when they stood beside the platform.

'May I remove your dressing gown?' he asked.

She hadn't expected for him to ask for permission and took it as an example. 'May I remove your shirt?'

He chuckled. 'Yes.'

'Then, yes, you may remove my dressing gown.'

She watched as he untied the belt at her waist, let it fall free, dangling at her side by the loops sewn at the waist line. He then lifted the material off her shoulders and glided it down her arms before he released it, letting it land in a pile on the floor.

Her hands trembled with anticipation as she unbuttoned the last of his shirt buttons, then tugged it free from the waistband of his trousers. His skin beneath her hands was warm, silky, as she slid them under the material on his shoulders. She pushed the material away, then tugged it off his arms, giggling at her own jerky movements when she couldn't get the material over his hands.

With his help, the shirt was freed and she did nothing by stare in awe at his fit and perfect torso. He was so broad, so muscular, so gorgeous.

'I want to see you, too,' he whispered, leaning in and kissing the side of her neck.

'Please,' she said. 'I'm growing anxious for more.'

He tugged at the string at the neckline of her nightgown. 'This is all part of more.'

'It is?'

'Yes, and there is no need to be anxious.' He kissed the hallow of her throat. 'All good things come to those who wait.'

She was massaging the bulk of his upper arms and, though what he said might be true, she was finding herself very impatient. 'How long will I have to wait?'

He bent down, gathered the hem of her gown and lifted it. She stretched her arms over her head as he guided the material up past her waist, breasts, arms and finally her hands, leaving her bare. 'The wait is over.' He kissed the top of her shoulder. Then her shoulder blade, before saying, 'All you have to do now is enjoy.'

She sucked in air as his lips went lower, over the swell of her breast which sent a wave of tingles so intense her toes curled. 'All right,' she whispered, too enthralled to really speak.

He lifted his head, staring at her for a breathless moment. 'You are so beautiful. So perfect.' Combing his hands into her hair that she'd left unrestrained, he said, 'So very beautiful. How did I get so lucky?'

Fate, she figured, had intervened because if there was a beautiful man, it was the one standing before her. She glided her hands up to his shoulders, then down, over his muscular chest. 'Oh, my lord,' she whispered, 'I am the lucky one, for I worship the ground you walk on.'

'I don't wish for your worship,' he said. 'Merely your love.'

'You already have it.' She stretched on to her toes to kiss his lips. 'As I have yours.' She had no doubts about that, even before his mouth captured hers in a kiss that was so captivating, she melted against him, lavishing in the feel of his heated, sculpted body.

He was a skilled, admirable, yet patient teacher. By the time they were lying on the bed, stripped bare of any confinements between them, she was a mass of wild, wicked desires and needs.

He loved her body with his hands, providing soft caresses and teasing strokes. Loved with his mouth, by kissing and tasting areas she'd never known could be so sensitive or kissed.

There was love in his eyes, too, as he explored her body, caressing her with nothing more than subtle, yet penetrating gazes that made her skin shiver with delight.

An intense, driving pleasure pooled between her legs and spiked intensely as he kissed her breasts, teasing her already hardened nipples with his tongue. She had lost complete control, but wasn't bothered by that, instead she accepted each delight-filled lesson he bestowed upon her.

It felt as if it had been hours, yet minutes at the same time, of incredible, sweet torture that left her trembling when he nudged her legs further apart and settled himself between them. Above her, keeping his weight off her with one arm, he gazed directly into her eyes.

'I love you,' he whispered, 'and will now take you as my lady. You'll be my lady for ever.'

'And you, my lord.' Of their own accord, for she had long ago lost possession of her body, her hips rose up, opening herself for his entrance.

He entered her with a smooth, slow motion that gave her time to stretch, to accommodate him inch by inch. She felt full, complete and womanly in an entirely different way than ever before.

The want, the desire to move, overtook her thoughts, and her focus settled on meeting his forward thrusts. Her fingers dug into the bulk of his arms as they jointly participated in the ultimate union of their bodies. A dance to which they moved to the music of their mutual mounting pleasure.

There were gasps, moans of gratification and cries caused by sheer pleasure, and that was all from her.

The intense, powerful pleasure inside her grew to a point where it seemed to momentarily stall, then it exploded.

His name left her lips, at least twice, maybe more, she wasn't sure. Her entire body was reacting to the indescribable waves of bliss that washed over her, again and again and again.

She opened her eyes in time to see a powerful strain across Henry's face, his neck, before he thrust inside her, deeply. Perfectly, because she felt his release. Felt how it rocked him as hard as hers had her. She clung to him, taking as much joy in his completion as she had in her own.

He collapsed atop her, but only for a split second, because he caught her shoulders and rolled her with him, until he was on his back and she was lying atop him, feeling his heart pound beneath her breasts pressed against his chest.

'I have to say it again,' he said, breathless and hoarse. 'You are an amazing woman.'

She tucked her head beneath his chin, closed her eyes and breathed, just breathed, because she didn't need to do anything else.

If there was one thing that Henry regretted, that he could change, it would be the sun. He would stop it from rising. There was no part of the night that he wanted to end. Yet, end it would.

He closed his eyes, focused only on extracting the utmost pleasure for both of them from the union of their bodies. She'd given of herself so freely, so passionately, he should have had enough satisfaction to last for years, yet here he was, buried deep inside her again. One of the many times they'd made love throughout the night. The final time, because after this, he'd have to collect his discarded clothes and leave her room. Enter his own, which would be far too lonely.

Solace came knowing that loneliness wouldn't last long. They would be wed in less than forty-eight hours.

Forty-eight hours. He let out a slow groan, both in pleasure at how her hips were meeting his, how her body was clenched tightly around him, drawing out every ounce of pleasure left inside him, and in knowing that the next forty-eight hours would feel like years.

She had her legs wrapped around him, keeping them locked together through every thrust, heightening the friction between them. It was almost too much, the pinnacle of his release too close.

As if her body knew exactly what his needed, it jerked and she gasped. Her eyes, her smile, displayed her pleasure as her orgasm overtook her.

His breath stalled as a grunt blocked his throat when his climax hit, racking his body with pleasure and shattering his last bits of control.

He found her mouth, kissed her until nothing but gratification flowed through his veins.

The aftermath, or perhaps it was simply their love, filled the air with an aura that said all was perfect, right in the world.

It was all perfect in their world.

In this quiet, stolen night.

A night that had to end.

He planted a final kiss on her lips, then rolled to the edge of the bed and sat up.

She followed him. Wrapped her arms around him from behind and laid her head against his back. 'I don't want you to leave.'

'I don't want to leave.' He rubbed her hands and forearms. 'But I have to. It'll be light soon.'

'I'm anxious for the day when we don't have to pretend,' she said.

Twisting, he looked at her. 'We aren't pretending.'

She laid her head on his shoulder. 'You're right. We aren't. Never have been.'

'No, we haven't.' He kissed the top of her head. 'I will see you at breakfast.'

Smothering a yawn, she released her hold on him. 'I think I'll take a nap until then.'

'You do that.'

He found their pile of clothes, put his on and laid her nightgown and robe on the foot of the bed. Rather than being snuggled beneath the covers, she was sitting up, with the sheet draped over her legs, leaving her glorious breasts bare for him to see in the faint light. He crawled on to the bed. Kissed each one, then her lips.

Then, pressing one finger against her lips, because if she asked, he would stay, he shook his head.

She waved at him and he left.

A few short hours later, he was at the breakfast table when she entered the dining room, looking more beautiful than ever. He rose and felt his heart flutter as she walked straight to him and lifted her face for a kiss.

He obliged, then held her chair as she sat.

'Your mother and Violet are not up yet?' she asked.

'I haven't seen them yet.' His mother had used the evening meal last night to plan their wedding and had insisted that everything would be ready. That all the two of them would have to do would be to say 'I do'. He was grateful for that in many ways.

After accepting a cup of tea, to which Suzanne added a spoonful of sugar, she asked, 'What are you going to do today?'

'I,' he said, looking directly at her, 'am going to show my Countess around Beaufort today. Not the castle or grounds, but the property. It will take most of the day, so I've asked for a picnic lunch to be prepared.'

She stared at him, resting her chin on one fist, her smile growing until it encompassed her entire face.

In that moment, Henry knew he was worthy of her love. Her heart was truly made of gold and her love was so pure, so untainted, that she could only love a man who had earned it.

Little more than a day later, Suzanne turned from the mirror, held the skirt of her gown, which was a shade of silver as close to a sparkle as a colour could get, out at her sides and looked at her friends. 'What do you think?'

'Think?' Annabelle asked. 'I'm speechless. It's the loveliest gown I've ever seen.'

Suzanne looked at Clara, waiting for her thoughts.

Clara shook her head. 'I've never seen a more beautiful bride.'

'Lady Beaufort gave it to me.' Suzanne turned to her reflection again. 'It's the gown she wore when she married Henry's father.' A bout of happiness made her eyes sting. 'It's strange, but I feel as if—' She shook her head, swallowed. 'As if I have a whole family.'

'You do,' Annabelle said. 'Everyone at Beaufort loves you. I saw that as soon as we arrived yesterday.'

'I love them, too,' Suzanne admitted, still amazed by how much she had come to care for everyone at Beaufort. 'I would never have thought that possible.'

'Of course it was possible,' Clara said, hugging her shoulders from behind. 'Possibilities are endless. Look at us. We are proof of that.' She giggled. 'Roger tells me that I was destined to marry him, because the name Clairmount says it was waiting for its Clara.'

Annabelle laughed. 'Well, if that's the case, then Mansfield was named so that I'd find my man there.'

Suzanne frowned, trying to come up with a match for Beaufort. 'I guess I was destined to find my beau at Beaufort.'

'And Henry found his beauty,' Clara said.

'That's for sure,' Annabelle said, 'and he's waiting for you downstairs.'

'There's nothing to be nervous about,' Clara said. 'Roger is tickled to be giving away the bride. He says it's practice for when Abigail is forty.'

'Forty?' Suzanne asked.

'Yes, he says she can't get married until then.'

Suzanne laughed and strode to the door. 'I appreciate him walking me down the aisle, but I'm not nervous.'

'Not even about the wedding night?' Annabelle asked.

Shaking her head slowly, Suzanne said, 'No.'

Clara gasped and stood, arms wide, in front of the door. 'Because you've already had it.'

'No,' Suzanne said, finding it hard to tell a white lie. 'One can't have a wedding night prior to the wedding.'

'But one can have…' Annabelle said no more, but her eyes did.

'Yes, one can.' Suzanne laughed. 'And it was everything you two said it would be and more!'

They all three laughed like school girls and were still laughing when they arrived at the upper hall, where her knight in shining armour was waiting for her. Today she would vow her love to him, for a lifetime, but she already was his and he was hers. They'd known how this would end from the start and they'd been right.

He took hold of her hand as she arrived at his side and held it, not only throughout the ceremony, but the day.

'Happy?' he asked, after the ceremony and meal, and while they danced to music being played on the harp.

'Yes,' she said, thinking about how he'd played the harp for her last night. He was as talented at that as everything else.

Annabelle and Drew danced closer, as did Clara and Roger.

'Drew and I were wondering,' Roger said.

'About what?' Henry asked.

'If this is over,' Drew supplied, looking at Annabelle. 'Three southern belles are probably all London can handle. There aren't any more, are there?'

Suzanne looked at Clara and Annabelle.

Annabelle shook her head. 'No, there were no more on my list.' With her eyes twinkling, she added, 'But I do wish Betty Ann Sinclair could see us now.'

'Me, too,' Clara said.

'Me, three,' Suzanne admitted.

'Who is Betty Ann Sinclair?' Henry asked.

'Just a girl from Virginia who would have given her

eye teeth to marry royalty.' She kissed his lips. 'I do hope she's fared well.' Looking at him, with her heart overflowing, she added, 'I certainly did.'

Although the music was still playing, the other dancers still sashaying across the floor, Henry stopped, scooped her into his arms, and carried her across the floor, out the door, leaving a wake of cheers and clapping.

'Where are we going?' she asked.

'My bedroom,' he said. 'Where you belong.'

'Where we belong,' she replied, and turned to wave at her friends.

Epilogue

Suzanne emptied the envelope, sorted the bound papers into three stacks and took a deep breath, trying to decide where to start. One. Two. Or three. They all three were new authors and she was excited to read each one.

Her sigh echoed around her and she drummed her fingers on the top of the table.

'What are you sighing so heavily about?' Henry asked, from where he was sitting next to the lit fireplace.

'I don't know where to start. One, two or three.'

'One,' he suggested.

'Why?'

'Because it's number one. Everything starts with one.'

'But the order doesn't mean anything, that's just how I pulled them out of the envelope.' She tapped each pile. 'One. Two. Three.'

He folded the newspaper he'd been reading and set it on the table beside his chair. 'What are they about?'

'All three are children's stories,' she said. 'Mr Winterbourne's letter says that the other children's books that I've acquired for the house are tremendous successes. Selling worldwide.'

'They are,' Henry said. 'I told you that from the report last month.'

She twisted in her chair to look at him. 'I know you did, but you could have just been telling me that.'

'Why?'

'Because I'm your wife.' When he'd first suggested that she become an editor for the publishing house, she'd declined, but he'd persisted. It had all started with Kathryn, who had asked if the lesson plans that she'd given her could be made into a book when she'd started teaching school in Hamburg, in the school Henry had funded after she'd suggested that the town deserved a school.

Mr Winterbourne had put the lessons into a book and it, too, was selling worldwide. As was her first book, about escaping the war, but Suzanne had lost her interest in being a writer. She liked helping others more and had encouraged Lady Beaufort to create a cook book with all the recipes from the cooks at Beaufort. Aunt Adelle's rum cake had been included in that book. It was time for the recipe to be shared with others.

That book also was selling well.

In the end, she'd agreed to become an acquiring editor and loved it.

Henry rose from the chair. 'Yes, you are my wife, but I wouldn't tell you the books are selling well if they weren't. You need the truth, the sales information, to know what to acquire and what not to acquire.'

She stood and walked towards him. 'I know, but you sometimes tell me little white lies.'

'Like what?'

'Like I'm not fat.'

He laid his hand on her protruding stomach. 'You aren't fat. You are carrying our baby.'

'I am, but I'm also fat.' She grasped her breasts with both hands. 'Even here. They are twice as big as they used to be.'

He grasped her shoulders and turned her about, so she faced the table again. Disappointment flooded her system. She'd already lost interest in the manuscripts and had been hoping for a kiss or more.

Feeling the release of the top button on the row that trailed down her back, she asked, 'What are you doing?'

'I don't think they are twice as big as they used to be.' He kissed the side of her neck. 'I'll examine them and let you know.'

She should have known he wouldn't disappoint her. After a year of marriage, he had yet to do that. 'You do know that we are in the library, not our bedroom.'

'Yes, I do.' He kissed her neck again, still unfastening buttons. 'And I know that no one will disturb us.'

'How do you know that?'

'Mother is at Violet's house,' he said.

Violet, upon marrying Carter, had moved into the house where Minerva and Bart used to live, after they'd been taken to Scotland. Minerva's brother had guaranteed no one would ever hear from them again.

Henry pushed the dress off her shoulders, let it fall forward. It caught on her breasts and he walked around her, carefully pulling the material away and letting it fall to the floor, exposing her lace-trimmed chemise. 'I may have let it be known that we aren't to be disturbed,' he whispered.

'You did?'

He trailed a line of kisses from one of her shoulder blades to the other. 'I did.' Using both hands, he then slid the straps of her chemise off her shoulders. 'Now, let's see if these are twice as large as they used to be.'

Throbbing with want, she pushed the straps off her arms, so he could tug away the material and fully examine her breasts, and more, because he wouldn't disappoint her there, either.

She was his Countess and he took very, very good care of her.

She, of course, took very, very good care of him, too.

* * * * *

If you enjoyed this story be sure to read the other books in Lauri Robinson's Southern Belles in London miniseries

The Return of His Promised Duchess
The Making of His Marchioness

*And why not pick up her
The Osterlund Saga miniseries?*

Marriage or Ruin for the Heiress
The Heiress and the Baby Boom

Get 3 FREE REWARDS!

We'll send you 2 FREE Books plus a FREE Mystery Gift.

FREE Value Over **$20**

Both the **Harlequin® Historical** and **Harlequin® Romance** series feature compelling novels filled with emotion and simmering romance.

YES! Please send me 2 FREE novels from the Harlequin Historical or Harlequin Romance series and my FREE Mystery Gift (gift is worth about $10 retail). After receiving them, if I don't wish to receive any more books, I can return the shipping statement marked "cancel." If I don't cancel, I will receive 6 brand-new Harlequin Historical books every month and be billed just $6.19 each in the U.S. or $6.74 each in Canada, a savings of at least 11% off the cover price, or 4 brand-new Harlequin Romance Larger-Print books every month and be billed just $6.09 each in the U.S. or $6.24 each in Canada, a savings of at least 13% off the cover price. It's quite a bargain! Shipping and handling is just 50¢ per book in the U.S. and $1.25 per book in Canada.* I understand that accepting the 2 free books and gift places me under no obligation to buy anything. I can always return a shipment and cancel at any time by calling the number below. The free books and gift are mine to keep no matter what I decide.

Choose one: ☐ **Harlequin Historical** (246/349 BPA GRNX)   ☐ **Harlequin Romance Larger-Print** (119/319 BPA GRNX)   ☐ **Or Try Both!** (246/349 & 119/319 BPA GRRD)

Name (please print)

Address   Apt. #

City   State/Province   Zip/Postal Code

Email: Please check this box ☐ if you would like to receive newsletters and promotional emails from Harlequin Enterprises ULC and its affiliates. You can unsubscribe anytime.

> Mail to the **Harlequin Reader Service:**
> **IN U.S.A.:** P.O. Box 1341, Buffalo, NY 14240-8531
> **IN CANADA:** P.O. Box 603, Fort Erie, Ontario L2A 5X3

Want to try 2 free books from another series? Call 1-800-873-8635 or visit www.ReaderService.com.

---

*Terms and prices subject to change without notice. Prices do not include sales taxes, which will be charged (if applicable) based on your state or country of residence. Canadian residents will be charged applicable taxes. Offer not valid in Quebec. This offer is limited to one order per household. Books received may not be as shown. Not valid for current subscribers to the Harlequin Historical or Harlequin Romance series. All orders subject to approval. Credit or debit balances in a customer's account(s) may be offset by any other outstanding balance owed by or to the customer. Please allow 4 to 6 weeks for delivery. Offer available while quantities last.

Your Privacy—Your information is being collected by Harlequin Enterprises ULC, operating as Harlequin Reader Service. For a complete summary of the information we collect, how we use this information and to whom it is disclosed, please visit our privacy notice located at corporate.harlequin.com/privacy-notice. From time to time we may also exchange your personal information with reputable third parties. If you wish to opt out of this sharing of your personal information, please visit readerservice.com/consumerschoice or call 1-800-873-8635. **Notice to California Residents**—Under California law, you have specific rights to control and access your data. For more information on these rights and how to exercise them, visit corporate.harlequin.com/california-privacy.

HHHRLP23

HARLEQUIN
PLUS

Try the best multimedia
subscription service for romance
readers like you!

Read, Watch and Play.

Experience the easiest way to get
the romance content you crave.

Start your **FREE TRIAL** at
<u>www.harlequinplus.com/freetrial</u>.